The Endless Colonnade

This specially prepared edition, issued in 1959, is for members of The Popular Book Club 9 Long Acre, London, W.C.99, from which address particulars of membership may be obtained. The book is issued by arrangement with Chatto & Windus Ltd., the original publishers

ROBERT HARLING

The Endless Colonnade

THE POPULAR BOOK CLUB
LONDON

MADE AND PRINTED IN GREAT BRITAIN FOR
THE POPULAR BOOK CLUB (ODHAMS PRESS LTD.)
BY ODHAMS (WATFORD) LIMITED
WATFORD, HERTS
S.859.SB.

1

AFTER three months' havering, I have decided to make a start with some kind of narrative. In writing I may find release from my memories. I do not know.

The events I shall try to record will live uneasily within my mind until I die. The memory of their violence still disturbs me, waking and sleeping. Apprehension is slow to disappear.

Yet I realize only too well that, in an age of violence, events which are strange to one man may well seem matter-of-fact to another. Therefore, lest I might be thought fanciful or over-imaginative, I will say something about myself. As a psychologist I usually want biographical notes for a case-history. Why should I except myself?

My entry in the current *Who's Who* is brief, almost complete and may suffice:

FROST, RUPERT HENDERSON, M.C., M.A., D.M., F.R.C.P.; *b*. Hampstead, 1912; *m*. 1937, Pauline Helen Conder; two *d*. *Educ.:* U.C.S., Hertford College, Oxford; U.C.H., London. Lt.-Col. R.A.M.C., 1942-45. *Publications:* The Psycho-Pathology of Paranoia; Aspects of the Urge to Power; A Thesis on Bondage. Contributor to Lancet, B.M.J., Practitioner, Journal of Mental Science. *Address:* 145 Wimpole Street, London, W.1; Gate Cottage, Higham, Suffolk. *Club:* Savile.

The only serious revision I have made for the next edition concerns my wife, Helen, who died last March, just over ten months ago. She had been ill for two years, a victim of Lutembacher's Syndrome, which still remains a too-obscure heart disease. We had been married for almost twenty years and in love for twenty-five. Medical students who are un-worldly enough to fall in love must learn to possess their years and hearts in patience. Such discipline, we are told when young, is good for the soul, or, at least, the character. Experience, on the other hand, has made me sceptical of all maxims concerning either.

7

More of Helen may appear in these pages. Some account of my two daughters. Joan, now nearly fifteen, and Peggy, just twelve, may also find a place, but dearly as I should like to write about all three, this record is mainly concerned with others.

2

EVEN to begin is relief. Something may come out of the words. The truth? That is always too much to ask of one man's record. One man's truth then? Even that is usually over-optimistic.

Yet it is hard to break the habits of a professional lifetime, and case-histories have been part of mine. One never gives up hope that they will give a lead. And now, the facts:

3

AFTER Helen's death, my practice persisted, but that is all. In my consulting-rooms and at St. Thomas's, where I am on the consultant staff, I was a medical automaton, a doctor without a purpose. And that, I have always believed, is an irreconcilable paradox.

Yet, cauterized by my bereavement, I was lost in self-pity and despair. I have heard it said that no philosopher triumphs over personal disaster or even discomfiture. Neither could I, a trained psychiatrist, find within myself the reserves to enable me to stand four-square against my loss. Such self-revelation might have proved galling, but I was beyond the reach of vanity or self-esteem. What I had tried to cure in others I found incurable within myself. I am not the first physician to find himself thus mocked. Recently, indeed, I have come to think that only the nearness of my daughters, with their inexpressible sympathy, saved me from deepest

8

melancholia. Fortunately they were both at Queen's College in Harley Street and I saw a great deal of them.

4

I HAD many letters of condolence, for during our years together we had made too many acquaintances and too few friends. Married couples who live out their lives in self-sufficiency are apt to neglect the contacts that make for friendship. That was my trouble after Helen's death, of course. I was too much alone. I see that now. People wished to be kind, but they had made their own circles and doubtless thought that I had also made mine.

Among the letters, however, was a brief note from James Westlake, a wartime friend. I had come to know him rather better than one usually gets to know another man in adult life, and our friendship had continued after the war in that desultory manner frequently more enduring and understanding than smoother relationships.

We had met in Italy. I had become mildly ashamed of my comparative safety at the base hospital in Naples and had asked for a transfer to forward troops. By determined string-pulling I had got myself attached to the Gunners in their advance from Salerno to the north. Westlake was adjutant to one of the regiments in that bitter warfare.

He had always amused and interested me, for he was the only man I have ever met, either in my private life or in professional practice, whom I would unhesitatingly have written down as a *normal* human being. As soon as I write the phrase, of course, I realize that such a description is enough to put him clean outside the bounds of normality. For one thing, he was—or seemed to be—free from those emotions which govern most men, and he always seemed unusually detached about himself as well as others. Nobody is ever *unusually* detached about himself (or herself), of course, but James Westlake made a very good shot at such objectivity.

9

The Mess never discovered him set on a course motivated by greed, ambition, envy, spite, jealousy or even general combat weariness or bloody-mindedness. His actions were invariably based, as far as we could judge, quite simply on his view of the likely benefit to the unit. Just that. A rare thing in the Service, as the Mess quickly agreed, especially the regulars.

Westlake took his detachment to unusual lengths, even to being detached about women. I gathered that he was a bachelor, and, although he obviously liked and was liked by women, and took them physically from time to time, he treated them all with a genial avuncularity, which in somebody scarcely over thirty—as he then was—is either pretty heavy going or extremely successful posing. Yet he showed no signs of incipient *gravitas* or of the *poseur*. In fact, he was sardonically good-humoured and, occasionally, almost hearty.

I gathered that he was some kind of farmer in the North, presumably with private means. He talked at rare intervals about his hunting, shooting and fishing, but not more frequently than he talked about books. He was that odd, but by no means rare, type of upper-middle-class Englishman: an outdoor man with mildly intellectual interests. He had that kind of bookishness which, I have sometimes thought, is almost part of a bachelor's equipment; a wide knowledge of writers of the past but slight acquaintance with contemporary work. In fact, he was almost old-fashioned. His manners were old-fashioned, and many of his values. Possibly even his sense of humour. Yet, by a vaulting paradox, he was the most efficient and up-to-date gunner in the regiment, and seemed possessed by a compulsion to cast out all established regimental customs. His advice, too, which was in frequent demand, was far from old-fashioned. Because he dealt in basic and probably universal values, his advice always seemed to have contemporary relevance.

In that Gunners' Mess he was known as "the enfant terrible", a nickname peculiarly well suited to him, for he had an unholy talent for seizing upon an unfortunate fellow officer's sincere comments on politicians, world affairs, books, buildings, even the progress of the war, and demonstrating these comments to be a rag-bag of poverty-ridden ideas. The whole Mess would

10

quickly find itself in an uproar, the victim exploding, a few convulsed with laughter, the others out for Westlake's blood.

They never spilled any, for he disarmed them by laughter, a denial of the worth of anything he had said, and a courteous apology to his opponent. Yet, although his retractions silenced his comrades, they were shocked. The English, I have often noticed, do not like cynicism in disputation. They prefer sincerity, however banal or pathetic. Westlake was something they couldn't really take: a congenital cynic, "an eighteenth-century relic" as one disgruntled subaltern called him. Nevertheless, the Mess had considerable affection for him, despite their suspicions. With a native acuity in judgment of men, they saw that he had no axe to grind, that he wasn't shooting a line, that he was merely keeping boredom at bay—from them as well as from himself.

I have written at some length about the paradoxical nature of James Westlake, partly because an interest in people has been an important part of my life's work, partly because he both attracted and puzzled me. Abnormal normality, so to speak, is very rare indeed. Then, too, he plays an important and, for me, eternally moving part in the record I am trying to put down.

5

AFTER the war we met a few times. I discovered fairly early on in the fitful peace that he sheep-farmed about three thousand acres in Cumberland, kept a pack of Fell hounds, hated London and only came South for the Derby, the Cesarewitch and the Summer Show at Burlington House. His interest in the Arts seemed to overlook private art galleries and even the theatre, but these might well have been secret vices, for he was uncommonly well-informed when conversation took in an artist or actor in the news.

When he did come to London he stayed either at Brooks's or with us in Wimpole Street, where we had—and I still have—a large top-floor flat above my consulting-rooms. He remained a bachelor, "confirmed but not convinced", he once said: a thin, dark, saturnine-looking man, somewhat above middle height with dark but greying hair, high cheek-bones, steady green eyes, a jutting bony jaw, and a thin-lipped sardonic mouth, frequently softened by laughter.

He returned our occasional hospitality by asking us all up to his place, first in 1947, and again in 1950 and 1953.

He lived in a stone farmhouse set just below one of those bleak Cumberland ridges from which no other building—apart from three of his own shepherds' cottages—could be seen to the far horizon. But his home life was far from bleak. Few other Englishmen could have been living in such comfort in those years. He was cosseted by a housekeeper, cook and a parlour-maid.

Helen and I both wondered about the housekeeper, a Mrs Sonia Harker. She was a Durham woman, aged about thirty when we first went up there, the widow of a naval petty officer who had been killed on one of the Murmansk convoys. She was a handsome, soft-spoken, curvaceous creature, who moved around the house with a smiling, half-proprietorial air. She ate with us, and, after the children had been bedded down, usually came in to sit with us in the long, low drawing-room. There she sewed, speaking occasionally in a gentle musical voice, offering her shrewd comments rather than uttering them. Then, around ten o'clock, she would gather her oddments, say good-night and disappear. Helen and myself became very attached to her, despite the invisible guard she put about herself. We often speculated upon her exact relationship with James, whose life, we decided, was as featherbedded as an oriental despot's.

Sometimes, from our bedroom, we heard—or persuaded ourselves we heard—sounds of laughter from the far end of the creaking farmhouse. But that, as Helen said, was James's own affair. Every man to his own recreations. And I was delighted to agree. My own were felicitous enough.

The farmhouse, too, was something of a puzzle. I had expected to find comfortable leather chairs, pleasant but solid mahogany furniture and a few black-framed wood-engravings. Instead, I found a formal dining-room and a fine drawing-room with several Regency pieces, including a spectacular

coromandel sofa-table, and an eclectic assembly of topo-
graphical paintings—Varley, Ward, de Wint and a Samuel
Palmer painting of the Weald, so enchanting that I have rarely
been so envious.

James was the supreme host, combining the essential but
contradictory qualities that make for such a rarity. He looked
after us with the utmost attention, yet was respectful of our
privacy. He was gay about serious subjects such as the post-
war chaos of the world and serious about light-hearted projects
such as excursions and picnics. And always he treated Helen
and the children with his own strange boisterous gentleness.
They, of course, adored both host and hostmanship. I also
think that his detachment intrigued them as it had always
intrigued me, although doubtless in different ways. Even my
younger daughter was plainly aware of the marked difference
of James's behaviour towards her from that of most other
men she met. And she openly approved his carefree yet solemn
courtesy. Also she approved his preoccupation with the welfare
of his Fell hounds, for he took his duties as Master extremely
seriously. The girls were delighted to join in the off-season
exercising and were inclined to think their parents strangely
unsentimental in their canine interests. I have rarely met a
doctor who was crazy about animals.

Perhaps I am digressing, yet the subtleties of James's personality and character had, as I have said, amused and
interested me for years. He was at once so obvious and yet so
elusive, and I would willingly prolong memories of those holidays at Atherston, his Cumberland farm.

6

JAMES followed his note of condolence with a postcard to say
that he would be in London in September, adding a postscript
that he would look me up. Meantime, if I felt inclined to travel
North for a week or so on my own, or with the girls, I was
welcome. But I was already trying to escape from the misery

by working fifteen or sixteen hours a day. In Cumberland I would have had time to brood, and that was a prospect I could not face. In a way I suppose I preferred my stupor of self-pity to the necessity for decision, even a decision as simple as asking my secretary to book three sleepers.

James broke that. He telephoned me from Atherston one evening at the beginning of September to say that he would be in London two days later. Could I lunch with him? I eagerly accepted. His companionship had always had a revivifying effect upon me, and I needed exactly that. "Scott's one o'clock, Wednesday, then," he said. "I have a few plans."

7

HE WAS seated in a corner by the window of the first-floor restaurant, reading the racing page of the mid-day *Standard*. He was unchanged. That is, he still gave out an extraordinary sense of freedom from those everyday cares that attend the lives of most of us. He was relaxed whilst most of us seem to pace some great treadmill of hypertension. Yet his mood did not spring from false optimism or bogus bonhomie. On the contrary. He was a convinced pessimist and mildly inclined to misanthropy. But there it was, obvious yet intangible, an immeasurable tranquillity, deriving not from complacency but from some kind of discipline he seemed to impose upon himself. Discipline upon ambition, fond hopes and all idealistic notions? Or freedom from the need to earn a living? I wonder.

I was glad to see him, not so glad to hear what he said.

"You don't look so well," were his first words after ordering me a large martini, smoked salmon and steak and oyster pudding, "but I suppose it's understandable."

"Probably," I said, revising his order to lamb cutlets.

"In fact, you look bloody awful."

Again I agreed.

"Why don't you go away for a while?"

"Then I shouldn't have my work. That's a drug, at least."

"You could have the drug of the sun instead."

"It's getting a bit late in the year for that."

"Not in Italy. You ought to know. September and October were always the best months there."

"It would remind me too much of the war."

"Not the way the Italians live now. Certainly not the way they eat or the way they're rebuilding. No other country in Europe's so quickly forgotten the war—or recovered from it. I was there last year. I know."

"Where should I go then? Florence? Too intellectual. Rome? Too fashionable. Capri? It always sounds such hell."

"I'm going to the Veneto."

"I should have thought you'd have to go farther south than that for the sun."

"We shall get the sun, although I don't particularly need it. We've had quite a spell in Cumberland this summer. No, old boy. We need culture, and I'm proposing to get it in a big way."

"Statues and ruins?" I asked, ignoring his use of "we".

"A few ruins, a lot of statues. You probably don't remember, but after the war I joined an outfit called the Anglo-Italian Palladian Society. I seem to remember that I even tried to get you to join to keep your Italian memories green."

I had a vague memory of his attempt. Helen had been keen but I had let the idea drift and die.

"Well, I joined," he went on. "Forgot the whole thing. Yearly subscription paid by banker's order, and an occasional booklet about porticos, pediments and God knows what all."

He noticed my smirk.

"Don't be so damned superior. It was interesting."

"And now you're going to see for yourself?"

"On the contrary. Now I'm going to see through somebody else's eyeballs. The Anglo-Italian pundits have laid on a trip to the better-known Palladian villas in the Veneto—that's where most of them are apparently—and I'm booked to go at the end of this month. You ought to come. You used to have more than a passing interest in Italian buildings."

"How many villas are there all told?"

"God knows. I gather we shall see about a couple of dozen,

15

plus a few Palladian palazzi in Vicenza. And a couple of churches in Venice," he added offhandedly.

"Those we know," I said, stepping into his trap. "In fact, we saw San Giorgia and Redentore together."

"So we did," he said, grinning.

I smiled, gradually coming alive again after a long night of shadows.

"I should quite like to see Venice again," I said grudgingly.

"Well, come along."

"But I'm not a member of your Anglo-Italian Society."

"I could probably fix it. In any case, even if I can't, we could meet in Venice. It's not a bad rendezvous. In fact, I know no better."

Gradually, under his influence, I became almost enthusiastic for the project he outlined so persuasively. Like all capable amateur (and most professional) physicians he was certain of himself, of his diagnosis and of his suggested cure, and his certainty communicated itself to the obstinate patient. We wrangled amiably about my supposed difficulties in getting away, but, by the time we were taking coffee, I was ready to fall in with his plans.

Two nights later he dined with us in Wimpole Street. His gift for exorcising the devils of sadness and regret transformed the family. Because they saw that the shadows had departed from myself—temporarily at least—Joan and Peggy were more carefree than I had seen them in three months. James was indeed a therapeutic visitor.

During the course of the meal he said that he had been to Chesham Place during the afternoon and made me a member of the Anglo-Italian Palladian Society.

"A-I-P-S spells apes," Peggy quickly pointed out in triumph.

"Apes it is," James agreed. "And speaking of initials, the Apes, needless to say, had a copy of *Who's Who* in the office, and when they saw all those handles to your papa's name they wouldn't rest until they had him enrolled as fellow ape. I even got a bit of reflected glory knowing such a panjandrum."

With such touches to vainglory, James made his way, and, falling in with his determination, I asked whether I was now sufficiently qualified to make the trip.

16

"All fixed."

Did we travel as members of a troupe or troop?

"Good God, no. We make our respective ways to Padua, and then only meet for the sightseeing trips. It's all been made as painless as possible."

"Do you know many of the characters who are going?"

"One or two."

"How are you going?"

"Flying to Milan, then train to Padua."

"Do I go the same way?"

"Same way, same day. I booked us both through. We leave on Friday the twenty-eighth. That gives you nearly three weeks to find a locum, or whatever psychiatrists find, and to put him in your place in your confessional box at the hospital and down below, I suppose." He pointed downwards to the floorboards and my consulting-rooms.

The girls were delighted and wanted to know more about the tour, then more about Palladio. Once again I was fascinated by the ease with which James dropped his open-air manner and became the near-donnish enthusiast. We sat at the table for nearly an hour whilst he talked of the Master and his buildings and even took out old envelopes to scribble half-remembered elevations of the villas.

I remember that Joan, with the directness of a fourteen-year-old, said at one point, "You know so much about Palladio and his buildings, James, I wonder you want to go and see them."

"Book knowledge!" James scoffed. "You know so much about Switzerland from your atlas, I suppose you'll never want to go to winter sports again?"

"Oh, no!" Joan said, aghast and delighted. This was the language of raillery she understood.

We all laughed, and James returned to his lecture, until my housekeeper, Mrs Seabrook, made it plain that we had been sitting at the dining-table far too long.

That I remember as our first unshadowed meal at home for several months.

8

So, THREE weeks later, I set off with James.

We left London Airport two hours late. The plane, from Milan, had been re-routed to Bovingdon, which presumably rates as N.W. England in these climatic conditions. Anyway, we were invited to drink in the bar "with the compliments of Alitalia", which we did whilst waiting, watching planes begin to take off as the mist cleared. This I remember clearly.

Indeed, almost everything from then on I remember vividly. Perhaps, after a time of lethargy and stupor, we come awake with all our senses keyed up.

James was at his merriest and most misanthropic, doubtless aware of my certain reaction to his moods. Gaiety was so obviously his true mood. Misanthropy was equally plainly his mood of affectation. He might occasionally object to the attitudes and pomposities of his fellow-men, but his malice was never more than verbal entertainment. And I was glad to be entertained.

The journey was uneventful. Mont Blanc was pointed out to us at the correct, breathtaking moment and a few minutes later (or so it seemed) we were banking to come in at Malpensa.

"We'd better take a taxi into Milan," James said, as we stretched our limbs on the tarmac, taking in the Italian sunshine. "Otherwise we'll miss the afternoon train to Padua. This airport is farther from a city centre than any in the world. Serves Turin, too, I believe."

I was content to leave everything to James. Although I had been mildly elated at getting away, I was surprised to find how swiftly I seemed to tire. Sleep seemed my greatest (indeed, my only) need.

9

MALPENSA must be twenty miles or more from Milan, but, with the fervent co-operation of our driver, we made a fast run into the city and to the station.

In his serviceable Italian, James explained that we had to catch the 1624 train to Padua. That gave us less than forty minutes. The driver's face set in demoniacal glee. We came out from the airport into the main road like a guided missile. James was content.

"Nothing like giving a continental taxi-driver a purpose in life," he said, settling back.

I took in my first breath of Italy in ten years. Cypress trees, olive groves, picturesque and run-down farm-houses, assertive wayside posters, and, above all, the blissful sun. Gradually I dozed, coming awake in fits and starts as the crises of our journey came upon us. Half an hour later I was hazily following James up the escalators from the booking-hall of Milan station, that fantastic memorial to the Mussolini era and national megalomania. We had made it by five minutes, James said. The train was moving in. We clambered on board and relaxed.

"Why the rush?" I puffed.

"I don't know," James said. "Usually I lead a quiet life, but when I come abroad I like a modicum of movement. Entering into the spirit of the country, I call it. No English stuffiness. You, too. Don't forget we've got the reception at the University tonight. Begin as you mean—or I mean—to go on. International bonhomie! Down with the English stuffed shirt! They're the war-cries."

"What reception?"

"Our Italian opposite numbers are acting host before the tour begins."

"Must we?"

"You needn't, I shall. But you ought to."

"Why?"

"Because it's no good getting involved in this kind of tour and then getting superior about it all. You've got to go in at the deep end. No dithering. Accept the black bonnets, and terrible clothes of the Englishwomen. Accept their intellectual interests. Accept their chitter-chat about their stay-at-home husbands, their work for the local church. Accept everything. You can relax tonight, but after that you're in it up to the eyebrows."

19

I smiled and agreed to the reception. But, I pointed out hopefully, I hadn't brought a black tie.

"No need. Informality is just the right note."

I shivered.

10

JAMES had booked us into the Hotel Jolanda, one of the two or three principal hotels in Padua, near the University and the Piazza Cavour, the official meeting-place for our daily excursions.

My room, overlooking the Via San Francesco, was too high and too large, built for an earlier age, but it was clean and comfortable. The external bedlam, however, was intolerable. Countless Lambrettas and Vespas spluttered in the streets like batteries of machine-guns. Taxis hooted at the cross-roads. Yet, after a bath and shave, I began to feel the way the continental traveller ought to feel and was almost looking forward to the reception.

Changing into a dark suit, I glanced at the folder James had thrust into my hand at the reception desk. "Padua, an ancient town of culture. Famous for its University founded in 1222 and today ranked amongst the most modern for its scientific installations." I read on: "The tomb of St Anthony in the Basilica . . . the Giotto frescoes in the chapel of the Scrovegni . . . the burial place of Petrarch . . ." and so on and on.

"All good cultural stuff," James had said, smiling his sardonic smile. And so it seemed. The bedside telephone interrupted my browsing and dressing. Mr Westlake was waiting downstairs, said a girl's voice in Italian.

Young men in roving bands, young women in pairs, and older, staider folk were moving in crowds along the Via Febbraio, the main street, as we crossed to the University. The town seemed possessed by a colourful, almost mediaeval air, which further stirred my rising spirits.

At the head of a huge stairway we were ushered, by a platoon of frock-coated footmen, into a large reception room. Here we were introduced by a small, neatly dressed Italian, first to himself, then to a larger and older Italian.

"Revisi, the little chap, is to be our guide," James said as we moved away. "The big fellow is the local president of the outfit."

We followed the main stream of the Anglo-Italian Palladian Society through a series of reception rooms, finally debouching into a library with pilastered bookcases and a narrow gallery. Here we were directed by yet another footman to small gilt and red plush chairs.

By then, as James had promised, I was in it up to the eyebrows.

Our large, bulging host started on a long and incomprehensible speech in Italian, presumably of welcome. This was followed by an equally incomprehensible reply in English by a thin, academic character with a stringy beard, a lilting Adam's apple and a would-be ingratiating giggle. My last thoughts, before my head fell like a gollywog's, were dominated by envy of James' apparent concentration. He jabbed me awake, to hear Signor Revisi finishing the third speech of the evening.

"Now for the bunfight," James hissed. "I've had enough architectural brain-washing to last a lifetime."

But, alas, he was wrong. We were directed into another series of rooms by what appeared to be a new series of hosts, a tall, majestic cleric at their head. By then the whole episode was taking, I thought, a macabre turn. Renaissance panelling, nineteenth-century chairs, grotesque skulls of one-time professors preserved under glass, merged into strange shadows under the half-lights from the sconces.

Then a woman's voice said, "Hello, James, isn't this absolutely fascinating?"

A young woman of about thirty, in a black dress with a small white collar, joined us. In the darkened room my hazy impression was that she was vivacious *and* pretty.

"Hello, Georgina!" James said gaily, but plainly determined not to be rushed into enthusiasm. "I can think of at least a dozen more exhilarating excursions," he added. "Besides, I'm hungry—and thirsty."

21

"Philistine!"

"Meet my friend, Doctor Frost. Mrs Sandford. Take care, Rupert, Georgina's an amateur of architecture. She's probably telling the truth for once and even enjoying this."

"Of course I am."

One of our dragomen pointed out Galileo's lecture rostrum. I was not impressed and was glad to hear James liken it to a jerry-built job from some sixteenth-century orange boxes. We moved on.

"Poor James!" Mrs Sandford said quickly and confidingly. "No historical sense at all."

"Very little," he agreed, "but a highly developed sense of proportion. This whole jamboree is getting out of hand."

"Too much starchiness?" I asked.

"The starchiness is in the organizers so far," he said defiantly.

"Early days for grousing, James," Mrs Sandford said gleefully in her curious, high-pitched voice. "We've still got the Anatomy Theatre."

"Why?"

"Because it was Magagni's."

"Who was he, for God's sake?"

"A great doctor, wasn't he, Doctor Frost?"

I nodded wearily as we entered what must be one of the oddest auditoria in the world; concentric galleries rising acutely around a chair and table. Magagni, explained one of our hosts, sat in the well, with the body to be dissected on the table. The rake of the galleries is so steep, that although the theatre held two hundred students, each had a perfect view.

"Unless all this ends in three minutes, I'm off," James hissed. By then, of course, my own medical interests were aroused, and I was trying to catch every word of the guide's brief lecture on the sixteenth-century Teatro Anatomico Antico di Fabrizio d'Acquapendente.

But at last we were done and returned to the reception rooms. There a magnificent buffet awaited us, with white-gloved stewards at the ready. We were immediately offered white wine, whisky, brandy, port and sherry. Canapés and cakes were disappearing at speed.

"Whisky and soda in an Italian university! Sacrilege!" James said, taking wine.

"I need some of those equally sacrilegious sausage rolls," cried Mrs Sandford. "Presumably they've been supplied as an essentially English tit-bit!"

At last, immodestly gorged, we moved to one of the long sofas in an adjoining room. A waiter with coffee and liqueurs followed.

"No university in the welfare state could lay on this kind of beano," James said.

"It would take a lot of time cooking the nationalized accounts if they did," Mrs Sandford said.

I sat there, pleasantly weary, envying them their vitality, wondering how long they had known each other, where they had met. Once again I began to doze. With great deliberation I put down my glass on a marble-topped table, lest mishap should mar the *entente cordiale*, and almost immediately fell asleep.

I have a vague memory of bowing, oh so gallantly, to Mrs Sandford at the gates of the university and wandering along a cobbled street, back to the Hotel Jolanda.

"Eight hours' sleep won't be enough if this kind of junketing continues," James said, following me through the revolving doors. "Shall I dig you out in the morning or shall we meet on the coach?"

My recent solitary habits were difficult to break.

"On the coach," I said, almost automatically.

Perhaps James, always more sensitive than he allowed others to suspect, had deliberately left me this escape.

"Good. Sleep well, old boy. I can't see how you won't." I bade him good-night and climbed soggily to the first floor to my room. Ten thousand Lambrettas couldn't have kept me awake.

11

I HAVE never kept a diary in my life: it always seemed an unnecessary chore when young; later a time ill-spent, when I could well be at my books, and, later still, an inexorable appointments book was diary enough.

Yet, for the first few days of that tour, somewhat out of character, I tried journal-keeping and did succeed in making brief entries in a notebook, but the effort was too much and soon died. I still have the earlier entries, including this staccato opening day:

SATURDAY. Dep. Padua 0930. Piazza Cavour. Gradual sorting-out of party. Luck of the draw—or luck of the early worm. Partnered by Mrs Sandford. Destination: Villa Molin near Padua. Splendid façade. Somewhat anti-climactic interior. Staircase and additions later and poor. On to Villa Duodo at Monselice. Magnificent ruin and situation. Lunched at Rovigo. Italo-American couple and Italian beauty. Gratuitous lecture. Afterwards Villa Badoer at Fratta Polesine. Rustic-Georgian down on its uppers, ripe for an English milord's restoration. Then Montagnana. Tea inside the walled city. Finally Villa Poiana, Poiana Maggiore. Now a tobacco firm. N.b.g. Interesting pierced semicircular arch, but no more. Arrived Padua 1900. More sleep.

So my journal says, barely but sufficiently, for each word recalls a long eventful day.

Dep. Padua 0930, for instance. Even that factual statement evokes the memory of waking into a world already noisy with Lambrettas and Fiats. I should have to ask for a room at the back of the hotel, I decided whilst shaving. There were probably rooms built round a well. What continental hotel exists without a well?

But meantime I was tolerant, unpossessed by traveller's spleen. For one thing I had wakened to a sharp knock on the door and the bustling entry of a dark-haired maid with my café complet. The joy of two rolls, butter, marmalade, black coffee and milk! Little enough to bring joy to a morning at home, but abroad, enough. Why can't we get similar rolls in England?

Then the brisk walk to the Piazza Cavour. I was coming alive, beginning to enjoy food, movement, life itself.

Our sortings-out by the coach in the Piazza Cavour were watched by a few old men and children. The rest of Padua

24

went busily about its Saturday affairs, unaware of the entertainment to be gained on their threshold: from the contrast in behaviour between the Italians and the English—the former already a group, the latter still apart—to the contrast in sartorial manners—from Harris tweeds and brogues to man-made fibres and high heels.

I was first amused by the sight of a young, fair, tousle-headed Englishman standing aside from the crowd, warily determined not to make a first fatal move that would involve him for the rest of the day in companionship with too bulky, antique or outlandish a partner.

There were others to speculate upon. The solitary women. Spinsters, wives, divorcees or what? The young men. Students, scholars, wolves or worse? The old men. Lonely hearts throbbing under hearty words? Widowers, bachelors, or ageing neuters rediscovering the Renaissance, lost since undergraduate vacations? And so on and so on. Time and gossip would show. Meanwhile, the almost canine sniffing of the English by the English was, as usual, fun to watch. Later the thaw would set in and then we should all be friends for life or promising to be.

Following James's advice, I climbed into the coach, past my more wary fellows. The only occupants were a middle-aged couple, dour yet self-contained, man and wife without a doubt. I took a seat by the window, three seats back from the driver. I would at least have one day's full viewing of the landscape of the Veneto.

My determined entry seemed to spark the mettle of others on the piazza, for they all began to crowd in. James, I noticed, had been ensnared by an earnest young woman. Signor Revisi, the small and dapper Italian who had made the introductions at the reception, arrived to speed things up. He had plainly expected to find us all dutifully encoached, ready for his guidance. He sharply, almost testily, rounded up the stragglers, encoached the lot, quickly scanned the passengers, then his list and remarked that only Mrs Sandford was to come.

I had preened myself upon my comfortable day too soon. The seat next to mine was the only seat now free. Mrs Sandford

25

would arrive and I should have to give up my boldly won vantage point. I simmered.

Then she did arrive, climbing into the coach in a post-haste rush of scent and swirling skirt.

"Ah!" she cried gaily to Signor Revisi, "nine twenty-nine!" Her greeting made us all seem like staid old maids installed at a railway station an hour before the train's departure, but James would have none of it.

"Come off it, Georgina!" he cried from the right. "You're late and you know it."

"I *am* sorry!" she said, standing by the door, peering deep into the coach recesses in the hopeless, but far from helpless, manner of pretty, short-sighted women who refuse to wear glasses until, at last, they must.

I was interested to see her in the clear light of day. My weariness of the previous night might well have caused misjudgments, but she was as pretty as I had remembered her, and unusually slim, I noticed, as I stood to offer her my place. I was also delighted to see that her white skirt was dangerously transparent in the sunlight shafting through the open door.

"I wouldn't hear of it!" she declared and made as if to place her handbag firmly against my chest to push me down. I subsided. She took the seat by my side. The door breathed shut. Revisi gave an order to the driver. We were off.

For several minutes we were all quiet, taking in the people and buildings of Padua. Old and new architecture was everywhere reconciled by arcading, I noticed, and began to wonder why the English (a nation of shoppers and shopkeepers under the world's most unpredictable sky) should have neglected arcading. The Ritz Arcade is pleasant but too brief a refuge. And window-shoppers in the Burlington Arcade always seem to find charm in the roofed walk.

In politeness I said as much to Mrs Sandford.

"But the English love shopping in the rain!" she cried out gaily. "Yet another heaven-sent chance for them to look even more miserable and blue-nosed than usual."

The forcefulness of her words caused a young-looking, grey-haired man I had already noticed in the piazza to swing round sharply in the seat ahead and look back over the leather neck-

26

rest. He seemed nervously amused, I thought. The red-headed girl at his side was also smiling. Not so the rather resolute-looking young woman seated by James. She moved in her seat as if someone had dropped a squib down her back.

James came to the rescue. "Georgina, your voice carries!" he said. "Frankly I like rain in England. Not for shopping, but for grass. My sheep like grass."

"I don't mind rain on grass!" she said, logically enough. "I just hate rain on pavements. But haven't you noticed, James, darling, how the rain seems to bring even more Londoners into the West End? I think they adore creeping down Oxford Street, steaming like boiled potatoes, don't you?"

"I try not to notice," James said.

"Oh, I do. I see them from my taxi and my heart bleeds for them. Quite needlessly, of course. They love it."

The pair in front laughed.

James gave up. Mrs Sandford went on more quietly, seeming almost to hug herself, "Oh, how lovely to talk about English rain under an Italian sun. Don't you think so, Doctor Frost?"

I agreed.

She held open the small booklet which each traveller had been given *with the Compliments of the Anglo-Italian Palladian Society,* and peered at the list of members.

"What kind of doctor are you?" she asked suddenly. "I didn't get a chance to ask last night. Are you a real doctor or one of those highbrow Ph.D.s?"

At the mention of "Ph.D." I saw the youngish grey-haired man suddenly turn again, obviously attentive.

"The usual kind, but I do specialize in psychiatry."

"That must keep you busy these days."

"Most days."

"Are you frightfully good at it? Should I know your name?"

She was one of those rare beings who ask personal questions with the certainty of getting answers. Doubt never curbs their assurance. And of course they are right. We all like an excuse to start an egotistical monologue.

"Like most medical specialists, I'm unknown outside the medical world," I said.

27

"You're not one of these hobby experts who knows more about Palladio than any other living creature?" she asked guardedly. "Isn't there a Doctor Keynes who knows everything about Blake?"

I laughed and shook my head. "Nothing like that, I assure you."

"Good. There's nothing more damping than making a fool of oneself talking to these secret experts, is there? I once lectured an old man about roses for an hour and he turned out to be a king-pin at Wisley. He didn't let on at all. Very naughty of him, I thought. But he was very sweet. I suppose you're an expert about people's minds and all that?"

"I have to try to be."

She spoke with a fey imperturbability that had me half-smiling, half-apprehensive with every sentence. Again she went off at a tangent: "It's art experts I can't stand. *You* don't talk about psychiatry to everybody you meet, do you? But so-called art experts do. How I hate arty-crafty know-alls!"

Again her voice began to rise, gaily and shrilly. The young couple in front, I noticed, especially the man, were now unashamedly devoting their undivided attention to Mrs Sandford. Later I had cause to remember this attentiveness, but at that moment I wanted only that Georgina Sandford should continue, scarcely caring what she said so long as she talked. Her voice had a quality that I can only describe as poignant eagerness, occasionally wildly affected and shrill, then immediately natural and quiet. The inconsequential comments rippled off her tongue, as if in a race against laughter. Then would follow the odd catch, almost brittle and, for me, as I have said, wholly poignant. Whatever balderdash she might talk during the morning, I knew that I would listen. I also suspected that beneath the apparent frivolity a shrewd mind was at work.

For one morning, at least, I decided I would be her willing victim. Would her chatter then begin to pall? How wrong I was!

Georgina Sandford rattled on. She had the rare gift of appearing to be so sure of herself that she skipped the step-by-step conventional preludes before making her assertions. Most of us prefer to know our audiences and something of their

28

probable reactions to our speculations, but Mrs Sandford went straight in, perhaps unaware that any statement she made was ever provocative. For her it was, quite simply, her own view. Anybody else was entitled to agree or disagree. No bones or friendship would be broken in argument.

Until we reached the Villa Molin, then, I was delighted to have her as my companion, talking about Italy and the Italians, England and the English. She loved them both, especially the former. "Plus their own particular slice of the sun," she added, laughing. "Perhaps that is what I love the most."

She had been in Venice for a week, alone. "The most intoxicating city in the world," she opined, "but one shouldn't be alone. I'm no crowd-lover, but I've been almost looking forward to this gang of culture-bashers. This morning I love them all," she said shrilly, moving her arm to take in the coach-load.

So, gaily, we came to the first stop in the day's excursion. I followed her from the coach. The young grey-haired man and his red-haired companion stood aside to let us descend. He had a rather boyish air, despite his prematurely grey hair, but he seemed over-deferential. He deferred to us, he deferred to his girl friend and took her arm with a tentative gesture, rather in the manner of a man who thinks he might easily be rebuffed.

The Villa Molin, designed by Palladio's pupil, Vincenzo Scamozzi, is boldly and beautifully sited, overlooking the Battaglia Canal, one of those straight, well-kept waterways of the Veneto. The exterior is impressive with a fine portico, splendidly reflected in the canal. It is said that Inigo Jones was influenced by the villa in his designs for balustrading the Queen's House at Greenwich. I could see his point.

These few facts I gathered from Signor Revisi's brief talk in the top-lit central room. Fortunately, he had the gift of compression. I had been too tired the previous evening to notice that. He loved the Palladian tradition, but he didn't over-indulge his love. He was also depressed by the interior of the villa. "For these things Vincenzo Scamozzi—and thus, of course, Andrea Palladio, his Master—is not to be blamed!" Revisi declared. With what loving grandeur he pronounced his heroes' names!

"Can you imagine an English guide rolling off the names of

Hawksmoor or Vanbrugh with the same loving effect?" James said afterwards as we walked through the gardens. "Not even a Frenchman, declaiming the names of Napoleon's marshals, could get such feeling into the names of what, after all, are just chaps."

"Just like you or me?"

"More or less."

The parterres and cypresses of the gardens partly restored our faith in Italy's appreciation of her own treasures. But these horticultural charms could be matched by countless one-acre gardens in English suburbia. The English have been spoiled by their parklands. Gardens abroad need to be fabulous to gain our grudging approbation. We both agreed on this.

Walking back across the rough grassland, behind the villa, James said:

"What d'you make of Georgina Sandford?"

"She's very amusing. Have you known her long?"

"Twenty years."

"That's a long time. She can't be so very old now."

"I knew her father. She's thirty-two."

"Is she now? I'd have put her at twenty-eight."

"I think I would, too, if I didn't know. Odd, isn't it, the way that women who've had the devil to cope with so often look years younger than those who've had it easy?"

"Has she had such a rough time, then?"

" 'Had' and 'has'."

"Tell me more."

"I can tell you about the 'has' part. Might save you from touching on a tender spot by mistake. The rest of the story would take too long. Tell you another time. She's married to a man I was at school with: Hal Sandford. Extraordinary bird. Outsize sadist in my view. She keeps pretty quiet about him. Rum as they come. Does she strike you as a likely crack-up?"

"Good God, no! Highly strung, living on her nerves a bit, but no more so than seventy per cent of women these days. No more than half the occupants of this coach."

"Do your patients have to twang like bloody harps before you think they're half-way round the bend?" James barked.

"She's no patient of mine and not likely to be," I protested.

30

He laughed good-naturedly. "I hope not, for her sake, if that's your usual bedside manner."

"You probably see her less impersonally than I do," I said. "And women have an extraordinary capacity for absorbing men's cruelty. She's an extremely resilient type, I'd say. She might seem the hysterical type, but I'd say she was fairly balanced. Has she any children?"

"Two. Both at boarding school in the best English tradition of fobbing-off responsibility for bringing 'em up ourselves." He spoke almost bitterly, an unusual thing for him to do, and I was intrigued.

"You think she ought to be looking after them?" I asked.

"I don't know. I was hoping you'd have views of your own."

"I've told you my views," I said. "At first sight I'd say Mrs Sandford is a young woman of common sense and a talent for charades or harmless exhibitionism."

"Bah!" James said in exasperation.

"I still think you're doing what too many people are apt to do," I said gently. "Making a case out of two or three known circumstances. If I wished to be harsh I might even say you almost sound as if you want her to be unbalanced. As I've said, she may be highly strung but certainly not dangerously so."

" 'Dangerously' is when they suddenly scream at breakfast, I take it?"

"Or in a coach in Italy."

He laughed and seemed to relax. I wondered why he was taking such a protagonist's interest in Georgina Sandford's state of mind. In any case, I was mildly piqued professionally. If she were as highly strung as James insisted that she was, I felt that I would have noticed and noted. Was he perhaps persuading himself along a line he wished to go? Such self-persuasion wasn't unknown. And if so, why?

"Tell me more about Sandford himself," I said as we walked back towards the house. In the distance I could see Signor Revisi rounding-up his charges.

"Very pleasant, on first acquaintance. A bit of a cold fish, I'd say. Tall. Good-looking in a blond teutonic way. Did quite well in the war, I believe. One of those private bloody armies.

31

Personally, I'm all for having one army in a war, not dozens of odds and sods, long-range bearded groups, short-arsed recce groups and God knows what all."

"How long have they been married?"

"About twelve or thirteen years."

Whilst James had been in Italy, in fact. Was that the rub? I wondered. Was she a schoolgirl he had mentally reserved for himself as his future wife only to find on (or before) his return that she had meantime married? That might have explained much of his detachment as adjutant in Italy.

We returned to the coach, and I waited eagerly for Mrs Sandford to climb in. I remembered her thin white jersey skirt, and I wanted to make sure she wasn't twanging like a bloody harp.

Unfortunately she followed a bulky Italian woman into the coach and sat down at my side as demurely and twangless as a tone-deaf nun.

Had she liked the Villa? I asked.

"I love all houses with gorgeous porticoes. If I were broke I'd buy a small box of a house in the middle of a field and put porticoes on each side. A miniature Mereworth without all that dreadful upkeep. I wonder what the Italian for portico is?"

"Portico," I said.

"How splendid to be so clever at lingos! I never was. My husband is. Put him on a desert island or in the middle of a jungle and in no time he's inviting the chief's daughter in to see his etchings."

Perhaps I should have taken my chance then to ask about Sandford, but I didn't. I wasn't on a busman's holiday, I told myself firmly. Not even for James.

Georgina Sandford prattled on during the next leg of our journey through the flat Veneto landscape towards the distant mountains, and still the young couple in front were avid listeners as were our other nearer neighbours.

Then Revisi suddenly crackled into the gossip of the coach from his microphone: "The Villa Duodo, which we shall reach in about ten minutes, is now no more than a shell of the villa built by Vincenzo Scamozzi"—again the resounding war-cry of a name—"but enough remains for us to see its beauty. You should also make a point of seeing the charming little church of San Giorgio, also by Scamozzi, adjacent to the villa."

Our driver stopped to ask the way of a group outside a café in the small sleepy town of Monselice. After listening intently and nodding a dozen times, he bravely swung the coach from the main street into a narrow alley with a sharp turn up the hill. Like most Italian drivers he seemed to welcome obstacles. We applauded his skill as he put the coach boldly up the narrowing ascent, bringing it to a halt on a broad terrace. We stepped down from the coach to find ourselves dwarfed by two immense columns each surmounted by a large stone lion wearing a cardinal's biretta. Instead of the gay incongruity with which this headgear should have invested the lions, they had instead a chilling authority. Beyond the piers rose the long approach to the Villa Duodo.

The crumbling villa forms two sides of a square with the small family church holding one corner. Decaying statues stand nearby like forlorn yet saintly sentinels. The villa, no more than one room wide, is poised with breathtaking bravado above the great valley, spinning away until lost in the misty horizon.

I made no attempt to explore the villa, but sat on one of the stone steps above the square, taking in the façades of the strangely beautiful group of buildings, drinking in the wondrous sunlight. Around me I could hear lamentations in Italian and English. Slowly I looked around. Behind me Mrs Sandford was making a careful way down the steep grassy path between the statues.

"Can nothing be done to stop the whole place disintegrating?" asked an aggrieved, high-pitched English voice from a group by one of the crumbling statues.

A small, plump Italian began to explain in English that a plan existed to turn the villa into a home for the aged. The Englishman, the thin, stringy-bearded pedant of the previous evening, was deeply shocked. "The aged! It's not possible! Once here they'd never leave the place," he whined.

"Perhaps that's the general idea," James said, joining them. "Don't we all want to get rid of the aged without overworking our conscience?"

33

The Italian shrugged his shoulders non-committally.

"Odd, isn't it?" James said. "Medical science does its best to keep us alive till we're ninety, ten million more mouths to feed are born every year and the food boffins say there won't be enough food to feed us all in sixty years' time."

"But how exciting to starve to death in a place like this!" Mrs Sandford cried gaily, passing the group.

She came to the steps where I was seated and sat down. "The view from the hillside is wonderful! You should go up."

"I may climb many other hills before I die," I said, "but I'm certain I shan't see any other buildings as strange and sad as these, under a sun like this. I'm staying here."

"Splendid!" James said, joining us. "Let us resist Georgina's excessive enthusiasms at all costs. Aestheticism is bad enough. God preserve us from athleticism too!"

"Perhaps you're right, James," she said. "This is bliss enough."

James looked very pleased with himself at that moment, I thought. He had put the Italian and the Englishman to flight and now he had Georgina's agreement.

We sat there silently, looking down on the villa, its stone face pocked and cracked, the slats of the great wooden doors as loose as a windblown barn's.

Revisi's voice called gently from the square. We rose regretfully. I walked with Mrs Sandford and James down the steep path to the coach. We were all quiet. I had missed the church, but not the sun.

12.

WE WERE to lunch in the small town of Rovigo, Revisi explained after we had reassembled. There were two restaurants of repute: *The Corona Ferrea* and *The Granariere*. He wished to make two mixed parties of Italians and English. Would we make a gamble and take our chance?

Thereupon, he came down the aisle of the coach and each of us drew a piece of pasteboard from his Italian straw hat. I drew a G. and regretfully noted that Georgina Sandford had

34

drawn a C.F. card, James, too, had drawn C.F. They were both
delighted, plainly finding strength in unity. My recent love of
solitude, I noticed, was slipping fast. Now my dominant feeling
was petulant regret that I was not to lunch with them.

But at the *Ristorante Granariere*, still following James's
advice, I went straight to the first table in the dining-room. A
young couple, the man about thirty, the woman somewhat
younger, were already there. He was dark. She was pale, her
pallor emphasized by her grey seersucker suit. He introduced
himself and his wife: Paolo and Margaret Brunatelli. She said
"Hello" with the easy freedom of a young American girl
straight off the campus.

Following Mrs Sandford's technique, I began to ask Signor
Brunatelli about himself. He answered in fluent English.
Relieved, I let him continue.

He was, it appeared, Reader in Architecture at the University of Florence. He had finished his studies before the Italians
entered the war—"that dreadful foolish day"—had fought in
North Africa, and, at the war's end, had worked as interpreter
for the American army. Then he had been given a post-
graduate scholarship to Cornell. There he had met his wife
from Hartford, Connecticut—and here they were. All that
experience seemed to add up to more than his apparent years.
He was probably thirty-five, but, unlike most Italians over
thirty, had kept his figure.

What did he think of Palladio? I asked, too innocently as
it turned out.

"The greatest architectural force of the last five hundred
years!" he declaimed boldly, and then, in calculated diffi-
dence, "Would you agree?"

"I am prepared to be convinced. . . ."

He smiled and began, but was immediately interrupted by
the waiter. We ordered our meal: scampi, lasagne Napolitane
and chianti for me, I remember.

Then Brunatelli was back to his subject: "We know that
he was born in my own city of Padua in 1508," he went
on, lecturing proudly. "We know of some of his movements,
some of his patrons, most of his buildings, but of his life
before forty we know too little, and it is what happens before

35

forty that is important to a man's career. Would you agree?"

I agreed wholeheartedly with his theory, but I was beginning to wonder whether my interest in Palladio would outlast the meal.

Fortunately Revisi came to the table and my rescue. He escorted a young woman of about thirty, one of those pale, sad, olive-skinned Italian women from the South, I surmised from past experience. I stood up with Brunatelli.

Revisi obviously knew the Brunatellis pretty well, for he spoke in English: "I bring Signora Colleoni with confidence to your table. She is a Neapolitan alone in a Palladian world."

"She is very welcome," I said.

"Especially if she can talk about anything but Palladio," Margaret Brunatelli added casually and cuttingly. I almost sat down in surprise at her candour.

"That is now for you all to find out," Revisi said pleasantly, smiling his charmer's smile as he turned and went.

"Won't you sit down?" Margaret Brunatelli asked imperturbably. She had an amused glint in her eye.

We were silent as Signora Colleoni composed herself at the table. She wore a black linen suit. Her hair was dark and curled and cut fairly short. I suspected that she was wearing shoes with heels too high for the day's excursion, but I had had no chance to see her shoes or her legs.

Brunatelli, unabashed by his wife's directness, returned to his monologue. "We were talking about my favourite subject —Palladio—signora. Now you have joined us we can talk of other things. Unless—" he pleaded hopefully—"Palladio is your favourite subject too."

"Io conosco poco il Palladio," Signora Colleoni said, recognizing another Italian. "Non è molto conosciuto a Napoli." Then she turned to me and said, smiling gravely, "I have already told myself many times this day that I am here with false pretences," she said, "I know little of Palladio. He is little known in Naples."

She spoke English hesitantly, but, like any pretty foreigner trying to speak a man's own tongue, her helplessness aroused only my masculine protectiveness. And she was far more than pretty, I thought, noting the fine small nose, the full, well-shaped lips and firm, pointed chin. Yet the eyes were perhaps the most memorable feature in the pear-shaped face: watchful, deep-set, dark blue, almost purple in their intensity of colour and shaded by heavy lashes, too thickly loaded with mascara for daylight and for sightseeing.

Those, I remember clearly, were my first impressions of Signora Colleoni. Those—and her neckline. Her suit, although simple and well-cut, plunged far too deeply at the neckline for lunchtime comfort. At least, for my comfort. In the moment of introduction I had noticed the white flesh and the deep shadows that shaped her breasts. Well, it was a pleasant if disturbing irruption into a sightseer's day, I told myself, trying to settle myself once more to scampi and Brunatelli's platform manner.

She aroused my curiosity almost immediately, even as Brunatelli again began to talk, too conscientiously, about Naples. For one thing, she seemed so sharply out of place in this kind of tour. It was easy to imagine her husband as a successful Neapolitan food factor or car distributor. Then, too, there were more disturbing elements in my curiosity. Signora Colleoni used a scent, like her mascara, too heavy for daylight, sunlight and Palladio.

Pleasantly bemused and titillated by this mildly explosive interruption, I let Brunatelli ramble on. He had the accursed academic talent for turning any subject into a lecture, and I was delighted to notice his wife's open yawn at a particularly long-winded reference to Ischia. But he was unstoppable, and in Signora Colleoni and myself he had two docile victims. He used us to the limit of endurance. Long before fruit came to the table he had returned to the subject of Palladio and I was back where I came in. By two-thirty and black coffee I was prepared to persuade myself that, architecturally, I was now one of the best-informed members of the Anglo-Italian Palladian Society. So too was Signora Colleoni—if she had been listening as carefully as her attentive expression had implied.

Punch-drunk from Palladio, I made my excuses and tottered out to search for James and Mrs Sandford.

I was still strangely disturbed, I noticed, wandering back along the main street. My arms and legs were vaguely uncoordinated. And Chianti alone wasn't the sole explanation. The memory of the curve of Signora Colleoni's breasts was too vivid and too recent for composure. Months of celibacy suddenly mocked me with an old crone's cackle.

James and Mrs Sandford were seated under the arcade of the *Corona Ferrea*. I told them something of my instructional luncheon, pointing out Brunatelli and his wife, now walking between the stalls and booths on the other side of the bustling square.

"He may be a bore, but he's quite good looking," Georgina Sandford said. "So is the young American wife. It's not fair. Good-looking men should be divided amongst the ugly girls."

"By divided, do you mean dissected?" I asked.

James guffawed. "And what about good-looking girls?" he asked, recovering. "Divide them up, too?"

"Ugly men are so often rich," she said. "They can buy their pretty girls. Wouldn't you agree, Doctor Frost?"

"Observation seems to bear you out."

"See!" she said to James, "I have medical backing."

"Don't quote me too often," I said absently. Across the square I had noticed Signora Colleoni returning to the coach. As I had suspected, her heels were far too high for cobblestones and ancient steps. Yet I had to admit her legs seemed made for high heels: long, beautifully shaped, exquisitely slim ankles. She walked well, too, like so many Italian women: straight back and assured steps. And without a hint of lordosis, that congenital failing of so many Italian women.

But those spiky heels were out of place, I told myself firmly. And if I am to be resolutely honest with myself, I also felt that they were more than a touch out of place. They were desperately ill-chosen for the occasion. I was mildly irritated by my own priggishness and Signora Colleoni's blindness to her inappropriate clothes and make-up. She should have known better, I told myself. She was plainly intelligent. But did I want a young and beautiful Italian woman to dress like someone following the guns across a Yorkshire moor? I asked myself. Fretfully I gave up.

"And is that your other table companion?" Mrs Sandford asked, following my gaze. I nodded.

"She looks quite a piece," James said with relish.

"And did *you* discuss Palladio?" I asked, changing the subject, unaccountably irritated by the world of meaning in James' words.

"No!" Georgina said. "We discussed sheep."

"You said you were a country girl at heart," James protested.

"I said I grew up in the country, which is very different. Anyway, it was an enthralling conversation, even if a trifle one-sided. I'm overjoyed it's been such a delicious and gorgeous year for sheep."

"Not exactly a country girl's language," James said.

"Your very words!" she cried.

She was so gay that I wondered how much Chianti they had drunk, but, as if to answer my speculation, James said, "We've drunk very little, old boy. A trifle touched by the sun. Come on. I see Revisi counting his sheep."

There was a general movement towards the coach. James hurriedly paid his bill.

13

SIGNOR REVISI took up his amplifier. The two villas we had already seen were post-Palladian, he said. Now we were to see two villas designed by the Master himself: the Villa Badoer at Fratta Polesine and the Villa Poiana at Poiana Maggiore. With good fortune we should be able to see them and return to Padua before seven o'clock.

This we did, thanks to his own efficiency and to swift, certain driving by our chauffeur.

The Villa Badoer is one of the prettiest small houses in the world, despite its setting in a small garden opposite a row of village shops.

A young woman showed us over the villa, now decaying. Only a millionaire or the Government could take on the task of restoration, she said sadly. She could do next to nothing. She did her best, but always things were too much for her.

We walked round the cramped grounds, photographed the

39

house, its pretty iron staircase, the pillared loggia. Then I was done and wandered slowly back to the coach. Georgina Sandford was already there.

"Too tiring?" I asked.

"No, too saddening. I hate to see beautiful houses in decay."

Others came drifting back. We climbed in, busily shepherded by the indefatigable Revisi. I was already weary. The busy morning, the continuing sun, the movement of the coach, the Chianti . . . all these were piling up on me, but Mrs Sandford was just beginning. As the coach started, she said in her shrill, eager voice, "Your work must be enthralling, Doctor Frost."

"Sometimes," I said, hoping that the conventional opening might hide a cursory interest and that I should soon be left to sleep. I should have known better.

"When is 'sometimes'?"

"When I help someone, I suppose."

The young couple in the seat before us were quiet, their heads suspiciously flat against the leather headrests of the seats. Mrs Sandford had already enlivened their trip once before that day. Now they were ready for more. And at my expense, I thought sourly.

"And how often is that?"

"Not as often as I'd wish."

"Three a week?"

I laughed. "It's not as cut and dried as all that."

"But they tell you their troubles. Can't you say 'Do this!' or 'Don't do that!' 'Stop making love to your sister' or 'Start hitting your mother'."

"Any other suggested treatments?" I asked, now wide-awake.

"Touché," she said with a smile, resting her hand gently on my arm. "But didn't I read somewhere that there are only seven jokes in the world? And only seven plots for a novel? Are there more than seven cures for misfits?"

"It's the thousands of sub-plots in novels and life that make for trouble—and interest," I said. "But I'd love to have your other five treatments. You've only suggested two."

She slowly ticked them off: "Take a cold bath. Take a

mistress. Take a holiday. Take the money in the till. There's four." She began to giggle, and then added in spluttering triumph: "And take Doctor Frost's advice. There you are. The seven basic treatments for mental disorders."

I could see the top of the young man's head in front: he was as immobile as a statue. Far too immobile for dozing. That was certain. James leaned across the gangway. "I can't help hearing your genius for over-simplification at work again, Georgina."

"Well, if I ever have to go to a psychiatrist I shall want some quick action," she said defiantly. "I shall keep the taxi ticking down in Harley Street while I dash in for a quick cure."

"Wimpole Street, in Rupert's case."

"Oh, I don't think I'd go to Doctor Frost."

"Why not?" James said, already forgetful of his serious intent and of his shocked companion. Already he was doubtless scenting the kind of entertainment he relished, the *enfant terrible* of wartime quickly reasserting itself.

"He looks too kind."

"Oh, I wouldn't say that," he said magisterially. "He gets a nasty glint in his blue eyes sometimes."

"All the same, I think he looks very kind," she persisted. "And by the end of this trip he'll probably know too much about me—thanks to you. No, I should want the ruthless James Mason kind of psychiatrist." She turned to me: "D'you know any like that?"

"No, alas. But I doubt whether they'd be members of the British Medical Association." She smiled. "Anyway, I don't suppose that kind of man would be much good for what I'd want," she said, mock-sadly.

"How d'you know what you'd want until he told you?" James asked.

"I have intuition."

"Bah!" said James. "Let me get back to sleep."

She settled back in her seat, laughing.

"Perhaps I will come to you then, Doctor Frost, if you'll have me and if things get really out of hand. How much do you charge?"

I laughed. This was a new kind of badinage for me, but she

41

had an encompassing gaiety. Even the young woman by James's side was more interested than she would ever have admitted, and the grey-haired young man was glancing back over the top of the seat as if he would have liked to join in the discussion.

"Usual specialist rates in my consulting rooms. Nothing if your doctor sends you to see me at St Thomas's Out-Patients' Department. Tuesdays and Fridays. Two till six."

"I'll come privately," she said, still laughing.

"Why wait?" James said. "Can't we all join in? It's been public enough so far."

The practice and science of psychiatry looked like taking quite a beating, I thought, and tried to sidetrack the conversation by asking whether she liked James Mason as a film star. It was a false move.

"I've only seen him in *The Seven Veils*. That's what gave me the idea of having a deliciously ruthless psychiatrist all to myself." Her voice was still audible to those in adjacent seats: "But I don't really think I need that kind of treatment, do you, James?"

Again this seismographic jumping between gaiety and seriousness.

"I didn't see the film," he said, shortly, almost brusquely.

She turned to me.

"No. Kindness is what I want."

"It's what we all want," I said. I was getting mildly out of my depth. Almost every answer I gave made me appear more of a medical clown. And if I refused to answer I should merely look a boor. Anyway, I was on holiday and slipping deeper and deeper into the holiday mood minute by minute. So what the hell!

"But there's so little kindness around!" she said plaintively, but still near to laughter.

"Nonsense," James said, good humour back again. "It's just sheer kindness on my part that I haven't strangled you for keeping me awake this afternoon."

She laughed and I relaxed. Within a minute they were discussing whether sheep were kind to each other. Within another minute I was dozing. As I nodded, I wondered why James had grown so harsh a minute before. But sleep overtook my speculations, and I slept until we reached the walled city of Montagnana.

As we stood up to make our way out of the coach, the youngish grey-haired man in the seat ahead also stood waiting. He nodded. I thought how tense he seemed to be, for I could not help but notice the way his teeth kept biting at his lower lip and the fierceness of his grip on the leather neck rest of the high seat. Within a short time I had cause to remember these superficial observations.

I had tea with James and Georgina Sandford in a café overlooking the piazza within the city. By that time we were all feeling the efforts of the day and our conversation was less touched by badinage. James and Mrs Sandford talked of Atherston, and, although I was interested, I had little to contribute. They seemed to have known each other all their lives. I liked listening to her strange and brittle voice, which seemed to suit my recuperating mood, but weariness continued to dominate my fitfully wakeful life.

I have but hazy memories of the rest of that day's sightseeing. I remember the sad state of the Villa Poiana and the astonished glances of a crowd of Italian peasants who lived and stored their tobacco crop in the villa and obviously could not understand why a group of well-dressed sightseers should clamber down from a coach in order to inspect their tumbledown home.

But the architects in the Society were fascinated by this early Palladian building and were anxious to make their drawings and take their photographs in the fast-fading light of the day.

Then back to the coach and back to Padua. I had a hot bath, dined in my new room—and then slept.

14

THE next entry in my ill-kept diary is shorter:

SUNDAY. New room in the Jolanda. V. quiet. Slept well. Early start. 0850 dep. Padua. Gloomy coach drive to Venice via Stra

& Mira. Motoscaffi via the Grand Canal. Il Redentore & San Giorgio Maggiore. Back to the Schiavoni. Mrs S. and J. most of the morning. Lunch Signóra C.

Brief as they are, the words are vividly alive for me. For one thing I was beginning to enjoy myself. All trepidation had vanished.

Long hours of sleep were beginning to have their healing influence. I was less tetchy. I was finding pleasure in hearing once again the novel sound of my own laughter.

My work has inevitably inclined me towards analysing myself as well as others. As I shaved that Sunday morning, I remember that I tried to trace the stages in my escape from melancholy. Sleep, I said airily, but I went steadily on. Soon I began to realize how much I owed to Georgina Sandford's gaiety and chatter. Something else flickered in my mind like a tiny flag.

I smiled as I realized that the deep V-cut of Signora Colleoni's suit had made its curative contribution, too. I had become as ascetic as the safety razor I held, I told myself as I stilled the flutterings of the flag. She made me aware once more of the blood within my veins. I looked forward to the day in Venice. How much I owed to James!

Meanwhile, I wondered fleetingly whether his interest in Georgina Sandford was quite as detached and avuncular as he had wished me to believe. Well, that was his affair. The days would show. To my professional eyes she looked sane enough. If only the rest of humanity had the same kind of slightly zany sanity, I thought. I repeated the phrase to myself as I shaved. I would bring it out casually in one of my lectures to the fourth-year students at St Thomas's. "Zany sanity." It had just the right touch of worldly levity for would-be internes.

A man can be too jaunty! I reached the coach to discover that the time was after half-past eight, that Georgina Sandford and James were sitting together up front and that I would have to share a seat half-way down the coach with Miss Desmond, James' partner of the previous day. I gloomily made my way along the aisle of the coach, past legs and baskets.

Then I noticed a spare seat by Signora Colleoni in the rear bench seat. But I was barred from her by the penultimate row

44

of seats, also bench type and the full width of the coach. To reach Signora Colleoni I should have to retrace my steps, climb out of the coach and enter by the side door at the rear of the coach. And all under the eyes of the staring Palladians.

Signora Colleoni seemed to be considering the whole scene as gravely and attentively as she had considered Brunatelli the day before. I looked up and caught her gently smiling eyes. Was she aware of my dilemma? I wondered as I half-turned, tripped over a plump female leg and received a voluble Italian apology. My nerve failed. Muttering an apology I went one step, turned and sat down by the side of Miss Desmond, hating her. And I was *not* the last-comer, it seemed. A tweedy English-woman of about forty now arrived in a panic and bustled into the rear of the coach, next to Signora Colleoni. Signor Revisi mopped his brow and we were off.

By that time my light-hearted mood of the early morning had gone. I felt as possessive about Georgina Sandford and Signora Colleoni as a querulous caliph. And here I was, parked with Miss Desmond, who began immediately to talk about Palladio.

God knows, Miss Desmond was harmless enough. She was just another of those Englishwomen who seemed destined to spinsterhood as if by some diabolic decree. She was almost handsome in a blue-eyed, fresh-complexioned way, but her face was a shade too long and her chin too forceful for young womanhood. Men are uncommonly wary of female jawbones, and Miss Desmond, alas, lived down to one's worst fore-bodings. Her views on any topic were expressed with the blunt-ness of a company sergeant-major.

She passed from architecture to medicine. She had a younger brother at Guy's who was proposing to specialize in gynaecol-ogy. She'd once thought of the profession herself, she said. Mine was the line she would have chosen. I groaned inwardly and yearned for escape. Would a swift vault over the inter-vening members of the Anglo-Palladian Society into the rear coach seat seem the act of a madman? I caught the appreciative eyes of the young grey-haired man. He was now in the adjacent seat on the opposite side of the gangway, still with his young woman of yesterday. She looked very pretty, I thought. Red-gold hair, retroussé nose and a brilliant jade green sweater and skirt. Very pretty indeed. How I was beginning to notice pretty women once again! Miss Desmond paused for breath. The young man said, "Rather a good idea, this Venetian trip, don't you think? I'm all for a little water after yesterday's dust."

With overwhelming gratitude for his well-timed intervention, I agreed wholeheartedly. He had a quiet, confiding voice, as if he weren't quite certain that anyone would agree with his views and might need persuasion, a frequent mannerism of dons and the higher ranks of the Civil Service, I have often noticed. He also bit into his lower lip after he had spoken. I tried to put him at his ease. He had been kind enough to rescue me from outrageous persecution. I could at least try to calm his nervousness.

"How do we travel when we get there?" I asked. "Motoscaffi? Vaporetti or what? They can't fit us all into one vast gondola, can they?"

He smiled.

"I rather gather Revisi's laid on a couple of motoscaffi."

Had he been to Venice before? I asked.

"I was here in nineteen-thirty. I was only eight or nine at the time, so don't remember much about it. And you?"

"In the war. Or, rather, just after the war."

Had he made his remark about his age to emphasize that his hair was prematurely grey? I wondered. That made him about thirty-three or four. Well, he looked about that, so why worry?

His companion, the pretty red-headed girl, leaned forward.

"He remembers the pigeons," she said, and then: "In St Mark's Square."

"So will you," I said.

She was remarkably pretty. And very young. Not more than nineteen or twenty, I judged.

The young man laughed, mildly self-consciously. "And that's about all. Apart from the gondolas and the gondoliers' straw hats and red hat-bands."

"Does one remember buildings from that age, I often wonder?" Miss Desmond said, leaning across, butting in.

"I've remembered our farm buildings since I was a tiny tot," the red-headed girl said, with a young girl's blushing over-eager manner. "I can even remember lying in my pram looking at the barn rafters."

"I mean *important* buildings," Miss Desmond said.

Miss Desmond, I thought, you will die a spinster. You will die no woman's friend. Nothing on this earth can save you.

"Our farm buildings *are* important," the girl said, pouting. "At least, I thought so—and still do."

"Of course they were, Elizabeth," the young man said, but she was already sitting well back in her seat against the window, affronted, hurt and out of things, temporarily at least. Her escort, disconcerted, surreptitiously groped for her hand. Miss Desmond, poor thing, hadn't meant anything tart. She just hadn't thought. She never had thought. And always, five seconds later, she would regret her dashed-off comments. Now she, too, abashed, looked from the window at the flat, canal-cut landscape. That left the young man and myself.

"My name's Greenaway," he said gamely, coming back into the picture.

I gave my own.

"I couldn't help overhearing yesterday that you're a medico."

"Of a kind. And you?"

"A scientist. Also of a kind. More truthfully I suppose I'm a Civil Servant."

Again that confessional touch as if he had to make everything clear straightaway.

"Interesting work?"

"I find it so." He reflected. Then: "Yes. Very."

"Is this trip hobby or holiday?" I asked.

"A bit of both," he said, somewhat ruefully I thought. "At the moment I'm rather overcome by all the architectural expertise we've got with us."

I agreed.

"Yet I've enjoyed it enormously so far. I was a bit alarmed when I booked."

"I was booked in, so I take no responsibility for anything," I said. "I'm letting it all flow over me."

"A sensible course," he said feelingly.

We were beyond Mestre. Far off, the squalid approaches to

47

Venice began to show across the flat landscape; oil storage tanks, gantries, dumps of every kind. Then we were on the causeway, the Ponte della Liberta, alongside the railroad. Excitement ran through the bus like a zephyr breeze. James turned and, by sign language, linked me with himself and Mrs Sandford for the sightseeing ahead. I nodded vigorously, and turned again to Greenaway, who was asking me whether I knew Florence and Rome. We talked travel until journey's end.

We left the coach in the Piazzale Roma and wandered off after Signor Revisi.

Miss Desmond had joined a vociferous plump Italian. Greenaway was holding the arm of his young red-headed beauty, who didn't seem as co-operative as a sensitive girl should have been. I wondered whether she was still sulking. James was waiting, his arm through Georgina Sandford's. The world seemed full of couples.

"How do you find Miss Desmond?" James asked.

"Didactic."

"Any chance of a cure?"

"Marriage to a dominant male might help."

"Better give her to my husband for a week," Georgina Sandford said.

"Don't!" James commanded, gripping her arm. She winced, and laughed as I pointed out that a week wasn't marriage.

"It is sometimes," she said, serious for once. "At least it's all you get sometimes. And all you want."

"Nonsense!" James said, stepping away sharply. "Where are these motoscaffi Revisi was nattering about?" He turned and walked off. Georgina caught up with him, put her arm through his and beckoned me with the other. Then she took my arm. I was touched. "No more 'Mrs Sandford'," she said. "My name's Georgina. I shall call you Rupert. All this stuffy 'Doctor-Mrs' stuff drives me mad."

"Me, too," said James. "I nearly called him 'Doctor' meself just now. Good, there's Revisi. Rounding-up as usual. I think he'd make quite a decent shepherd."

Georgina laughed. "You're as English as an old dew-lappy sheepdog yourself, James."

He smiled. The momentary cloud had gone, but I was left wondering. I had never seen James so close to losing his normal equanimity.

Revisi was standing on the quayside, arranging, declaiming. We clambered into the first launch. As soon as Revisi had numbered twenty or so we were waved away. I looked astern to see Signora Colleoni with a group of Italians, patiently awaiting embarkation in the second launch. She was wearing a dark grey suit and yellow shirt with a full byronic collar. A white raincoat rested between her folded arms. Her heels were still too high, yet she looked serene and statuesque, strangely remote from her companions. Then we were caught into the breathtaking enchantment of the Grand Canal and Signora Colleoni was lost to sight. But not for long. I was beginning to look out for her.

After the second launch had also disembarked at the Il Redentore quay I saw her again. Revisi had begun to lecture, easily and informatively. Standing on the broad stairway of the approach, he pleaded with us to take note of the double pediment of the façade and especially the pedimented doorway. Within, we were to be sure to see the Ascension by Tintoretto. I glanced around at the strange assembly we made there on the wide step. Signora Colleoni was still gravely attentive.

Few of the others gave any outward signs of their cultural quest. I had half-expected to find my companions a more distinguished company than an average group of sightseers at York Minster or Cheddar Gorge. Not a bit of it. The men, English and Italian, had the same double chins, the same paunches; the women the same thick ankles and shuffling walks. With exceptions of course. James, Georgina, Greenaway, his redhead, one or two of the young men, a few of the Italians. Perhaps, after all, it wasn't a bad ratio of international distinction.

A side glance showed me that Signora Colleoni was still alone. I followed her into the church as we broke up after Revisi's little lecture. She walked magnificently, her hands folded before her, holding the white raincoat. But surely those heels were still too high for sightseeing, I told myself, but my conviction was weakening. Her legs were too beautiful for

49

any kind of criticism, and I was glad to find how accurate had been my distant appraisal from across the square at Rovigo. They were more beautiful than I had thought. I was strangely delighted by this reassurance. I had half thought that a woman so rounded must inevitably have too-rounded legs, but she was tall for an Italian woman, probably five foot six or seven. I was curious to know more about her.

After Il Redentore, we crossed to the church of San Giorgio Maggiore, and slowly drifted through the interior in a daze of subdued pleasure. Revisi had carefully planned our visits so that although we missed any formal service, yet each church held something of the aura of devotion. Revisi had made certain that we should not waste time inspecting dead architecture. Yet, is there any dead architecture in Venice, as there is in, say, Berlin or even Paris?

As we returned to the launch an hour later, Georgina said, "I don't think I've ever spent a more heavenly morning."

James agreed. He was quieter than before. As they stood in the stern of the launch he held her arm, closely, almost protectively. Unlike Greenaway's companion, Georgina showed every sign of welcoming the gesture.

We crossed to the Schiavoni quay and disembarked at the private jetty of the Danieli.

"I thought we'd lunch here," James said, as we stepped ashore on to the red carpet, helped by the liveried hotel footman. "What d'you say, Rupert?"

"I'd like to explore."

"Oh, but you must lunch with us!" Georgina cried. "I'll just powder my nose. You both wait here."

"We've got noses to powder, too," James said.

"Meet you in the bar."

Washing, James said, "If you feel like exploring, I should, old boy. Pity not to. I'll make your peace with Georgina."

"One drink and I shall."

I had my drink and, resisting Georgina's blandishments, went out into the sunlight. After the collective morning I wanted a solitary interlude. We were to meet outside the Danieli at four o'clock for a visit to the church of San Francesco della Vigna before returning to the coach. But the afternoon's arrangements were flexible. Anyone could drop out. I had heard several of the members planning excursions to the Lido. Too crowded by far on a Sunday, James avowed. Others were planning to visit the Museo Correr. "That shuts on Sunday afternoons," James said with seeming authority. I would drift, were my last words to James and Georgina. I might see them on the launch. Otherwise I would return to Padua by train that evening and meet them at the Piazza Cavour the following morning. "Next to Miss Desmond, of course!" Georgina had gaily called.

I went out from the Danieli to the Schiavoni quay and began to walk slowly towards St Mark's, and its milling Sunday crowds.

I was lost in wonder as I walked. The blue and healing sky, the wide sweep of the quays, then the piazzetta with thousands of sightseers and millions of pot-bellied, arrogant pigeons. Hackneyed, undoubtedly, but just what the doctor ordered. Doctor James for Doctor Frost, in fact.

I crossed to the corner café overlooking the Molo. Here I should have all the views: quayside, piazza, palazzo, Cathedral, boats and crowds. Like a longtime dweller in a dark tenement, I wanted, with unholy greed, to seize all the colour and movement in this revel of the world.

I sat down at a canopied table and stretched my legs. Palladio could be an exhausting Master. A waiter unwillingly detached himself from an argumentative trio and came across. I ordered a mushroom omelette, green salad and a small bottle of Chianti. More gondolas and launches arrived at the adjacent steps, disembarking Americans, Scandinavians, Germans, French and English. There they stood, feeding the overfed pigeons whilst their bounty was photographed for the family album and the folks back home.

In a rush of rare pleasure in the present, I looked around, gulping in all that I had so nearly missed. Perhaps I took in a deep breath of air from the near lagoon. Perhaps I smiled. Whatever the reason, my open mouth came to with a lockjaw click as I stared straight into the calm and smiling eyes of Signora Colleoni, seated two tables away.

Whether my earlier frustrations on the coach journey gave

51

me a split-second of unaccustomed resolution, or whether I was at pains to disprove any suspicion that I habitually viewed my surroundings open-mouthed, I found myself suddenly rising from my chair and moving between the busy tables to her side. Nothing is more calculated to give a man resolution than the need to restore his *amour propre*. Would she lunch with me? I asked decisively. It would be an honour and a pleasure for me.

"But I do not talk of Palladio," she said, smiling, neither accepting nor declining my invitation.

"There are other subjects, especially in Italy," I said. Could I hold to my resolve or would I falter and fade out under those serene and smiling eyes?

"These two days I sometimes do not think so," she said, still smiling, and then, "It is kind of you to ask me. Will you come to my table? I think we have the same waiter."

I went back and took up my hat and returned to her side.

"You eat very little," she said. "I hear your order."

"Will you have a bigger meal, then?"

"So much bigger. I have ordered scampi, risotto, fruit and wine. I am Italian, you know."

"I will eat slowly."

"I, too, eat slowly. You will have to talk to me."

"Tell me three subjects that interest you."

She reflected for a moment and then said slowly, watching me: "Vestiti, vacanze, films, parties."

"No serious things?" I asked.

I was slightly shaken by her honesty.

"I think all these things are serious things."

I laughed. "All right then. What are your really serious subjects?"

She thought for a moment and said slowly, "Money, comfort, children. I think those are my most serious subjects."

She was certainly honest, disconcertingly so.

I noticed a wedding ring and two rather flamboyant diamond rings on her long, fine hands. The waiter returned with croissants and butter. I also ordered scampi for myself and a larger carafe of Chianti.

We began to talk about the previous day's excursions and

the villas we had seen. Then she said, "Is this a holiday for you?"

"A kind of holiday. My wife died six months ago and a friend thought this would be a rest cure."

"I am sorry to hear that. And is it a rest cure?"

"The best I could have wished for. And is it a holiday for you?"

She thought for a moment before answering.

"For me, too, it is a kind of rest cure," she said, and then, after a long moment, added, "I am apart from my husband. What you call 'separated', is it not so?"

I nodded, and asked where she had learned to speak English so well.

"Not well, but enough. I learn in Rome. I was a secretary soon after the war, and the best money was for those who knew English."

"Did you work with the English?"

"No, the Americans."

The waiter came with scampi and the Chianti.

"And you married an American?" I hazarded.

She smiled and slowly shook her head. "No. Like all good Italian girls I marry a Roman. And now I live in Naples."

She vouchsafed no more, as if this were the full story of her life.

We ate in silence for a while. Then, with a sigh as if the heat oppressed her, she stood up and took off her thin jacket. Within the confines of her yellow linen shirt her breasts were as brazenly outlined as a cover girl's. She sat down again, at ease, but I was as disturbed and excited as a teen-age wolf. I imagined she knew enough about men to know something of the excitement she had provoked, yet her eyes were as serene as before, wholly bereft of obvious provocation, I would have said.

"How did you come to venture on this trip?" I asked, trying to regain my tottering composure.

"A friend told me about it. She thought I should come. She knows that I needed the rest cure I speak to you about. And she thinks I am less than half-educated—like most Italian women. She says it will be good for my mind."

"But why?" I asked, as amused by her candour as I was disturbed by her body.

"Because, she says we Italians live too much in the present and ignore our past."

"But the past of Italy goes a long way back beyond Palladio."

"My friend says a beginner must start somewhere," she said, simply. "And that to study Palladio will mean to start in the middle, which is a good point to start at."

As she smiled, she took one of the scampi between her white teeth. Poor Scampi! You didn't stand a chance, I thought. And would a man stand a better chance?

"And are you enjoying what you see?" I asked.

"Not a whale of a lot," she said.

The phrase was so bizarre coming from her lips that I laughed aloud as I asked, "Why not?"

"I do not understand enough about the beginnings of architecture," she said. "It is like starting to learn to play the piano by playing Rossini. I have missed the early things, the five-finger exercises. I was too busy fighting to stay alive."

"But none of us is an expert."

"There is always Signor Brunatelli!" she said, and laughed aloud, her head back, her throat long and white.

I laughed too. I had forgotten him. He seemed years ago.

"Perhaps he could give us a lesson on Palladian first principles every morning between eight and nine," I said.

"Not for me. I am lazy—sono pigrissima—and always in haste in the mornings. I get to the coach only just in time."

"Me, too, especially this morning. It was too early."

"But are you not an expert?" she asked, suddenly serious.

"Good heavens, no."

"But you looked very wise yesterday."

"Looking wise is part of a doctor's equipment."

"Ah, that is what you are. Of course. A medical doctor?"

I nodded and said, "Why 'of course'?"

"Yes," she said reflectively, half-smiling again, resting her head on her upturned palm, considering me. "Yes. I see that that is right."

I laughed. Signora Colleoni was an enlivening but oddly

54

disconcerting companion. A fish probably has much the same reaction, when played by a civilized sportsman, as I had then: I was baffled, intrigued and determined to go on. And I was mildly disconcerted by my own faulty appraisal of her character and personality. Her silence and apparent gravity on the previous day had suggested that she might well be a serious-minded young woman, despite her high heels and fine but too-obvious clothes. Her interests might not be exclusively concerned with the arts, but she would talk seriously about Italy and the Italians or about clothes and food. A gift for silence often creates this false impression. Now I could see that Signora Colleoni was far from serious-minded. In fact, she seemed to be unrepentantly frivolous.

She dabbed her mouth with the napkin and took a mirror from her handbag. The outline of her lips was unimpaired, but she retouched them from a bright red lipstick, and then powdered her small disdainful nose. She carefully replaced her handbag on the nearby chair and smiled into my face, suddenly and openly, placing her hands, one upon the other, on the table-cloth, seeming to hold herself for my inspection. You have been aware too long of your effect on men, I thought, trying to return her smile. Or was it that I was inexperienced with women who had spent their lives in the study of men or even, perhaps, in just liking men?

"Have you any children?" she asked.

"Two daughters: twelve and fourteen."

"Sad ages for daughters," she said. "From the age of ten girls must work for the rest of their lives."

"Men, too," I said.

"Not in the same way," she said. "Many men like their work. Few women ever do."

"Perhaps they should all find rich husbands," I said.

"That is not the answer," she said quietly and, it seemed, from first-hand experience.

"Have you any children?"

"None."

The waiter came with the risotto and omelette.

"Can you talk of your wife?" she asked quietly. She seemed to have the gift of sympathy.

55

"I think so." I hoped it was true. I had scarcely spoken of Helen in six months.

"Did you, do you love her?"

"Yes."

"And she loved you, of course?"

"I think she did."

"Was she beautiful?"

"Handsome," I said. "A good head. Fine eyes, grey and large."

"Was she fair or dark?"

"Fair."

"And slim, of course."

I nodded. "But why 'of course'?"

"Because Englishmen like slim women."

I smiled and shook my head. "Not all Englishmen. All Englishwomen want to be slim, but that is a different matter."

"All American women, too," she said. "It is strange, is it not, this wish to deny one's shape?" Then she asked hesitantly, "Was it an accident?"

"No, a little-known heart disease."

"And her name?"

"Helen."

"And your own? All I know from Signor Revisi is that you are Doctor Frost."

"Rupert. And yours?"

"Bianca Maria Cordelia Colleoni," she said, playing the vowels from her tongue like a song.

"And your friends call you . . . ?"

"Bianca, Rupert."

I laughed. She was always a move ahead.

She put on a pair of dark glasses against the sunlight.

"A pity to hide your eyes," I said.

"That is a bold thing for an Englishman to say," she said mockingly.

"The English have only become tongue-tied in the last two hundred years. Before that we were a bold race. In the boudoir as well as on the battlefield. Then the first kind of boldness disappeared. Nobody seems to know when."

"And you are an old-fashioned man?" she queried, her eyes alive with gaiety and mockery.

"I sometimes think so," I said, "but not, alas, in the way I have just been explaining."

"Yet there is an old-fashioned appearance about you," she said seriously. "You are like an Englishman in one of those old-fashioned prints I have seen in tailor's shops in the Via Condotti in Rome. What is it about you? Not just because you are tall."

"My face?"

"Perhaps," she said, her head on one side. "Your long and sad face. Your stern look—just like an English Victorian papa in an Italian novel. Even that funny cap you wore in the motoscaffio."

I laughed and said, half-questioning, "And you are as modern as the day itself?"

"No. I may look like that, but all women are old-fashioned. No woman invents anything to make things go more quickly. Not even in the kitchen. Men do all these things. Only men and children are modern." Her fluency in English was swiftly returning.

I thought on her remark as the waiter took our plates and reappeared with a basket of fresh fruit. Just when she seemed at her most frivolous she would say something half-serious; always a disconcerting trick. I cut into my apple slowly. Already I was finding Bianca Maria Cordelia Colleoni the most unexpected measure in my unexpected cure.

"Will you go to San Francesco della Vigna this afternoon?" she asked, cutting into a large pear.

"I would rather explore Venice with you," I said, the rewards of my earlier boldness now being so apparent.

"And I with you," she said easily, not looking up.

We slowly ate the fruit and then drank coffee.

For me the crowds around us had receded as the crowds doubtless recede for the players in great amphitheatres. Now only Signora Colleoni, the sun and the sea remained. And I had the intoxicating sensation of being, once again after many months, alive and almost well.

Bianca made a further re-examination of her scarlet lips,

57

again perfecting their perfect outline. I paid the waiter and we stood up to go. She placed her jacket and raincoat over one arm, and slipped the other arm through my own. I was delighted and excited by the spontaneity of her gesture. I had never known this swiftness and apparent naturalness in intimacy. Despite the long years of my professional experience and my so-called maturity, I was beginning to realize that I was virtually a juvenile in this strange new game in which I now seemed to be so willingly involved. To my surprise her first words as we walked were, "I think you are funny, Rupert."

"But why?"

"Because you are so serious."

"Not always."

"No, not always, I think."

"Don't you yearn to speak Italian?" I asked, changing the subject.

"I can talk Italian with my compatriots on the coach," she said. "Sa parlare italiano?"

"Pochissimo," I said truthfully.

She laughed and said slowly: "Vorrei fermarmi con te a Venezia per l'ora del tè, e se vorremo anche per la cena."

Well, that was a plan that also suited me. Tea in Venice, then by gondola to a restaurant for a late dinner and the train back to Padua. And I was delighted by her phrase "se vorremo anche"—if we liked each other—and determined that for my part we should like each other. I savoured the phrase again: "se vorremo anche" and smiled. She, seeing my reaction, also laughed.

We walked slowly across the Piazza towards that narrow opening beneath the clock tower leading into the narrow Merceria, surely the most enchanting shopping street in the world, but closed, alas, on Sundays.

15

BY THE end of that day I knew that Bianca was already, for me, the most enchanting and captivating creature in the world.

In these thoughts I found no disloyalty to Helen. She had been the only creature in the world. She had been the only woman in my life I had ever truly loved. We had grown up together. I had often thought, and we had often said, that we seemed as close and well-suited to each other as any two people are ever likely to be in this world of endless solitude and loneliness. Physically, mentally, even spiritually perhaps (though I have never felt the need for so-called spiritual experience) we were attuned, one to the other, and because we both realized that such a relationship is, alas, too rare, we had tried to cherish and renew its vitality day by day, keeping watch over incipient complacency, that most lethal disease in marriage. To explain all this fully would tot up to many chapters in another kind of record, out of place here. Dearest Helen was dead. Our lives were over. I have no belief that I shall ever see her in some shadowy paradise beyond the grave.

There, in Venice, as I walked with Bianca and inevitably mused on these things, I knew that Helen would have wished me to snap out of self-pity and despair, and, I also suspected, she would have smiled had she been able to see Bianca, the first woman I had fallen for in her own eternal absence.

I have also thought a great deal about these things since that time; during these recent months. Perhaps I am not honest when I say I had no sense of disloyalty to Helen. I had thought of her ceaselessly since her death and, in the way of those who have recently lost someone unusually near and dear, I had found that I sometimes spoke aloud to her, almost jokingly, putting a proposal to her memory or asking advice of the image I carried in my memory. There was nothing disquieting in this: such behaviour in such circumstances is universal, I think, part of the process of rebuilding the life of the one who lives on. There is nothing dangerous or unhealthy in the habit; rather the reverse, if, gradually, the one who lives is thus revived.

I now see that in the first strange hours of my relationship with Bianca I was mildly shamefaced, so to speak, towards the memory of Helen. All widows and widowers with felicitous memories undoubtedly share this sense of guilt. Yet I had never been so explanatory towards myself, or to the image of the living Helen, after spending an hour or a night with a

59

woman in the Middle East or Italy during the war. But that was easy to understand. I had needed the physical release. Years afterwards, Helen had been amused and interested, wanting to know something of these loveless interludes and partners. There in Venice, after months of desolation, I suspected that I needed more than a loveless interlude or partner and, as the magical afternoon and evening progressed, as we walked about Venice, or sat overlooking the great piazza from a small alcove in Florian's, I sensed that I was walking open-eyed into an experience as serious as any in my life, notwithstanding its beginnings in raillery and laughter.

The afternoon merged into dusk, and as we walked and ate, and laughed and talked, this knowledge gradually possessed me. By midnight, when I left Bianca at her hotel after travelling back by one of the late trains from Venice, I knew that I was bemused and captivated by her beauty and her ways. And as she raised her lips, still brilliantly red and quite unimpaired after the long day, I thought, perhaps, that the relationship was not, after all, to be as one-sided as all would-be lovers dread.

I kissed her and spoke already as a lover. How clearly I remember my insistent command, "Let us be early in the coach so that we can be together. It is crazy to be with others. Together we might even master the secrets of Palladio."

Bianca's laughter rang out gaily in the Paduan night.

And then, as I turned to go, she called my name. I went back and she raised her lips to be kissed again, and, as I did, she placed my hand against the full curve of her breast. Then she was gone, within the swing doors of the hotel. And I was walking along the Via d'Italia as giddy as a youth in the first madness of the blood.

16

I SUPPOSE the time was about a quarter after midnight when I got back to the Hotel Jolanda.

I took my key from the night porter and turned towards the lift. The attendant swung back the gate. A voice said "Hello, Doctor Frost!" and Greenaway stood up from one of the nearer armchairs in the foyer which opened out from the hall. He came across. Dearly as I wished to be alone, I greeted him sociably, for he looked rather tired and drawn.

"What about a nightcap?" he jerked out tentatively, and again I saw the tooth bite into the lower lip. He seemed over-nervous for someone so set upon conviviality.

My first instinct was to say I'd had quite a day, and I have often wondered since how events might have been changed had I followed my instinct. But something about his tentative man-ner, his acute nervousness and his obvious belief that I would turn him down, persuaded me to agree, despite my long and intoxicating day. Perhaps, too, something in my Scottish ancestry prompted me to more mundane human contact after those magical preceding hours.

He was pathetically delighted by my acceptance, and I went back with him into the hotel lounge, where an unfinished drink stood on one of the many low tables. He called the night porter and asked what I'd have. I said whisky. He asked for two. "And soda," I said. "Lots."

"Have a good day?" he asked. "You turned in culture after lunch, I gather. I looked for you, but you'd vanished."

I nodded and asked about San Francesco della Vigna.

"Not bad," he said, "but not one of the Master's best. And a bit tucked away. I don't like hiding good things under bushels. What did you do?"

"Explored Venice."

"You were right. I should have done the same."

"And how did your companion—Miss . . ."

"Castle. Elizabeth Castle."

"How did she like the church?"

"Not at all."

The night porter brought our drinks. I made mine long. Greenaway kept his almost neat. He hadn't yet finished his earlier drink and kept the glass. We were silent until the porter left us. Then Greenaway said, "I was rather interested by something you said yesterday which I couldn't help over-hearing."

"Prompted by Mrs Sandford, I'm afraid I said lots of things, mostly in self-defence."

He smiled. "You said there wasn't enough kindness in the world."

I nodded.

"I understand you're a well-known psychiatrist?"

"Scarcely well-known. At least, not in the Gilbert Harding sense."

"Eminent, then."

I shrugged the cliché away.

"I wondered what you meant by kindness," he went on.

I had thought too often on the subject to hesitate.

"Help," I said. "As simple as that. Help from one human being to another. I have a personal belief that we could all do a lot more with very slight effort."

"What stops us?"

"Selfishness. Short-sightedness. Pig-headedness. And quite often, of course, shyness."

He considered this remark for a moment or so and then he said in a sudden but yet carefully considered manner, "You could help me, Doctor Frost."

Then he sat looking at me, both hands gripping the raised tumbler containing his unfinished whisky. Then he put the tumbler on the glass top of the low table with a clatter. He stammered out an apology and then did the same thing again.

Meanwhile, I was, in the seconds after his appeal, groaning inwardly with scarcely hidden fury. Another consultation on the cheap. The woman at the dinner table. The wife of a colleague. The friend of a friend. I was surprised and irritated, as much by my own misjudgment of his character as by his gaucherie. He hadn't looked the type, but there he sat, "twanging like a bloody harp", as James would undoubtedly have said.

"It's possible," I said, fairly coolly and pointedly. "But these things can't be decided in a minute."

He didn't apologize. Yet ten minutes earlier I would have judged him to have been a man of some sensibility. Indeed, he scarcely seemed to pay any attention to me now that he had taken his plunge. He said with a rush: "You might at the same time help many other people. Even millions." He giggled

62

nervously, looked away and then gazed at me with a defiant, unsmiling directness. His blue eyes had an intensity I didn't care to see.

My irritation was changed to apprehension by his remark and the change in his appearance. Remembering the half-filled glass on the table on my arrival, I wondered whether he might have been drinking steadily throughout the evening. But apart from his nervousness, the strange slipped giggle and the staring pale blue eyes he seemed sober enough. Then his manner changed again and he said in the most matter-of-fact manner: "Would you care for a stroll round the piazza? It's a strange, even remarkable experience. Right out of the Middle Ages." He put down his empty glass and took up his fresh drink and finished that in a gulp and stood up, waiting for me. If he wasn't yet drunk he soon would be, I thought, watching him carefully. He no longer bit his under-lip, I noticed. He was, for a moment at least, a man of some determination. Yet it was a bogus, made-up air of resolution. He gave out a sense of expected defeat. He wouldn't have been surprised had I sat tight, told him I was tired and would prefer my bed to a stroll. Perhaps his pathetic defeatism defeated me, for I found myself finishing my drink and standing by his side.

"You can leave those there," he said, pointing to my cloth cap and camera. "You won't need 'em."

"I like a cap at night," I said lamely.

He smiled and took me by the arm, almost jauntily.

We went out of the Hotel Jolanda, turned left into the Via Roma, thence into the Piazza delle Erbe.

The great piazza was now deserted and I saw immediately all that Greenaway had meant. The Palazzo della Ragione towered above and along one side of a piazza as wide as Parliament Square, but here were no intervening islands of concrete or grass: instead, a wide and sweeping cobble-stoned townscape, lit fitfully by a few electric lights strung on a cable high above the ground. The shadows and dark entries to the alleyways, on the far side of the great square, made a forbidding background to this scene. Many Italian streets have this same ominous nocturnal quality for the Northerner. The Middle Ages, as Greenaway had said, were at one's elbow.

63

"I love this building," Greenaway said, pointing to the Palazzo. "Fourteenth century, and a roof span of two hundred and sixty feet by ninety. What about that for science?"

We began to cross the piazza diagonally.

I did not respond to his enthusiasm, impressive as I found the building. I was too wary.

"What would you say is the greatest help one man can render another?" he asked genially, as if about to start a disputation concerning relative values.

"It may sound banal," I said, "but don't these things always depend on circumstances? I might loan one man a hundred pounds to save his business and persuade another man's wife not to leave him and his children. Either action might save a man's reason or self-respect. There is an infinite number of answers." He laughed shortly.

"That's not an answer to my question. I said, 'What is the greatest help one man can render another?' 'Another man'," he repeated. "No business, no wife, no children. Just one man to another. One soul, if you like."

"You're still wildly over-simplifying," I said—very patiently, I thought. "Men need different things. The answer is infinitude itself. We have to take so many things into account. Birth. Education. Environment. Wealth. Health. The lot, in fact."

"With all those things stripped away?"

"Very little is left. Certainly no man that you or I would recognize," I said simply. By now I was wideawake, beginning to enter into the spirit of his enquiry. "We are the sum of those things. At least, you are to a psychologist. Less so for a physiologist, of course."

"There is still a core," he said doggedly. "His mind."

"His genes, if you like. That's the physiologist's and eugenist's territory. The mind is mine. Or so I like to think. I know all these things are indivisible and interdependent, and that the mind is all the things I mentioned, plus a thousand others—but . . ."

He interrupted me. "To save the mind, another's sanity, isn't that the greatest help one can give another?"

"If one can. It is a rare experience in medical history. At

least, rarely authenticated. Ultimately, a man can only save himself. It may sound almost biblical put like that, but a great deal of psychiatry is in those terms. Another man can often help by indicating a possible course of action, but . . ."

He stopped for a moment and took my arm, almost light-heartedly. "The perfect answer!" he said. "My answer, in fact. The answer I need. Now, Doctor Frost, help me to save mine."

By then I knew he wasn't drunk, but I was less certain of his mental state. To humour him I said, smiling, "It may be too late."

"It may be at that," he agreed, so seriously that my small joke died on the midnight air.

"You're joking!"

"I am as serious as any man you will ever speak to, Doctor Frost. I am at a crisis in my life, and how I decide may well affect the world."

He really is unbalanced, I thought. Yet his quiet, matter-of-fact words held no touch of madness: yet neither have the words of many murderers or megalomaniacs, and a million lesser lunatics. Then, just as I would decide in my mind that he was sane I would see again what had become a most disturbing mannerism: the nibbling at his lower lip. And, as with all tics this had its fearful fascination: I began to wait and watch for it so that my mind was only partly occupied by his words, bewildering and disturbing as they were.

Even in his fantastic subjectivity, Greenaway seemed to understand something of my bewilderment, for he went straight on: "As I told you this morning, I am a kind of scientist. I was trained as a scientist. My academic career was what is usually termed brilliant. Now I am attached to the Ministry of Supply. I've worked there for fourteen years, from half-way through the war until now. I have made three or four attempts to leave the Ministry for industrial research, but each time I have been persuaded to stay. I didn't want to leave. I'm not particularly ambitious in a material or financial sense. And I liked my work. After each resignation I seem to have found myself with a bigger income and higher status." Almost as an afterthought, he said, "It isn't true, you know, that all civil servants are underpaid. I am paid extremely well. That is by the way. The real reason I wished to leave was that I was becoming weighed down by the extent of my know-how—the new world religion. In my particular field—I'm a physicist—I probably have knowledge, or rather access to knowledge—no single man has the knowledge—which not more than half a dozen men in the world can have. I don't like that. The weight becomes intolerable. I've tried to explain that to my superiors, but they laugh. They're apt to think that any man who has a particular kind of scientific brain is a bit batty anyway."

"What is your particular task, if you can talk about it?" I asked.

His answer was, more or less as I recall it, to the effect that he had been working on the problem of a new kind of outer casing for the hydrogen bomb. "As you may know"—I remember this part of his statement clearly—"the Americans were somewhat disconcerted by the effects of their uranium bomb two years ago. They hadn't reckoned on the gigantic nature of the strontium-ninety fall-out. Neither had any of us, for that matter. All that was caused by what is now considered a fairly old-fashioned outer casing for the bomb."

He was gradually becoming the lecturer.

"Go on," I said dully, scarcely understanding a word.

"Well, that was the fission-fusion bomb. We're on to something new, a new outer layer, based on a series of shaped inward-travelling blast-waves."

I am somewhat hazy about the exact words, but that was the gist of his explanation. In my ignorance I may well have confused his jargon, but I remember, at that stage, catching him up on his use of the word "we".

"You say 'we'," I said. "Isn't that in itself an admission that yours is only a part of the knowledge?"

"We are all part of each other," he agreed. "As Donne said long ago. My knowledge is part of yours. We do not learn at school in a series of vacuums, do we?"

"Then where do *you* come in, then?"

He misinterpreted the intentional sarcasm of my emphasis of his importance and went on casually: "My main task is to correlate the practical results of the Woomera Testing Grounds and Christmas Island with our more theoretical work back at Cambridge and Harwell. I was in Woomera twice last year and in Christmas Island earlier this year."

He was fairly well up in the hierarchy then, I thought, if he had travelled thus far. The appearance of scientists is so often deceptive. They are not so concerned with outward appearances as business men or, for that matter, many medical men.

"And you're finding it a strain—the know-how part of it," I said soothingly, not really believing my honeyed words. "Well, it's understandable." By then I was beginning to realize that Greenaway's trouble wasn't as simple as all that.

"Of course I find it a strain," he replied easily, "but that's scarcely the beginning of it."

We had again reached the far corner of the piazza and stood for a moment. Would I now get an account of hypertension, lack of understanding or what?

"Have you ever been down any of these alleyways?" he asked suddenly.

"Not here."

"Just like sets for *Romeo and Juliet*. The narrowness, the shadows, the overhanging storeys. The atmosphere of violence near to hand."

We turned and began to pace back across the piazza. "Go on," I said unwillingly.

He seemed to relax as he talked about himself. The twanging seemed to start once he had to start thinking about other things. "No, my trouble is more complex, Doctor Frost. Like all scientists, I'm involved in this great dilemma of the indivisibility of science. Indivisibility. A word you used yourself just now. No one nation has a right to this exclusive knowledge. It is knowledge for the world. Your own profession practises what it preaches. The Salk polio vaccine, whatever its possible shortcomings, has been given to the world. A certain cure for cancer, if discovered tomorrow, would be published as soon as possible, wouldn't it? No nation would keep it for itself. Cancer now kills millions and will probably kill millions still unborn. Yet knowledge might stop those deaths. Mine is the problem

67

in reverse, so to speak. The secrets I am party to will kill millions. Yet I am not allowed to publish them. Yet publication would save life."

"We do not live in a logical world. Otherwise we shouldn't have invented God—or a series of gods. We have to explain the mess somehow."

"I am a scientist," he said. "I live by logic. To me it is logical that I should give the world any knowledge I possess."

"How many besides yourself would tell the world?"

"I think the Russians are sincere," he said, quite simply. "I think they would, given a chance."

"You believe that—even after Hungary?"

"Even after that. It was a bitter yet logical step. A surgical necessity."

That way lay anger and argument, and I left it. Instead I said quietly, "I've never found the Russians particularly internationally minded. Even in my own specialized field—where knowledge is never a dangerous thing—they're not particularly forthcoming."

"You may be right," he said. He brushed his hand across his brow. "I thought I knew. Perhaps I begin to have doubts, too. Perhaps that is the trouble. I don't know."

We turned again.

"What *don't* you know?"

"I know nothing at all in the world!" he said, quietly, almost giggling again as he said his mocking words. By then I was engrossed and wished to know more. I had had too little experience of this other modern malaise. Most of my patients are the victims, or think they are the victims, of money, sex or social maladjustment. I had had no experience of the scientist at war with his soul. How different from soldiers at war with war?

"What is your problem at this moment?" I asked. "I mean, have you a particular problem on your hands arising out of these doubts?"

"Quite simply, it is this," he said quietly. "I have with me microfilms of diagrams of small but essential constituents in new equipment we have installed at Woomera. Radical and unusual stuff, believe me. Diabolical stuff, too. Or it could be.

I am proposing to hand them into the keeping of another power on Thursday of this week."

"Have you ever done such a thing before?"

"Twice. Once in England, once before in Italy."

"When?"

"Both last year."

"And you are unsuspected?"

"There is no reason for me to be suspected."

"Men like yourself are often unaware of suspicion."

"That may be."

"And what has changed you now? Religion?" I sneered.

He smiled and said, "Never that. I was brought up in a highly religious household. In fact, I was reared a good Catholic, but when I became a man I put away childish things —without regret." He was silent for a moment and then said, "Elizabeth Castle changed me." His scientfic detachment left him as he mentioned the name. He became as flustered as a lovelorn boy. He bit his lips, put his hands in the pockets of his jacket, took them out, swung them ostentatiously at his side. An exhibition of extreme tension.

I almost laughed aloud at the preposterous answer. That red-headed slip of a girl playing a fateful part in a nation's security. Yet wasn't this the way the world moved, had always moved? Every history primer showed that.

"How?"

"I have never known anyone like her."

"Does she know anything about your views on handing over your country's secrets?"

"Good God, no!"

"Shouldn't you tell her, if you wish to know her better?"

He shrugged.

"What is her great power over you?" I went on.

"That I am in love with her."

I almost laughed to hear this willy-nilly mixing of emotional clichés and metaphysical abstractions.

"And she with you?"

"I don't know."

"Wouldn't it be a good idea to find out?"

"That I propose to do."

"When?"

"Tomorrow."

"And does the destination of the microfilms depend on her answer?"

"Not exactly," he said. For the first time he seemed somewhat uncomfortable and evasive in his answer, but he retained touches of that maddening complacency which afflicts so many of those who are caught into the great secrets of our time, aerodynamical boffins, research chemists, physicists, even psychiatrists . . . the modern mumbo-jumbologists, as I have heard them termed.

"What, then?" I asked.

"I think I have made my decision."

We both stopped in the middle of the square.

"And that is?"

"I shall ask Miss Castle to marry me." The tooth bit into his underlip. Uncertainty returned. He wasn't very optimistic concerning his chances. That was clear.

"And then everything in the garden will be lovely?" I said brutally. "What about your earlier essays in treason? Where do they come in?"

"I don't see it like that."

"You're preposterous!" I said.

After all, I wasn't there in a professional capacity, although Greenaway might persuade himself that I was.

"Not exactly," Greenaway said, imperturbable again. "Wasn't it Nietsche who said, 'That is your truth, this is mine'? I see things differently from you. That's all."

"What help did you want from me?"

"You have given me the help I needed."

"How, for God's sake?"

"You have helped to sort things out for me. I have made a start. I needed someone to put my case against. I have never talked of these things in just this way." He reflected for a moment and then said, as if surprised by the discovery: "How extraordinary. I've never told anyone on my so-called side of the fence any of these things. Astonishing!"

"You've doubtless talked to your contacts in this dreary game."

"Not very often. And that is different—they share my own convictions."

"You're only scratching at the surface if you think you have sorted things out by this kind of conversation," I said. "It's not even a preliminary consultation."

"Perhaps I am a little confused," he said suddenly. Again he drew his hand wearily across his brow.

In that moment of his confusion I began to see how mentally sick he really was. The sudden reactions: the nervous tics followed by the bogus bold front, the overweening vanity, the confusion, finally the collapse. The everlasting pendulum of the schizothyme I had seen so often. All within these twenty minutes.

"And what about the man you're supposed to meet on Thursday?" I asked.

"I know, I know."

"And your return to England with your prospective bride?"

His tooth fidgeted at his underlip as if he had a sore there.

"And the fact that your treason will find you out?"

"Don't!" he commanded quietly.

He put up his right hand. "I know all this. Sometimes, for a moment or so, things have seemed simpler. There seems a way out. Perhaps, somewhere, there is a way out. I thought for a moment yesterday that you were the way."

I could no longer think of him as the pleasant young grey-haired man on the coach. He was too near becoming an unwanted patient.

"Have you ever been psychoanalysed?" I asked him gently.

"Yes," he said, suddenly defensive.

"When?"

"Three years ago."

"By whom?"

"By someone you wouldn't have heard of. He had no medical degree. He wasn't fashionable."

"Who?"

"A Doctor Ludwig Beinhardt."

"Doctor of what?"

"Of Philosophy. Of Heidelberg."

"No medical degree?"

71

"None."

I forgot my profession for the moment.

"But why? Why? Why?" I asked, and then apologized.

"Who knows?" he said forlornly.

"You'd better see me in the morning. Come to my room at eight-thirty. By the way, how did you know I was out this evening?"

"I rang your room when I came in at ten o'clock and then sat waiting for you," he said simply.

To that I had no reply. We walked back to the hotel without another word. I left instructions to be called at half-past seven.

The clock at the reception desk revealed to my unbelieving eyes that we had been crossing and re-crossing the piazza for not much longer than half an hour and that I had left Bianca less than an hour before.

We took the lift to the second floor, now mostly occupied, I had heard, by the English members of the Anglo-Italian Palladian Society. There we bade each other formal goodnights.

Yet despite these long hours of climax and anti-climax I slept immediately. Such are the effects of action, movement, escape from self!

17

OF MY early morning consultation with Greenaway there is little enough to say. I had breakfasted and shaved before eight and then sat brooding over his troubles which, it seemed, he had succeeded in partly off-loading on to myself, his unwilling confidant.

I was furious. The sun was already strong and I would have preferred a more leisurely awakening and genial contemplation of the day ahead. Instead, Greenaway had driven all such self-indulgence from my mind. From time to time I thought longingly of Bianca, but twinges of professional conscience drew me back. After the too-short night of forgetfulness I was involved with another's tragedy.

72

As far as I could judge from the evidence of the night before, Greenaway showed unmistakable signs of schizophrenia. But medical considerations were not my only worries. Other thoughts helped to dull the morning sunlight. Now that I knew of Greenaway's earlier treason, wasn't it my duty to let the authorities know immediately of his present intentions? Shouldn't I make a positive move to stop him in this madman's progress? Miss Castle's yea or nay scarcely came into the matter.

But how did the average tourist set about letting Scotland Yard or M.I.5, or even the Ministry of Supply, know that he appeared to have another Fuchs or Nunn May on his hands? I wondered gloomily, pouring myself another cup of coffee. Would a cable do the job? TO MINISTER OF SUPPLY STOP HAVE ACQUIRED SECRET AGENT STOP PLEASE COLLECT PADUA SIGNED FROST? Or would just a walk to the local police headquarters do the job?

Well, it might make an entertaining weekend competition in an intellectuals' magazine, but for me it threatened to be an altogether new kind of headache. I sat there, cursing Greenaway and wondering whether to order more coffee.

My gloomy meditations were interrupted by a firm knock on the door. I called out, and Greenaway stepped in. He looked as refreshed and boyish as he had in the coach on the previous day. His pale blue eyes were intensified in colour by a blue shirt. His grey suit was as trim as if a valet had had it for an hour that morning. I made to stand up, but he waved me back to my armchair.

"You were extraordinarily kind to me last night," he said calmly. I might have given him a couple of theatre tickets or rendered a similar social service.

"I'm very glad," I said limply.

He sat down on the bentwood chair by the table and took up a spoonful of sugar from the bowl on the breakfast tray. At that moment, despite his grey hair, he looked about twenty-five.

"But what happens next?" he asked.

"I'd been wondering that myself."

"I've rather put myself in your hands," he said.

"It's a primary requirement when asking for help."

"Has it occurred to you that I might have done that deliberately?"

"I usually leave speculation until a later stage in consultations."

"Touché," he said and smiled.

He replaced the spoon, put his hand inside his jacket and took out a long narrow manila envelope, typical OHMS issue. He held the envelope for me to take.

"These are the oddments I was speaking about last night," he said quietly. "I think it would probably be a good idea if you were to hang on to them."

Almost involuntarily I held out my hand, took the envelope and put it in the inside pocket of my own jacket. How innocently one accepts the contributions to one's destiny!

"A good idea for whom?" I asked.

"For me," he said. "For everyone."

"For me?"

"Yours is the only questionable position," he said, again smiling.

"Till when do I hold this?"

"Till I ask you to return them."

"And when will that be?"

"In London probably."

"Not where—when?"

"Next week, probably."

"But it can't end there," I said solemnly. I was increasingly unhappy and uncertain with these new developments.

"No," he agreed. "It can't end there. But shall we cross that bridge when we come to it?"

"You know what I mean," I persisted. I wanted things as clear as language could make them.

"I think I do. What has happened before, you mean?"

I nodded. "Plus the fact that I shall probably not return this envelope to you personally?"

"It is quite a bridge," he said, biting his lower lip for the first time that morning.

"Yet it will have to be crossed."

"Not all bridges have to be crossed alone," he persisted.

I did not answer.

"Others will help me," he said, almost defiantly, the schizothyme's pathetic belief that he has a special place in society evident again.

"Possibly," I said, "but there are some bridges that have to be crossed alone."

"Thanks for maintaining my metaphor, or is it simile?" he said, laughing. "That's the devil of a scientific education. After seventeen one never considers even the language of Fowler, let alone Shakespeare."

I laughed. His charm was infectious, but I was determined to remain serious. The whole thing was more serious than anything I had ever touched. I hated each advancing moment and commitment.

"Why have you made this decision?" I asked.

"Because it is no longer mine alone," he said, watching me. "By speaking to you I made part of the decision your responsibility. Then, too, Elizabeth will make it easier."

"She is very young for something like this," I said as gently as I could.

"Do you think so? She's nineteen."

"To me that is very young."

He bit his lip. Then he said miserably, "So it is to me sometimes."

"Why did you speak to ME?" I went on.

"Because I gathered that you were a psychiatrist and I could see for myself that you were the kind of man I might talk to."

"Those aren't reasons enough."

"They were for me."

"Why didn't you consult a responsible psychiatrist three years ago?"

He shrugged. "Beinhardt was recommended. You know the kind of thing—a friend of a friend of a friend."

I did! Only too well!

He stood up as if the day were done. One of the characteristics of the schizothyme is that the insurmountable problems of one moment are seen to be quite simple of solution the next. Psychopaths, of course, have this outlook in common with men of outstanding gifts, especially military commanders. The psychopath, however, with his profound conviction that Providence, Fate, life, will aid him, is apt to let things rest. The military commander knows better.

"We shall be seeing each other," Greenaway said, smiling. He stood by the door, slim, boyish, with not an apparent care in the world.

"I wish you good fortune in your venture with Miss Castle today. Is it today?"

He nodded. "You are very kind," he said as he went out.

I sat on for several minutes after he had gone. Somewhere in the town a clock chimed nine. I was puzzled by Greenaway, and apprehensive. For fifteen years I have dealt almost daily with psychopaths of one kind or another. Many I have come to know as friends. Indeed, it is my deep conviction that no physician can hope to begin to understand his individual patients unless he begins with some kind of compassion for mankind itself. His compassion may be partly fury with the idiocies of the human condition or a resigned acceptance of its quotidian round, but he must have some feeling other than that of the detached, so-called specialist. As Donne said, and as Greenaway had echoed, we are all part of each other. I could see so much of Greenaway's viewpoint: the idealism that had been sidetracked, the youthfulness that had refused the world's compromises and had thus become involved in its own, the one-world philosophy of the scientist. I might have sat there too long, but another knock on the door brought me back from my wanderings. James's voice called, "You there, Rupert?"

I growled a reply and let him in.

"I thought we might walk down to the coach together. Seems ages since we saw you last. Where did you get to? We tried to track you down for dinner last night but no luck."

"I dined in Venice. I met Signora Colleoni there early in the afternoon and we spent the evening together."

He looked puzzled.

"Remember? The Italian woman I lunched with in Rovigo. I think I pointed her out to you."

"The good-looker a bit too smartly dressed for this kind of outing? That the one?"

"She might be," I agreed slowly, and unwillingly.

76

"Anyway, a pleasant evening?"

"Very."

We went down and out into the Piazza Cavour.

"What sort of day did *you* have?" I asked.

"We stayed on in Venice, too, for quite some time. Very pleasant. Georgina takes a lot of handling. Too little authority in her life."

"I thought you said she had too much."

"Did I? Not enough of the right kind, I probably meant. Her mind's as undisciplined as a child's."

So was Greenaway's, I thought, and wished I could have discussed his case with James. By then we were at the coach. Georgina was already inside, in command of a front seat. She acknowledged our arrival with a mock regal wave.

"You'd better sit with Georgina today," James said. "My temper's getting a bit frayed with her non-stop nonsense."

"I don't believe it for a moment," I said, "and in any case I've arranged to sit with Signora Colleoni." Did my admission sound somewhat sheepish? I wondered.

"Oh, did you now?" He considered me quizzically, but said no more.

I let him go first and move forward to Georgina. Bianca was half-way towards the rear of the coach. Greenaway was at the back, preoccupied with a good deal of arranging and rearranging of cushion, books and raincoat for Miss Castle. As I sat down, he looked round, nodded and smiled. He was being over-attentive to Miss Castle's comfort. And she was accepting his devotion too complacently. I saw trouble ahead.

Meantime Bianca, smiling and serene, was guarding the seat at her side with piled-up jacket and raincoat. I took them and rearranged them in the luggage rack, and then sat down and took her hand in my own. I was soon caught away into a more felicitous mood than the one Greenaway had thrust upon me.

77

18

THAT morning we were to visit the Villa Lazara Pisani and the great State property, the Villa Pisani at Stra, both eighteenth-century buildings and both within easy motoring distance of Padua. After that—by midday, Revisi said—the day would be our own. Neither villa was the work of Palladio, he added regretfully.

The Villa Lazara Pisani is comparatively small, no larger than a small English manor house, with later loggias and wings. The *chinoiserie* decoration of the interior is enchanting, and it was a pleasant surprise to find that the house was not a bare memorial to other days, but the comfortable and charming home of an Italian noblewoman. We were allowed to wander at will throughout the house.

"This is what I have really been looking for," Bianca said, as we drifted through the rooms. "So few Italian homes have any real charm—like this!" She moved her arm to take in the room.

I had often noticed the same fact myself and did not oppose her statement.

"What is—was—your home like?" I asked, hesitantly.

"Moderna . . . frivola . . . proprio come tu crede che io sia, forse," she said gaily, her mood changing once again, on the instant.

"God forbid!" I took her hand.

"It is true, Rupert," she said. "And I think you think I am those things. Even if you do not know you do."

We were alone, standing in one of the upstairs bedrooms, a pretty room painted in the palest of pastel greens with ancient carpets and gay curtains. A typical guest-room from an English country house, I thought with insular complacency.

"Tell me, isn't it so, then?" she asked.

"Nonsense!"

She laughed. "You are kind—and funny!" she added as an afterthought. Other members of the Society were down below: in the reception rooms or wandering through the loggias. Only a few still seemed to be about in the upper rooms.

"I'm sure you made a very comfortable home for your husband," I said.

"Not very. In fact, I think it was terrible. Especially when I see a place like this."

"What was wrong?"

"Così chic, così all moda."

I ignored the deprecation and said, "And what about your present home?"

She smiled. "The hotel?"

I smiled too, not pressing my question, too caught up in present happiness. Part of the pleasure of the early days of love is surely in the prospect of a gradual unravelling of the other's life by an infinity of questions and answers, posed, answered and parried over many dining-tables, through many wanderings. To me, then, it seemed a future of delight and pleasure. A limited future, I admitted, but my desires and hopes were also limited—then.

After an hour in this beguiling house we were gathered together by Revisi and driven to the Villa Pisani, scarcely a villa but a palace, decaying and forsaken, more like a film set than a museum.

There we were marshalled in an inner hallway whilst Revisi arranged our entrance fees en bloc.

"Here," he said, whilst waiting for the tickets, "we shall see many pieces of considerable historic interest."

By then I was beginning to understand something of Revisi's explanatory remarks. Such a statement from him was extremely tepid. When he had something exceptional to show, his enthusiasm was unrestrained, but I had noticed before that he was too good a patriot to damn, irrevocably, anything Italian. The English can vie with each other in the subtleties of understatement: not so foreigners: it is an exercise that either eludes them or has no appeal. We made our way through room after room of boring mediocrity in furnishing and decoration. James came across as I stood examining a gilded crest, whilst Bianca examined a chimney-piece.

"What about lunch?" he asked.

"We're going into Venice," I said on the instant.

"So are we. May see you," he said, accepting my evasion.

79

"We'll look out for you. Come and meet Bianca."

We talked together, all decrying the Villa Pisani, until the tramp of feet through the uncarpeted State Rooms died away. We followed slowly, almost wearily. Museum boredom is a malady all its own.

Georgina had vanished. The moribund museum had plainly been too much for her. Then, far off, we saw her sauntering alongside the man-made canal that unites the palace with its stable block, a quarter of a mile away.

"Must see Georgina doesn't fall in," James said, leaving us. "She's not to be trusted near water. May see you both in Venice."

"Your friend is very English," Bianca said, watching him stride off.

"Perhaps he is. Yes, I suppose so."

"Is he a very good friend?"

"Thanks to him, I met you."

She smiled. "And are we going to Venice? I did not know."

"I said so, to keep you to myself. James suggested lunching with Georgina and himself."

"They are married?"

I shook my head.

"But he is in love with her."

I laughed. "Is he?"

"Yes," she said seriously. "I have watched them together—from the time I saw you speak to them in the piazza at Rovigo. I should like to talk with them sometime, but not today."

I nodded, but absent-mindedly. Ahead, perhaps thirty yards away, amongst the trees, I had seen Greenaway and Miss Castle. They were standing together and he was talking, very seriously. Then she turned and began to walk on. He followed and put his arm about her shoulders as if to turn her towards himself, but she disengaged herself, somewhat petulantly, I thought, and they walked on, apart, dismally apart, neither speaking.

I took Bianca's hand and led her away, towards the water. She, too, had noticed the sad little scene.

"You spoke to him in the coach yesterday?" she said.

I nodded. "You know all my movements."

80

"All those I could know since we met," she said, unabashed by confession of her forthright interest. "I wanted to know more about you. That is all, but that is reason enough, Rupert, isn't it?"

"Reason enough for me," I said. "The young man I met first on the coach. I spoke to him then. And again last night and again this morning."

I was astonished, hearing my words, to realize how recent and frequent my conversations with Greenaway had been. Nearness to Bianca made all other meetings seem remote. I had been forcibly reminded of that when James had spoken to me in the villa half an hour before.

"The young grey-haired man does not seem to be making very good progress," Bianca said, smiling. "The girl is very young."

"No younger to him than you to me," I said. "How old are you?"

"I am thirty-one. And you?"

"Forty-five."

"An interesting difference," she said.

"A generation almost," I said. "How old is your husband?"

To my surprise she said, "Rupert, let us not talk about these things. Please."

I took her arm and we walked slowly towards the stables.

"I am very sorry, Rupert," Bianca said as we walked. "I will tell you at another time. Now I am too happy."

That was reason enough for any man, I thought, and was silent and almost content.

We approached the stables. Greenaway and Miss Castle reappeared, through the trees, crossing our path, a dejected-looking pair. Greenaway nodded vaguely. The girl walked ahead. Poor chap, I thought. Thumbs down . . . and then what? In my happiness my sympathies were wholly with him—at least as far as his emotions were concerned.

The stables were disappointing. A pretty elevation hiding cramped equestrian quarters, now falling into decay. The spaciousness and grandeur of stables in great English houses— Woburn or Badminton for instance—made those of the Villa Pisani seem pathetically penny-proud.

81

We turned and walked slowly back along the wide grass verge of the other bank of the overgrown canal.

"Shall we go back to Padua or on to Venice?" I asked.

"No, let us get the bus to Venice from here. One comes every half-hour, I heard somebody say."

We walked through the hallways out to the dusty road, towards a distant bus stop in Stra.

19

I HAVE been told, by Venetians and Englishmen who have wintered there, that Venice can prove the most chilling and despairing of cities. Cold winds and the damp air from the Lagoon seek out the bones of those foolish enough to remain after the autumn sun has gone. But in the late summer Venice is the sunniest and gayest city in the world.

Again that day, Monday, we lunched overlooking the Canale di San Marco and San Giorgio Maggiore. Again the sun gave the world its blessing, silvering the waves beneath the gondolas at the Molo, regilding the texture of almost every façade in the square.

Our chatter was as carefree as before, but now strangely touched, for me at least, by a sudden tenderness and desire. Months of continence and constraint receded. I was as different from the weary medico James had brought to Padua as a man could be.

We lunched lightly: spaghetti, chianti and blackest coffee. Afterwards we walked towards the Molo's edge, past the two giant columns, threading a way between sightseers, pigeons and peanut vendors. At the water's edge we evaded the gondoliers' enticements, turned and began to walk slowly past the seaward face of the Doge's Palace, past the postcard kiosks and the grape stalls, away from the hordes, along the Riva degli Schiavoni. Crossing the first of the bridges, I was tempted to try for an afternoon passage by steamer to Torcello or even the shorter trip to Chioggia, but we wandered on. I even gave thought to a project for journeying out to the Lido to swim, but still we wandered on, finally leaving the quayside for the narrow alleyways that run between the hotels that face the Schiavoni.

We began, once again, to talk about our meeting and ourselves, and perhaps emboldened by the unaccustomed chianti and the dazzling sun, I said, "And now, Bianca, fifty hours after meeting you, I am in love."

"With Venice, with love or with me?" she asked, smiling.

"With you," I heard myself declare boldly and without reserve. I heard my words but scarcely recognized the speaker. Shades of generations of London Scots must have recoiled from such abandon, but I plunged on. Bianca was less disturbed.

"But that is as it should be, Rupert," she said quietly.

"But it *is* a bit soon," I pointed out.

"No sooner than my love for you," she said.

We stopped at the entrance to an alleyway and kissed, and then turned blindly into the shade of the narrow thoroughfare.

"All my teaching tells me to beware of haste," I said, protesting, so that we might talk yet more.

"No teaching and no teacher knows about love. Surely you know that, Rupert. For some it comes at leisure, for others in haste. For others never. For us it is here. And now what shall we do?"

She made these declamations in the most matter-of-fact manner, her voice scarcely above a whisper.

"What *shall* we do?" I echoed.

"La cosa logica è di fare l'amore," she said, her eyes alight, tenderly mocking my conventional rhetoric.

"Here?"

"C'è troppa gente," she said gaily. It was too public.

Always she seemed possessed by this gaiety, which was for me the most unusual and intriguing of her charms. Like most psychiatrists I have spent most of my working life in close contact with gloom or dealers in gloom. Gaiety is far removed from the consulting-room. Perhaps that is why physicians and surgeons are reputedly fairly frequent visitors to night-clubs. They must have some escape from the proximity of death and despair. If gaiety was Bianca's mood, boldness was my own, and I said, "Then we must find a room. We must. In a great city like this there must be hotels."

"Perhaps."

"Why perhaps?"

"The holiday season is not yet over. Hotel rooms are hard to find in Venice in September."

"Today is the first of October," I said doggedly.

. She laughed aloud. "Oh, Rupert, how English you are! Perhaps you are right, and that little fact will make a big difference."

"We must look—and ask."

"We must tell them that an English doctor wants the room for an examination!" she laughed mercilessly. "And you will make me open my mouth and show you my tongue, Rupert?" She took my arm gaily, laughing, laughing. But my own mood was too desperate for laughter. I was too near and still too far from my desire.

How clearly I remember how my pace quickened! And then slowed as we came suddenly and wholly unexpectedly from the alley into the small and peaceful piazza before the Church of San Zaccharia, that sombre relic of the Renaissance set amongst the shadows behind the Schiavoni. The visual impact of the contrast was startling and slightly daunting. I doubted whether we should find the kind of pensione we wanted in these areas. Beyond the church was another alleyway.

"The only hotel we shall find from now on will be sordid," I said, twenty-five years of medical training rushing out.

Bianca laughed. She seemed possessed by a giddy recklessness. "They will have beds," she said. "You can inspect the sheets, Rupert, whilst I take off my clothes."

I laughed, too, wondering whether chianti had a delayed effect upon women. But where? Where? Where? was now a rampaging question in my mind.

We went deeper still into the maze of alleys.

"Venice has as many hotels as London has buses," I said at one point.

"Perhaps, like buses they have all driven away," Bianca joked, but for me the joke was bitter.

We briefly discussed the likely merits of two or three tumble-down houses that might have offered rooms, but Bianca brushed them aside. We would know the right one, she seriously announced. It would be smaller, more squalid and smell of the Venetian drains. And the doctor would be revolted. She revelled in mockery of my seriousness, almost doubling up with laughter as she saw my rueful smile. My innate Anglo-Scots caution drove her on and on.

20

WE BOTH saw the Pensione Greci at the same moment. From the outside it was another of those thousand minor palazzi once sited so colourfully above the side-canals of Venice, now down on their uppers.

The house was obviously far gone in decay. Threadbare sun-blinds, once brazen Venetian red, were now a washed-out rust and hung, like ancient sailcloth, upon the Byzantine-Gothic windows. Stucco curled from the terra-cotta walls like peeled-off rind. Even the faded signboard hung from its rail like a loose rafter.

Nevertheless, we boldly crossed the Ponte dei Greci and entered the small, stone-flagged courtyard. My spirits rallied slightly at the sight of the freshly whitewashed steps, but flagged again within the marbled hall. An air of utter hopelessness seemed to possess the house and its musty airlessness settled like sodden sacking upon my shoulders.

A small rickety table was set to one side of the hall, with a dog-eared register and a stained metal inkwell. Behind, on the damp wall, hung a lopsided key-rack.

We stood there for three or four minutes, Bianca relaxed and smiling, myself fretful and impatient. As I began to speak of my distaste for the place a short, thick-set, big-faced woman, with atrociously dyed red hair, appeared on the first floor railed gallery, and stood looking down upon us, wiping her hands on what I was relieved to see was a clean apron. By that time I was so against the Pensione Greci that the woman's demeanour seemed immediately intimidating, but Bianca smiled, and, on the instant, the woman smiled, a quick grin that split her face like a puncture. She came down the two flights of stone stairs, still grinning.

We wanted a room, Bianca said.

"For how long? A day? A night? A week?"

"Today and tonight," Bianca said.

"That will be three thousand lire. With breakfast."

Relief flooded my spirits. I forgot the house and its forbidding mistress and gladly handed her the notes. She opened the register, asked me to fill in the counterfoil and took down two or three keys from the wall-rack. Fortunately, I had my passport in my inner pocket. Replacing it, after entering the details in the register, I felt Greenaway's OHMS envelope. Perhaps it was a measure of my changed mood, but I gave it scarcely a passing thought. I was already unperturbed by the responsibility of having such high-flown secrets in my possession. Few residents of the Pensione Greci would be interested in the remoter realms of atomic and metallurgical research, I thought. Certainly not its two most recent guests.

We followed the woman upstairs to the fifth floor. She seemed to have the energy of a demon, stumping up the stairs a pair at a time. The narrow staircase with its thin iron handrail and delicate Gothic balusters spiralled steeply upwards. There were apparently three or four rooms on each floor, each opening on to a circular gallery. The interior was far smaller than had seemed possible from the Via Greci. I wondered who had built the house three hundred years before. A Venetian merchant? A pirate sailor of the Adriatic? A money-lender of the alley-ways?

Almost breathless after the climb, we were shown into a surprisingly large and pleasant room. Although furnished with little more than a large brass bedstead, washstand and a wardrobe listing well to starboard, it was clean and free from the dankness of the hall.

I crossed to the window. Scarcely more than an arm's length away was a leaning campanile. Suddenly I realized where we were. In my eagerness to get inside the Pensione I had forgotten that I had wandered often in this part of Venice just after the war. Surely this was the leaning tower of the Greek Orthodox Church, San Giorgio dei Greci?

"Of course," said the genial redheaded ogress.

Below was a small tree-shaded quayside with gondolas, barges and a couple of craft more like skiffs. Opposite were newer apartment houses, gay with well-tended window boxes.

Behind me the woman spoke to Bianca.

"She says there is a choice of another room," Bianca said.

"Shall we look?" I said. "I like it here."

"And so do I," Bianca said, and turning thanked the woman, who stood proudly by the door, grinning widely. At my phrase she plucked one of the keys from the handful in her fist, gave it to me with a bobbing flourish and left us, closing the door with a decisive bang and humming loudly as she went down and down.

I silently apologized to her departure for my misjudgment of her face and frowning welcome. Already my fears that our walk might end in anticlimax had gone for good. I was delighted with the room, bedazzled by the unexpected pleasures of the day. The white walls and red tiles, the brass bed with its butcher-blue cover, the marble-topped washstand and tin bidet now seemed a poetic assembly. Certainly no poet could have wished for more. I took Bianca in my arms.

"Sono venuta per vedere il dottore," she said gravely, gently freeing herself and standing back. "I understand he lives here."

Then, we were in each other's arms again.

"He is an English doctor you have come to see," I pointed out.

"No other kind will do."

"It is frequently necessary for patients to undress for English doctors," I said, unbuttoning her white blouse, beginning to make my unfamiliar way about her clothes. She stood quite still, unhelpfully watching my seeking hands. Then as last she was free. And on the instant her beauty possessed me like a spell. I poured out all that lovers have always said in their moments of discovery, but she stilled my words, tugging at my tie, laughing, dancing on the sudden cold tiles.

"Your clothes, Rupert, are what you call . . . an interruption. And the tiles are cold. Meet me in bed."

Within a moment I had joined her within the jangling bed, gamely settling itself to its ancient duty.

"Are you prepared for this?" I asked, medical awareness at last appearing, perhaps a trifle tardily. "Scientifically prepared, I mean. I am not."

"You need not have one tiny worry, Rupert," she said, placing her arms about my head, drawing me down. I began to kiss her very gently.

"Did you have any Italian girls in the war?" she asked dreamily, as I caressed her.

"Now and then."

"Were they what men call good in bed?"

"Efficient is probably a better word. What is your word?"

"The Italian word is 'brave', Rupert. Isn't that a nicer word?" She laughed, faraway, adding with her usual logic, "But you would not have liked them inefficient, would you, Rupert?"

I laughed.

"Are you efficient, Rupert?"

"Love-making, like quarrelling, needs two," I said.

"I am here," she said. "You are here. Why do we wait?"

Thus we were engulfed.

21

WE WENT down into the town for supper sometime after nine o'clock. By then we had decided to stay the night in Venice and return to Padua the following morning in time for the coach at half-past nine.

In one of the small shops of the sidewalks I bought shaving-cream, a razor and a bar of soap, the Pensione Greci having proved as soapless as any other continental hotel.

Life is probably at its most exciting in a time of acute contrast. Thus, for many men, life never recaptures the excitements

88

of wartime with its dangers and pacific lulls. So, then, I moved in a world of new excitement. To buy shaving-cream after the magic of our afternoon merely pointed the fantasy of the day.

Emotionally, nothing so swift and cataclysmic had ever swept me up in this way. My love for Helen had been the gradual development of a boy-and-girl romance into tenderness and marriage. I had been involved in swift wartime physical affairs, but now I was caught into a love-affair utterly satisfying and, it seemed to me, genuinely sincere and reciprocated. Yet I could not shake off the sense of unreality that had attended our time together. I knew I was living through this fantasy, yet I could scarcely believe my knowledge.

Afterwards we walked slowly through the maze of the town towards the Rialto. There in the open air, by the bridge, overlooking the Grand Canal, we dined, hungrily, thirstily and merrily. Although her tongue was as artful and her humour occasionally devilish as before, Bianca had now a new tenderness. From time to time she spoke in Italian, the words tumbling out like melodies.

And afterwards, as we walked slowly back to the pensione in that delaying, masochistic manner of lovers who know that a secret world of enchantment and excitement awaits them at journey's end, I began to talk—as all lovers must talk—of the future. And Bianca seemed only to wish to listen.

22

WE AWOKE early, no later than six the next morning, the sun moving into the room like a beneficent but unrelenting conscience.

We turned towards each other, the bed jangling to our movements, and lay there for an hour, whispering, loving, laughing. Then, about seven, we began to panic and arose, washed and dressed, and crept downstairs.

Our patrone was already at the door, sluicing down the steps.

"Good-bye!" Bianca called. "And thank you!"

"Good-bye, and good fortune," the woman cried, grinning. "But what about breakfast?"

"At the station. Perhaps we shall see you again," Bianca called.

"You will! You will!" the padrona cried and waved her hand-broom in farewell.

Venice is such a place of sun and leisure that one is apt to forget the thousands who must minister to the daily needs of a million pleasure-seekers. Now, as we dashed across the Schiavoni to the Zaccharia vaporetto station, we were caught into their movements. We caught the vaporetto in good time, but at the station had twenty minutes to wait for the train to Padua. The buffet was open. Never did rolls and coffee taste so well.

From the station at Padua we took a taxi to the Jolanda by way of the Grande Italia. In the taxi we talked only of the day ahead—the coach journey, the villas and the fact that we should be together.

23

As I entered the Jolanda, the clock above the reception desk registered ten to nine.

I went straight up to my room, took a quick shower and was buttoning a clean shirt in the bathroom when I heard a peremptory knock on the door.

I shouted "Uno momento", thinking the girl was probably making another attempt to deliver my breakfast after an earlier failure. Instead, in the bathroom mirror refracted from the wardrobe mirror, reflecting the door, I saw Greenaway enter the room. His boyish look had gone. He was drawn and white and looked more like a man in his sixties than his thirties. Now for a period of commiseration, I thought.

He said, without preamble or apology for the intrusion, "Frost, I've lost my nerve."

"What on earth do you mean?" I asked, coming out from the bathroom, in my shirt, glad to have an excuse for moving round the room, hunting for cuff-links, tie and braces.

"Just what I said. I've lost my nerve. Isn't that enough?"

"But what have you lost your nerve about?"

"This whole thing."

"And what do you propose to do?"

"I don't know."

"Now, look!" I said firmly. "Do you mean you've suddenly become aware of the damn silly things you've been doing during the last year or so, and that you're now afraid of the consequences? Or what?"

"I've lost my nerve about today. My meeting."

I had forgotten about that in the turmoil of my own emotions.

"Today, was it? Well, don't go."

"It isn't as easy as that."

"Why not?"

"If I don't turn up, they'll come looking for me."

"Well, go back to England."

"There's Miss Castle. I was responsible for bringing her out here. I paid her fare, everything. I feel responsible for her."

"Isn't she old enough to look after herself? You think she's old enough for marriage."

"She turned me down!" he said, blurting out the words. They were possibly the crux of the matter, I thought, and not the *non sequitur* they might have seemed.

"Well, it was on the cards," I said as gently as I could.

"But she means everything to me," he said pathetically.

"Well, let it rest and try again sometime."

"No, it was final. As final as anything this side of the grave. It turns out that she doesn't even particularly like me," he added with a bitter laugh.

"Lots of love-affairs start with these setbacks."

"Not this one. This isn't a setback. This is it! The lot!" He made a cutting movement like a man with a billhook at a hedge.

"Well, what about today?" I said, pulling on my trousers. "Can I help?"

"What would you suggest?"

"I suggest you go if you feel you must, but give a miss to

the chap you're supposed to meet and start back for England this evening. Get to Milan and see if you can get on an overnight plane. Otherwise go by train. That's my real advice."

"What about the papers I gave you yesterday?"

"I'll keep those."

"Why? They're my property."

"No, they're not. In a final count they probably belong to the Queen. At an intermediate point they belong to the taxpayer. As a taxpayer I'd rather take the responsibility for keeping them than hand them back to you."

He made a sudden grab for my jacket hanging over a chair, but I took his arm and swung him away. He sprawled across the room, falling against the small table, then across the bed. He was the younger man, but in no shape for any kind of argument. In any case, it had been a half-hearted, petulant protest rather than a do-or-die attempt at manhandling.

"Don't be an ass!" I said, as if talking to an outrageously foolish student.

"I'm sorry," he said, and then, dolefully, "What am I to do?"

"I've put the choice to you," I said. "Now make up your own mind, for God's sake."

"If I come along today, will you hang around?" he begged. "I couldn't stay here. I'd go mad. I shall have to think about going back. I see that. Meantime, I have this rendezvous. I suppose I shall have to skip it."

I tried to control my exasperation by exaggerated formality. "With whom are you to make this rendezvous?"

"Two men will be dressed as friars," he said. "That's all I know."

My heavy formality vanished. I laughed in disbelief. "It's not possible!"

"Oh, I don't know," he said, suddenly defensive. "It's not a particularly conspicuous garb in Italy, and we're going to a kind of school run by monks, aren't we? One of the villas on our list for today."

"What Order do these monastic types belong to—or claim to belong to?"

"Franciscan."

"What colour are they? Their habits, I mean."

"Tobacco brown."

"Well, then, you'll know what to look out for and dodge. Do they know you?"

"They probably have a description."

"Has anybody contacted you here?"

"I was told of this rendezvous at the reception the other evening."

"By whom, for God's sake?"

"Someone I don't know and wouldn't know again. He came up to me and spoke to me. At first I thought he was one of the university people. Perhaps he was. Afterwards I thought it might be someone on the coach, but I haven't recognized anyone."

"Why didn't you have to hand over the papers to him?"

"Things never seem to be as simple as that in this bloody business," he said. "One always seems to be part of some ghastly daisy chain. I suppose nobody is ever allowed to get to know anybody else in case they both start acting like human beings."

He sounded so lugubrious in his self-pitying volte-face I almost laughed. Instead I said, "Who d'you deal with in England?"

"I've only had about half a dozen meetings in my life," he said. "I suppose I've met about three different people all told."

"How did you start?"

"A long-ago acquaintance from my undergraduate days at University College, London. I was a bit of a firebrand there, but I'd rather got out of it until all this started three years ago."

He seemed keen to go on talking but we were interrupted by a knock on the door. James's voice said, "Ready, Rupert?"

"Nearly. Come in."

James entered boisterously. He seemed surprised to see Greenaway present.

"D'you know each other?" I said, changing my passport, papers and Greenaway's envelope from the blue jacket hanging over the chair to the fawn jacket of the suit I proposed to wear that day. I introduced them and, on a sudden decision, added lightly, but with an undertone not to be mistaken by Greenaway: "James, Greenaway here is in a bit of a fix. He's

supposed to be meeting a couple of holy men today and he
may want to give them a miss. They're not quite what they
seem, apparently. Can't tell you any more. If necessary you
might help to trip them up."

"You've come to the right chap," he said. "I once had a holy
man as form-master. He was a very unholy holy man. Revenge
is sweet, saith the Lord. Thanks for the chance, Greenaway."

Greenaway seemed puzzled by the air of facetiousness that
now moved in the room, and he said, somewhat lamely, "I'm
very grateful to you both." He turned to James: "But not too
forceful a revenge, please." He was trying hard to enter into
the spirit evoked by James, and I was suddenly desperately
sorry for him.

"Subtlety is my middle name," James said.

"Furioso will be Revisi's middle name, if we don't buck up,"
I said.

We went out and down by the stairs. James was now
enchanted by the name Furioso and continued to repeat
"Furioso Revisi" like a moronic chant until we were half-way
to the Piazza Cavour.

He interrupted his chant only to question Greenaway: "No
more information you can give us about these holey-boley
fellows of yours, Greenaway? I mean, are they fat or thin, old
or young, bishops or curates, or whatever the local rank?"

"They're friars," I said. "Franciscans. At least, they'll look
like that. Brown habits. You know the kind of garb."

James glanced sideways at me. I frowned, trying to signal to
him to lay off. I knew him too well. This was the kind of
project he could so quickly and mercilessly take to farcical
extremes. Greenaway merely nodded.

We had walked so swiftly to the Piazza Cavour that we were
amongst the earliest arrivals. I took James' arm and held him
back. Greenaway got into the coach as if it were a tumbril and
made his way into the shadows of the offside. Bianca was
already in the coach. What the hell! I thought, and blew her
a kiss. She waved back.

"Who're you blowing kisses to, for God's sake?" James
asked, astonished. "Your Italian popsy? Things are moving
pretty fast there, aren't they?"

94

"Pretty fast."

"Good for you. Where the hell's Georgina got to?"

"I can't see her in the coach," I said, and then hurriedly, "Look, James, take it easy about these monkish types. It's pretty serious stuff. I'll tell you one day. Probably this evening if I can."

"Why not now?"

"There's no time, and perhaps I should ask Greenaway first, although I can't think his permission is really necessary."

"Why all the mystery?"

"Skip it," I begged.

He skipped it.

There is an office of the Wagons Lits Company in the Piazza Cavour, almost opposite the parking place normally taken by the coach. On a sudden decision I left James, crossed the square, went in and asked if an overnight train ran from Padua to Rome. A young, smooth Italian said, immediately, "Yes, at forty minutes after midnight."

What were the chances of a couchette for Friday evening? I asked.

Usually all right, he said. He could let me know within an hour. He'd have to check with Venice.

I said I would come in later that afternoon and hope to pick up tickets.

Pleased with my own resolution, I returned to the waiting coach and climbed in. Bianca beckoned and I made my way to her side.

Greenaway had taken a place by Miss Castle's side, two seats in front of my own. They were both silent, Greenaway's despondency as plain as a thunder cloud.

24

THE Villa Anselmo is set in the typical country of the Veneto, about twenty miles from Padua. The nearer poplars and the distant hills are the only irruptions into the great plain.

We drove into the grounds between high stone piers, sur-mounted by two great casts of hounds. I looked towards Greenaway. He was listening, somewhat absent-mindedly, I thought, to Miss Castle, now chattering gaily, as if oblivious of the agony she had brought to her companion. Greenaway craned his head above her red-gold hair, looking out across the low-lying fields to a line of distant poplars. I sensed and shared his apprehension. But why? I asked myself, and could not answer.

The villa was built in the middle of the seventeenth century, and in the manner of Palladio, by an unknown architect. It is a majestically severe building and might well have been a proto-type for Vanbrugh's Seaton Delaval phase. The setting of the villa, in what appears to be a vast saucer rimmed by distant, low-lying foothills, enhances both its austerity and stateliness.

The villa had been in the Anselmo family for generations, Revisi explained, as we approached the magnificent portico above wide stone steps. Indeed, it had been contended that the building had been designed between 1745 and 1747 by Count Leonardo Anselmo, scholar, aristocrat, dilettante, merchant, traveller, and friend of Francesco Muttoni. He reeled off the record like an inventory of glory.

"The Anselmos have continued in this great tradition," Revisi went on. "Count Luigi Anselmo is a friend of poets and painters, a patron of their arts. And it will probably interest our English friends to know that Count Luigi is also a great sports-man. He has one of the finest packs of hounds in Northern Italy. He has, also, what is perhaps too rare amongst great Italian landowners, a social conscience."

"Hear! Hear!" said one or two Italian voices, whilst the English tried to look like a group of benevolent thrusters over fences.

I looked round to see whether Revisi's recital had interested James, but he was talking gaily to Georgina. Meanwhile, Revisi was still enlarging upon Anselmo's munificence.

"You will also see here," he was saying, "a seminary for orphan boys conducted by the Church. All this, Count Luigi has permitted to be conducted in the Villa Anselmo. This seminary is now one of the most famous places of youthful learning in Northern Italy, and visitors come from many countries to see the school at work and play. Already, several of the boys from Anselmo have won high awards in our universities. They are also skilful footballers," he added with a smile. "And of this latter fact, the Count is especially proud."

Everyone laughed or smiled. Except perhaps Greenaway, and myself, watching Greenaway. In any case, I thought, Revisi probably meant soccer and I had played another code.

"Will you forgive me if I leave you for most of this visit?" I asked Bianca, as we disembarked from the coach. "I have one or two things I must talk over with James."

"But of course," she said. "I shall try to get back into the good books of my compatriots. I have been neglecting them and some of them begin to look at me with frowns."

"I am trying to book to Rome by sleeper on Friday," I said as we disembarked.

"You are very efficient," she whispered.

James came across. "I've told Georgina to look after herself this time," he said. "What do we do? Follow Greenaway like a couple of those Scotland Yard flatfoots who follow the P.M.?"

"Just hang around is my only advice. I'm out of my depth, too."

In a field to the rear of the villa, now towering above us like a gigantic stage set, boys were playing soccer, one team in red shirts, the other in white. They made lively splashes of colour against the background of trees.

Greenaway stood with Miss Castle. Georgina and Bianca stood together. James and myself set ourselves at the edge of the group now gathered around Revisi, waiting for his lead. Revisi, for once, seemed nonplussed: as if his careful planning had gone awry. Then, to his obvious relief, the door within the great portico opened and two friars in the white habits of Dominicans came out. After a moment's hesitancy, as if daunted by what they saw before them, they began to descend the steps.

"Ah, Signor Revisi! I am sorry!" cried the older man in Italian, leading the way. He beamed upon us all and within ten seconds they were both surrounded and caught up in the questions of the Italians in the group. The British seemed forlornly out of things, except one of the inevitable English spinsters, now more determined than ever to exercise her Italian.

The younger man, after having allowed his superior two minutes' grace, began to talk in fluent English. Skilfully and swiftly he brought everyone into a lively chattering group. Gradually the whole party was shepherded up the stone steps to the great hall of the *piano nobile*. Here were the famous frescoes by Giuseppi Angelo and Tiepolo, the younger friar announced proudly, unable to resist a flash of pride and possessiveness by proxy.

Opening out of the hall was a suite of comfortably furnished sitting-rooms, which could be glimpsed through arched entrances, the sofas covered with splendidly flamboyant pillar-box-red blankets.

"Where is the school?" someone asked in a high voice as we wandered around the hall, peeping into the rooms barred from us by red ropes held in gleaming brass fists.

"Below, in the rooms off the old arcades. Le vecchie stanze per i servi," the young man said. "We shall see them later if you are interested. But beware which arcades. On one side are the kennels and hounds of the Count Anselmo. Meanwhile here is the sala with the world-famous frescoes by Tiepolo."

We trooped outside to the sala. Three football games were now in progress. Blue, green, red and white hoops and yellow shirts dotted the distant pitches. The scene was as gay as a Dufy painting, and, in a sacrilegious moment, I thought the whole scene had more vivacity and charm than the great frescoes of "The Seasons" we had been enjoined to admire.

I had been trying to keep a careful watch on Greenaway, but it was difficult in that shambling throng. When I did see him he appeared to be more relaxed, walking close to Miss Castle and listening intently to the white-robed guide.

Thus we all stood in a group in the sala, self-consciously examining the frescoes, making suitable remarks, stealing side-long glances at the beautiful sweep of this valley of the River Po. Even the most determinedly culture-conscious English tourists would rather look at landscape any day than at a painting of landscape, and so it was then. I was amused to

98

watch them leave the frescoes and cross to the balcony, gazing at the far hills and the nearer games of football. Then the friar called to us, directing us from the sala to the upper bedrooms, all superbly furnished.

"Not much monasticism here," James said. "I suppose this is where the Count takes refuge."

"And now to the classrooms for those who are interested!" announced the friar. We all began to straggle down by one or other of the two staircases leading down to the loggia, thence to the vaulted kitchens and out into the arcade.

The seminary was a credit to the Order; a series of white-painted barely furnished rooms with sky-blue ceilings and sliding blackboards, each opening out on to the low terrace.

The women and one or two of the younger men were quick to praise the achievements of the Dominicans and the functional gaiety of the rooms, but James was not to be ensnared by non-essentials.

"School is hell, whatever the surroundings!" he declared in a loud whisper. "Nobody's yet invented any background that makes it bearable."

I nodded agreement, although my own form-rooms had been pleasant enough, despite the fact that they had lacked a rural vista of twelve or fifteen miles.

In the mêlée of sightseeing I had temporarily forgotten Greenaway. In a sudden spurt of conscience I swung round to seek him out, but he was nowhere to be seen. Miss Castle had also gone. James was unperturbed and tried to calm my fears.

"He's in good hands," he said. "In his place I'd have taken that red-headed popsy off into the woods, too." But my face must have shown my alarm, for he added hastily, "But I'm forgetting. What d'you suggest we do?"

"Look around!" I said and stepped quickly out of the group and hurried back to the loggia, James following dutifully. From there, I thought, we should be able to scan the surrounding playing-fields. Greenaway couldn't have got far. From that vantage point we ought to be able to spot him and Miss Castle.

From the balcony we quickly sighted them, perhaps two hundred yards away, well beyond the first football pitch and walking between the two farther games towards the distant grove of poplars. They were deeply engrossed, a foot or so apart, paying no attention to the games around them. Greenaway was gesturing with his right arm as if explaining something of serious consequence. They had presumably walked round the pitch, beyond the goalposts and nets, and then alongside the touchline, towards the trees. I was momentarily relieved. Surely there was nothing unusual in such an escape from the crowd. Wasn't it, in fact, a more natural reaction by the young than hanging around? Most of us had done the same thing at one time or another in our visits. Even the architecturally devout often got well away from the buildings in order to see the villas in their true settings. Too often, alas, beautiful buildings were now in dismal surroundings.

But Greenaway wasn't looking back at the villa. To me, watching from a distance, it seemed that he was pleading for his love, even perhaps his life.

James had also spotted them, but now he was looking farther afield. "Look!" he said suddenly. "This *is* a bit of luck. As Revisi Furioso so truthfully explained, this is quite a sporting establishment. Look!"

From the cover of the poplars beyond the most distant football match, a pack of light-coloured foxhounds appeared, complete with huntsmen and whipper-in, exercising on foot. It was an unexpectedly English sight in that Italian valley. For James the sight was plainly a vision of supreme pleasure and nostalgia. "This is a treat!" he almost shouted. "Just like home! I'd forgotten the Italians were sometimes real sportsmen."

But my own eyes were fixed on two brown-habited friars who had walked into the frame my eyes had made of huntsman and hounds. For the moment I could not relate them to my hazy sense of apprehension. Then the association clicked into place. Vision and memory merged as the figures moved slowly from the grove of poplars towards the boundary of the playing-fields, towards Greenaway and Miss Castle.

"The idiot!" I exclaimed to nobody in particular.

Apparently Greenaway hadn't seen the friars. He was too intent on his story to Miss Castle.

"Put me in the picture," James begged. "*Why* is he an idiot?"

I didn't answer but stood there, fascinated and frustrated,

100

watching a by-play seemingly impossible to stop. The gap between the Franciscans and Greenaway narrowed, step by step, as the friars skirted the far game and advanced towards the young couple now in the strip of no man's land between the two games.

Even from that distance, I could persuade myself that I saw Greenaway's start of surprise as he was suddenly faced by the friars. He put his arm in front of Miss Castle as if to thrust her out of the scene, but, in the same instant, with the smoothness of prearranged plan, one of the friars spoke to her, took her protectively by the arm, and began to escort her slowly back towards the house. For a second or so she hesitated in bewilderment and turned towards Greenaway for explanation, but he was already deeply involved in his new conversation, talking earnestly, even expostulating, with the taller friar who remained with him. He turned as Miss Castle spoke to him and pointed towards the villa. Then, as if in sudden accord, or perhaps as a result of sudden resolve or collapse, he turned away with the friar and began to walk towards the trees.

"We must go over and break it up!" I said, instinctively but unthinkingly, as I turned to dash down the stairway.

"Three hundred yards at least," James said, more practically. He followed me down the steps. "And it means crossing two football games. We shall be very popular. What's your time for the furlong these days, Rupert?"

"Something under the hour."

"Mine, too. We might make it before nightfall if we cut across the games. Shall we?"

I knew he was letting me down lightly. Few men in their forties could have been in better physical shape than James, conditioned by his year-round life in the open.

"We'll have to. Play's at the other end," I said.

"It'll be back soon," James said judicially. "I've been watching 'em. Well-matched teams. Hadn't you noticed?" I shook my head to save my breath.

We came out into the kitchens, then out to the yard below the loggia.

"Just a moment! It's a chance!" James called suddenly, standing stock-still.

He put his hands to his mouth and gave a magnificent view hallo, then another. I was so startled by the sudden volume of noise in my eardrums that I leapt a foot in the air.

"A triumph for lungs trained on the fells," James said proudly as the echoes of his cries died away. From our view-point, slightly above ground level, I could see the hounds break away and start to race across the field towards us on a wide front. They took everything in their stride, spreading confusion and disquiet. Within a split second they had ruined the far football game. Boys were suddenly helpless and aimless as the hounds fanned out across the pitch, into the game, between their legs. Play died in mass bewilderment and laughter. The football disappeared. Then the hounds were up with the friar and Greenaway. The friar made as if to turn, decided against it, vacillated, turned again too late, tripped himself in the folds of his habit, floundered and went down under the rush of hounds. The boys, recovering, began to chase the hounds, now well into the two other games. Greenaway helped the friar to his feet and then, after a moment's hesitation, broke away, following the schoolboy teams in pursuit of the pack.

"This is no place for us!" James said swiftly. "Up to the loggia again."

A minute later we were standing, two innocent Englishmen in a mixed Anglo-Italian group, all plainly captivated by the comedy of confusion being played out before them, for the hounds, followed by shouting, laughing, madcap boys, were now well into the nearer game.

In the medley, I had lost sight of Miss Castle and her Fran-ciscan escort. They must have skirted the touchline of the nearer field, I judged, and be fairly near the villa. Then I caught sight of her, almost dancing with gaiety and laughter, watching boys, hounds, huntsman, whipper-in, referees and linesmen from all three games caught in the wild, fantastic frolic. I remember my fleeting thought that she seemed more at ease against this background of high jinks than walking in constraint with Greenaway.

By then, without the remotest sign of control or direction from the huntsman and whipper-in, the hounds were in yet greater confusion. For the onlookers the scene was overwhelmingly hilarious. Sixty-odd boys in multi-coloured shirts were racing aimlessly but enthusiastically amongst twenty-five couple of hounds. Monastic referees and linesmen, their habits tucked into their cordelli, were enforced participants in the widespread farce. Nobody seemed able to make a first attempt to restore order. Indeed, almost everyone, except the huntsman and whipper-in, seemed to revel in the confusion. All the members of the Anglo-Italian Palladian Society had left their cultural sight-seeing and were standing on the terrace, some lost impiously in laughter, others wide-eyed and nervous at this uproarious pandemonium.

I noticed that Greenaway had unobtrusively rejoined the group below. A moment later Miss Castle was again standing by his side, still almost breathless with laughter, unashamedly lost in delight.

I could see that even Greenaway was smiling, although his smile seemed somewhat strained. I wondered how he would explain away the unusual episode in which she had been unwittingly involved.

At last, as the huntsman and whipper-in began laboriously to round up the packs, James and I went down and joined the chattering, mirthful crowd on the terrace. I wandered across to Greenaway, took him by the arm and drew him aside.

"Why did you disappear like that?" I asked.

"It's not really any concern of yours," he said, defiantly. "As I told you: if I were with Miss Castle you were excused."

"You met your Franciscans, I noticed."

He nodded gloomily. "It wasn't quite the rendezvous that had been arranged," he said limply, his defiance collapsing like a crumpled bag.

"How did it differ from the official rendezvous?"

"We were supposed to meet by the poplars on the far side of the football pitches, the boundary of the playing fields. I'd forgotten all about it. I was just wandering."

"I find that difficult to believe. You were near enough to the official rendezvous when you did meet."

"I hadn't noticed," he said pathetically. "I really had forgotten all about the rendezvous. I swear I had. I was too far

103

involved in what I was saying to Miss Castle. Please believe me."

"Then why didn't you go off in another direction?"

"I honestly don't know."

"What did your Franciscan have to say?" I asked peevishly.

"He gave me a password."

"Which was?"

He laughed sheepishly. "Pro bono publico, of all impossible phrases."

"Why so impossible? It's what you all believe, isn't it? Anyway, what happened then?"

"Like a fool I involuntarily returned my password. An equally damn silly word—portico. I've been living with it for a month. Then he asked me for the message I had for him. I said I hadn't one. He was very surprised and said there must be. At first I tried to brazen things out. Then I suppose I began to get scared at what I'd let myself in for and started playing for time. It didn't cut any ice. Then I said I didn't understand. He began to get annoyed and I began to panic."

"Is that why you walked off with him?"

"I suppose it must have been. I had a wild idea of trying to sock him. It was time I wanted. We'd just started an argument and then those damn fool dogs rushed us."

"You ought to thank every one of them personally."

"It was quite amusing—and opportune, as it turned out, of course. Did you have anything to do with it? The war-cry and all that, I mean? What do they call it? View hallo or something?"

"A fortunate coincidence. And now what?"

"God knows."

By then Revisi was rounding up his unwilling charges and bidding prolonged farewells to the priests. I walked across to Bianca and took her arm, and we joined the crowd surrounding the youthful footballers, who seemed as loth to return to their game as we all seemed to depart. I could see why. Apples, boiled sweets and chocolate were being distributed as if from a large yet invisible cornucopia. The boys were delighted, escorting the sightseers to the coaches with disarming courtesy.

As we left the Villa Anselmo, the coach swinging out into the road between the high piers of the entrance, two Franciscan friars were also leaving. Like two devout men of God they stepped aside in the dusty road, their heads slightly bowed. They were on the near side, my side, of the coach and Greenaway could not see them. One was enormous, I noticed, the other almost wizened, yet neither was an old man.

Bianca was still chuckling. "That was one of the most funny things I have seen in many years," she said. "When I am unhappy I will think of those little boys and the dogs and the friars, all in that wonderful mix-up. Did you ever see anything so funny, Rupert?"

"Never," I said, smiling, but my smile was warped by fear for Greenaway. I could not believe that this was the end of the troubles he had invited to himself. The faces of the two brown-garbed men standing in the dusty road were resolute and solemn. And Greenaway would not have such luck again. Fortune smiles on the brave, the old saw says, and most sayings, I find, are frequently confirmed by modern psychiatry. And, alas, nobody could call Greenaway brave.

We disembarked soon after midday for the picnic luncheon. By then we were in a side lane, on gently rising ground, well away from the main road between Padua and Vicenza, nearer the long line of low hills we had seen from the sala of the Villa Anselmo.

Descending from the coach, I looked around for Greenaway. As if following my thoughts, James came across. "What about our young grey-haired friend now?" he asked. "Do we let him be?"

I nodded. The bogus Franciscans could scarcely have followed us here, even though they might have a detailed itinerary of the tour and might even know Greenaway's daily movements. Surely Revisi hadn't planned this particular halt in this particular spot two or three months before? I thought. And who was the unknown contact in the coach, I wondered, watching the Society break up into groups and pairs. Certainly I should have found the task of spotting a probable informer well beyond any talent I might have had for intuitive deduction. The Italians and the English were typical cross-sections

105

of their national contributions to the tourist trade, as I had noted several times already. Plump men and women, young men and women . . . where would one look for an informer? And did an informer carry a recognizable mark of a lower order of mankind? I doubted it.

"Let Greenaway make his own arrangements for the rest of the day," I said, thinking that a picnic in these romantic surroundings might even help him in his proposals to Miss Castle. But had I the right to let any girl in for the tribulations of a romance with so treasonable a character? But there seemed little enough chance of that.

James broke my speculations, asking whether we should all lunch together. I agreed, dearly as I wished to be alone with Bianca.

I watched James return to Georgina, now setting out her meal, and then crossed to Bianca to ask, tardily, whether she objected to this foursome. She laughed. "They are kind. Your James is nice. So is Georgina. And we shall be alone all next week. Let us stay with them."

The picnic, higher up the slope amongst the pine trees, was a great success. Georgina was at her most preposterous, with her inconsequential comments on the tour and the tourists. And the Hotel Jolanda had packed two mouth-watering picnic baskets of fresh rolls, smoked ham, bel paese, cake and fruit. Plus, of course, two bottles of chianti.

Bianca sat and smiled, saying nothing, relaxed against an outcrop of mossy rock, laughing frequently at Georgina's sallies. I was amused, sitting there, to remember a fellow-student's advice from long-ago: "It's impossible to hide women's legs on picnics, Rupert. So let's take only the prettiest legs along with us." How true a comment! I thought, my eyes moving from Georgina's long and slender legs, still strangely those of a young girl's, to Bianca's, more sensuous and rounded, reminding me disturbingly of our long night in Venice, now already a century away. And when our eyes met I knew that Bianca, too, shared these thoughts.

At two o'clock Revisi's whistle recalled us to the coach. "None too soon," James said. "I was just beginning to nod, despite Georgina's monologue. At this moment I'd swop all the villas of the Veneto for forty winks on this grassy slope."

"To your feet, Philistine!" Georgina cried, scrambling up.

Meanwhile, Bianca unnoticed had collected cups and saucers, napery and cutlery, and replaced them in the baskets as swiftly and neatly as a peasant housewife.

We scrambled down the slope to the lane. I was relieved to find Greenaway already there, talking to Miss Castle and Brunatelli. Greenaway looked so solemn that I wondered whether he and his girl-friend had been landed with the pedagogue for their picnic, but I overheard Brunatelli lecturing them upon the view from the ridge where he had taken his meal, he said. I wondered where his wife had gone. Greenaway nodded glumly. Miss Castle looked fixedly away, her mood determinedly far off.

Poor Greenaway!

But the visits of the afternoon drove thoughts of Greenaway's dilemma from my mind. We visited both the Villa Barbaro and the Villa Emo, and the memories of those houses vividly remain.

The Villa Barbaro, at Maser, said Revisi in the coach, would be visited by the great courtesy of Contessa Luling-Volpi. "This is undoubtedly the most beautiful of all Palladio's villas," he went on. "Designed in 1560 for the brothers Barbar, one a Doge, the other an archbishop, the Villa Barbaro took eight years to build. You will find the building of the utmost simplicity: two storeys with single-storey arcades lying back on either side. Here, too, you will find the most fabulous of frescoes by Paolo Veronese, fabulous chimney-pieces, and, of course, the fabulous fountain by Bittona . . ." and so on and on.

Revisi's words were, for once, an understatement. The villa and its setting, the furnishings and decorations translate the visitor to a golden age. I wish, indeed, that this were a record of another kind, so that I could indulge my growing architectural interests and write at length of the Villa Barbaro, one of the half-dozen most beautiful houses in the world.

Time and again my mind goes back to that afternoon as to a

time of enchantment taken clean out of this mundane world. I remember so clearly walking with Bianca through the rooms of this miniature palace, then out to the grotto, then round to the stables to see a group of carriages and dog-carts, gleaming and polished as if for use on the morrow. Then down to the exquisite little Palladian church, and back to tea in the villa, to which we had been invited by our hostess. White-gloved footmen handed round cakes and ale. Entertainment on a truly mediaeval scale, as James said.

Afterwards, nodding in the warm coach, we drove to the Villa Emo at Fanzolo, another design by Palladio, less spectacular, but a house of considerable charm with a ramp approach to the pedimented front in place of the more conventional stairway. We were there until the cooler evening breeze began to stir amongst us as we walked through the arcades and gardens.

That day I remember as our most arduous day of sightseeing. The long day in the open air, the absorbed wandering through loggias, gardens, arcades and driveways, began to take their toll in the coach on the return journey. Heads began to nod and soon the coach was as quiet as a midnight dormitory.

Bianca rested her head upon my shoulder. Her hand reached out and clasped my own. I wondered what Miss Desmond and some of Bianca's compatriots might think of this private *entente cordiale,* but I was too caught up in happiness to bother with the outside world.

Only the sight of Greenaway cast a shadow. He sat on the opposite side of the coach, staring ahead as we drove swiftly through the darkening roads. Miss Castle had fallen asleep. Her head rested docilely upon his shoulder. I suddenly felt an overwhelming wave of compassion for the man, but at such times we are invincibly alone. No man can help. I might wish to help, offer to help, but ultimately he was alone.

Sometime before seven o'clock we came into Padua, to the Piazza Cavour, a silent but cheerful coach of sleepy sightseers. Farewells were heartfelt but weary. Remarks about the next day's journey to the Villas Malcontenta and Rotonda were made between yawns and sighs.

James and Georgina wandered off, waving a fond interim farewell. "May see you later!" James called. "We shall probably be dining in the piazza."

"I will call for you in two hours' time," I said to Bianca as she rubbed her eyes awake.

"Yes! I will be more of a companion then, Rupert. I promise. Now I will take a taxi down to the hotel."

I left her and went into the travel agency. Two tickets for the following night awaited me. I walked slowly back towards the hotel. At the Caffé Petrocchi I stopped for an espresso and a cognac and sat there for what seemed a long time, lost in a trance of happiness, watching the crowds, anticipating the pleasures of my bath, my dinner and the evening ahead. And was I, I wondered, putting off my return to the hotel and a hot bath lest I should run into Greenaway again?

25

BUT I was scarcely back in my room before I heard the two peremptory knocks I now recognized as Greenaway's.

He burst into the room, pale and tight-lipped. "All my stuff has been searched!" he said, the words exploding in the room like Christmas crackers.

I almost smiled to see his petulance, but said, as gently as I could, "Well, it was to be expected, wasn't it? I haven't given it much thought, but on your own admission you're not dealing with children."

"I know, I know," he said wearily, "but that doesn't get us anywhere."

"Then go back to London, as I told you. That is your best course. In fact, your only course."

"It's too late now."

"You could probably get to Milan by train tonight. From there you might still be able to get a cancelled flight on an overnight tourist plane. Or you could probably go straight through by train if you don't mind travelling hard."

"I've got an air passage booked for next week," he said doggedly.

"That won't help you now. Why don't you try the air people? They're usually very helpful?"

"I'm having dinner with Miss Castle."

"Then send her a note."

"I can't. Things are bad enough with her, anyway. I don't want to finish them for good."

"Well, then, relax for this evening. But for God's sake do something definite tomorrow morning."

He nodded, and then changed the subject.

"You're determined to hang on to those papers?" he asked.

"Absolutely."

"Even if I proposed to return to England tonight, would you still hang on to them?"

"Even then. I think they are out of your hands now, completely."

"They might bring you into some kind of danger," he said.

"I'll chance that."

"Supposing they realize you have them?"

"How can they, whoever they are, unless they've seen you coming into this room. Who are 'they', by the way?"

"God knows," he said hopelessly. "That's one of the most awful things about it all. The anonymity. The impersonal demands. The unexplaining authority."

"Surely that's why you came to love them in the first place, wasn't it?" I said bitterly. "One of them is probably on the coach with us."

He brushed that aside. "I know no more than you," he said wearily.

"Then why should they know I have your papers?"

"No reason at all."

"Did you mention it to them, those two holey-boley characters this morning?" I asked, suddenly suspicious.

"Good God, no, but they have a grisly talent for putting two and two together."

"Which two and two. They haven't seen the two of us together."

"That's true."

110

I was perturbed. "You're sure you said nothing?"

"For what my honour's worth. Nothing."

"Well, go out and enjoy yourself and see me in the morning. Here at half-past eight if you like."

Once again I was inexplicably sorry for him. "Tell the maid to bring your breakfast in here if you like," I added. "We can try to work out some kind of plan over coffee."

"You're very kind."

"Skip it."

"Nevertheless, you are."

He seemed to pull his shoulders back and to make a sudden resolve to be more cheerful. It was a sad sight.

"How are things with Miss Castle?" I asked.

"Couldn't be worse. She can scarcely wait for me to go. I'm sure she counts the days."

"Why not go tonight, then?"

"A man lives in hopes."

"Perhaps things will look up tonight. In any case, I wish you luck."

"Thank you, but I've lost hope."

He looked so youthful and doleful, standing there by the table, that I put my arm about his shoulders. Despite my hatred for his kind of treachery, my own happiness gave me some compassion for him in his misery.

"Pull yourself together," I said, and wondered how many more platitudes of comfort I should utter before he left. Always in moments of high emotion, platitudes seem, alas, the only language of mankind. Yet perhaps there is sense in that, too. We are thus kept earthbound, at least.

Greenaway muttered thanks and left the room. I was overcome by a sense of utmost frustration. His despair and self-pity shadowed my own happiness.

I ran a hot bath and tried to smooth away the world's sad face in that most ancient of soothers. Gradually I dozed. When I awoke it was a quarter to nine, and I had to shave and dress at breakneck speed. Fortunately an Italian taxi-driver can always get the traveller to a destination on time, however late his departure. But it was a needless rush: Bianca was unready.

We took two hours over dinner, laughing, talking, planning

111

our days-to-be in Rome. Neither of us seemed to regret that we should miss the second part of the tour. The prospect of Rome and escape into our own day-long, night-long companionship held us in a feverish enchantment.

I went back to the Grande Italia with Bianca and to her room. For an hour or more we lay on the single bed, whispering, laughing, loving. Shouldn't we ask the management, even at this late hour, to change her room? she asked. Hotel managements in Italy were so understanding.

Resolute, at last, I dressed and went, making my half-bold, half-sheepish way past the night-desk and the polite "Good-night" of the porter, out into the Paduan night.

The past twenty-four hours had been as strenuous as any I had had since the end of the war, I decided as I fell into bed. Sightseeing and lovemaking seemed to add up to fulsome days and nights. Within a minute I was asleep.

Sometime in the night I seem to recall waking momentarily as if a breeze had stirred the curtain or the door, but this I shall never know for certain.

I remember only that I awoke several seconds before the maid brought breakfast and was thus spared the shock of her usual bustling reveille. She brought in my tray and put it on the bedside commode. Leaving, she said, "Una nota, Signor", and picked up an envelope from the threshold of the door and brought it to the bed. I recognized the envelope as part of the Hotel Jolanda's stationery, but the writing was strange to me and I poured myself a cup of coffee before ripping it open. Several one-thousand lira notes tumbled out. I put them on the coverlet, took the first celestial gulp of the day and began to read the letter. There were two small half-quarto sheets, each carrying the die-stamped heading of the hotel, each covered on both sides with the neat handwriting of an experienced note-taker. The first sheet was headed 3 a.m.

As I read, I put the cup down on the tray, knowing that my body was already growing cold. Even as I read on hurriedly, I heard the loud cry of the maid and her stumbling footsteps along the corridor, and already I knew, without the shadow of a doubt, the reason for her cry.

Dear Frost,

I write to you because you have been kinder to me than anyone I have known during the recent years, and you are the only person I feel that I could talk to as a friend. I wish I had met you five years ago. Briefly, then, I have decided that I cannot go on. Long before you read this note I shall have died by my own hand, perhaps in my right mind, perhaps not. Who among us ever knows? I think that this is the only way out. If I return to England I face indictment, a ghastly trial, long imprisonment, professional and moral degradation. These things are beyond my resources. Things might have been different if I could have found some happiness with a woman, but here again I have never been successful. I got off to a bad start, as so many boys at boarding schools are apt to do. Too much of one's own sex at the age of puberty is a bad thing. I think women recognize these things in men without knowing they do. I think Elizabeth Castle did. Anyway, there it is. You will understand these things. At least, you will have met them before and will neither be shocked nor condemn.

Please return the papers I gave you to my chief, Professor Richard Hankinson at the Ministry of Supply on the 16th of this month when he returns from Australia. Not before and not after. My parents live in Shropshire. You can send them a cable or, if you're feeling especially brave, ring them at Fairfold 213. B (for Benedict) F. Greenaway. My mother is rather frail and my father will not leave her, I know. So he won't be tearing out here. In any case, I have never got on with him particularly well. Incompatibility of temperament and all that. And he never forgave me for renouncing his beloved faith. There is no one else. Apart from one or two frustrating attempts at friendship I have been rather a solitary.

I am sorry to leave you with the necessary clearing-up. It will probably spoil your projected visit to Rotunda and Malcontenta. This letter is for you alone. I have already written and left another on my dressing-table here for the coroner or whatever is his Italian equivalent. That should be enough of a smokescreen. On no account show this letter to anyone—but I see that its contents make that impossible. Burn it, please. Thank you.

If I may now give you the same advice that you gave me, I think you should return to England as soon as possible. I think you may possibly be in some danger yourself.

I am terribly sorry to leave you in such a situation, but I

must be honest. I did not like the look of those pseudo-religious figures I met today (sorry, yesterday. Three-fifteen, I notice by my watch). They look too purposeful. So do be careful, please. That is my only prayer, for it is as an unrepentant unbeliever that I take farewell of you and wish you well and thank you. I find I have more money with me than I shall need on the journey I now undertake. You may find it useful. Good-bye.

FRANCIS GREENAWAY

I raced through the letter, and sat there in bed, stunned and saddened. I was near to tears of sorrow, fury and frustration as I got out of bed and pulled on my dressing-gown. Steps again thudded along the corridors. I put my head out of the door to see two maids and a man in a dark suit walking in the determined manner of all mortals *en route* for an accident. I called to the second maid in Italian, asking what was wrong. She waved her arm distractedly, crying, "Una accidente, Signor."

"Silenzio!" hissed the man.

"Can I be of help?" I asked. "I am a doctor."

He turned quickly, mollified, and said, "Please, please."

I followed them along the corridor to Greenaway's room. The clerk opened the door. Greenaway was slumped into an arm-chair, dressed in grey flannel trousers, blue pullover and open shirt. By his side, on the dressing-table, were a blue envelope, a tumbler, a hip flask of whisky and a small bottle of white tablets, precisely arranged. I glanced at the label which carried a note of dosage. Barbital or Amylobarbitone, I judged. A dozen of those in a tumbler of whisky and he would have been dead before the dawn. I glanced at the envelope. It was addressed TO WHOM IT MAY CONCERN.

The three Italians—the tubby, panting clerk with shining bald head and a thin trickle of a moustache, and the two stolid, black-haired maids—stood within the room like a dumb chorus.

For the clerk's benefit I took up Greenaway's wrist for five seconds and then slowly shook my head. The trio crossed themselves quickly and one of the maids mouthed some kind of litany.

"A doctor in the town should be called," I said.

The hotel clerk nodded vaguely.

114

Already he could see a hectic day ahead, overloaded with trouble and officialdom.

I should be glad to be of what help I could, I said. "For the moment," I added in my groping Italian, "nothing more can be done. And nothing must be disturbed, of course. There will be an enquiry."

The clerk moaned his agreement.

I could not decide whether his gloom was for himself, the reputation of the hotel, or the dead man. Meantime, I took a sheet from the bed and placed it over poor Greenaway's body as the clerk ushered the girls from the room. I followed. No one else was about. The English, despite the girl's outburst (or perhaps, being English, because of it), had kept to their rooms. Most of them were probably heavy-limbed after the previous day's exertions, and, to those already awake, the hurried footsteps and brief hubbub had doubtless seemed no more than the usual boisterous opening of a day in the life of an Italian hotel.

I went along to James's room.

He was shaving. "Hello, old boy, anything wrong?" he asked, taking in my dressing-gown, unshaven face and perhaps my dolorous expression.

I told him briefly of Greenaway's death.

He took the news calmly. He had only met the young scientist on the previous morning in my rooms, and he had seen death too often to utter unfelt, conventional phrases.

"Any reason you can put to it?" he asked.

I took the armchair and told him to carry on while I talked.

He used an old-fashioned cut-throat razor. Even during the war I had always been fascinated and horrified by his expert handling of the instrument. As he moved the blade about his cheekbones with accustomed skill, I told him all I knew about Greenaway, from Sunday's midnight confessional in the piazza to that morning's letter, which I now took from my dressing-gown pocket and began to read aloud.

At the end he said, "And you've still got the papers?"

I nodded.

"Where are they now?"

"In my jacket pocket in my room."

115

"Should you have 'em there? Perhaps Greenaway did tell these chaps he'd handed them over to you."

"Possibly. But I prefer to believe he spoke the truth, and didn't tell them."

"What will you do now?"

"I suppose I shall be wanted at the inquest. I shall have to hang around."

"Do they have inquests here?" he asked, getting the razor under his nose. "I seem to remember they have a magistrate's enquiry first, or something like that. They don't go in for inquests the way we do. At least, they didn't ten years ago."

I vaguely remembered something along the same lines. We should see, I responded gloomily.

The question of the funeral would also arise.

"Do suicides get funerals here?" James asked, as if determined to deprecate all foreign customs.

"They must get a final resting-place somewhere."

Inconsequently, I suddenly remembered my rail tickets for Friday night. I should probably have to cancel those and try to get tickets for Saturday night. Surely the whole affair, with all its dreary consequences, ought to be over by then.

"I had arranged to go on to Rome on Friday night," I said slowly, watching James.

"And skip the second week of this tour?" he asked.

I nodded.

"You won't go now, I imagine?"

"I may have to put it off till Saturday, but I don't see why I shouldn't go then," I said, trying to quieten the defiant note that seemed suddenly to have crept into my words. "All this ought to be over by then."

"Mightn't it be a bit tricky?"

"Mightn't what be a bit tricky?"

"Wandering around the ruins with those valuable bits of paper in your pocket. If they're all Greenaway claimed, mightn't somebody want to dot you on the head and walk off with 'em?"

"I don't see why. Nobody, except yourself, knows I've got the papers. They'll be as safe with me in Rome as they would be in Wimpole Street. I don't know anybody else I can deliver them to. This chap Hankinson, Greenaway writes about, doesn't get back to London for another fortnight. I can just as easily get back to London from Rome as from here. More easily, in fact. And I can't see what difference the extra week will make. And if Greenaway did tell these characters anything, I might even be covering my tracks more effectively by getting to Rome as soon as possible."

"Couldn't you cover your tracks best of all by getting to England now?" he asked.

"I'd still have to wait a couple of weeks for Hankinson's return."

"You could put 'em in your bank until he did return."

I fell silent with the realization that I was protesting far too much. I knew it, and James knew it. How ironical, too, that James should be pressing me to return to London in the same manner, almost in the same words, that I had used towards Greenaway!

James finished the last tricky spot on his bony chin, washed his face and took up the towel.

"You must decide, of course," he mumbled from the depths of the towelling, "but to my mind those papers seem to be too vulnerable wandering around in Italy."

I was nettled. "They won't exactly be wandering around on their own. They'll be in my care."

He took up his shirt from the back of a chair.

"Now, don't take this amiss, Rupert, but shall *I* take 'em back?" he asked, pulling the shirt over his head.

"When?"

"Today."

"I wouldn't dream of letting you. They were handed to me. I know that Greenaway mentioned the possibility of danger, but I don't believe a word of it. He was a highly strung, over-imaginative young man at the end of his tether. He was also deeply involved. I'm none of those things and I don't see why I should put anybody else to any trouble—or in any trouble, for that matter. In any case, I think Greenaway was mildly hysterical."

"Could you put them in a strong room in a bank here?"

"What about all the questions and red tape? Would you?"

"Frankly, no."

"I could even post the envelope to myself in London. I've thought of that. Again, would you?"

"Frankly, no, old boy. I've also got the average Englishman's contempt for foreign mail services. Not that our own get any better, of course."

"Perhaps I could deposit them with the local consul," I said. I crossed to the table and took up James's copy of Muirhead's Blue Guide to *Northern Italy* and checked the entry for Padua. "No British consul mentioned here," I said. "Probably the nearest is Venice, and I may not be in Venice when I want them again." I shut the guide and replaced it, perhaps defiantly.

"Probably not," James agreed.

"You'd go straight back?" I persisted, wanting to get James's views quite straight.

"I don't know. I probably would in my own circumstances." He pulled on his trousers and began to button his braces slowly and deliberately. Then he grinned. "In your shoes I might think a bit differently."

"You mean Bianca?"

"Isn't that what *you* mean?"

I nodded.

"Well, then," he said, "you must make up your own mind, old boy. And why not? In your shoes, I'd probably be in Rome right now."

"You're being very charitable."

"That's one word for it," he said, laughing. "I might use another, not in the English-Italian dictionary. Anyway, it's your problem, old boy, and God knows you're a responsible enough citizen. Or you were until this Bianca popsy arrived on the scene. She's quite something. Know much about her?"

"A good deal."

"Enough?"

"I think so."

"You won't get hurt?"

"I don't think so."

"Will she?"

"I doubt it."

"Then everybody's happy, including J. Westlake, farmer and

118

stockbreeder. I wish you well. Hadn't you better get ready, old son? And what will you do about today's jaunt? Pity to miss Malcontenta and Rotonda."

"I don't see what else I can do. An Englishman ought to be here when the local medico arrives. And I'm the logical chap."

"Can I be of any help?"

"No, frankly. You go off. It'll be a dreary day. I can promise anybody that. I've had it a score of times before. It will have its own ghastly professional interest, seeing how they do things here, I suppose. I seem to have missed it ten years ago: or else I've forgotten. What about Miss Castle? Who's going to tell her?"

"I will. I'll see her at the coach and tell her Greenaway's not coming this morning. There's nothing much she can do here, in any case. Later on, probably after lunch, I'll break the real news to her. And to Revisi. I don't suppose the hotel people here will be shouting it from the housetops just yet. According to what you've just said, the young redhead wasn't exactly crazy about Greenaway, and I don't see why we should upset the enjoyment of fifty other people."

"Far from it. But Miss Castle may feel she ought to be upset now it's too late. It's apt to be a normal reaction to this kind of situation."

"Probably, but she'll soon get over it."

James poured himself a cup of coffee. Then he said, with a slow smile, "I hope it doesn't sound too cynical, but I'd say there's no better morale-builder for a young woman than death from unrequited love on her behalf. Wouldn't you agree?"

"I haven't quite got your macabre sense of humour," I said, "but there's probably something in what you say."

"Speaking as a psychiatrist, in fact, you'd agree?"

"Regretfully, both as a psychiatrist and as a so-called man of the world."

He nodded and went on: "I take it that Greenaway's real trouble was that nobody loved him. Not even himself. I've always held the view that a man, any man, must like at least something in himself, even his social connections or the way he does his hair. If he doesn't, he don't stand a hope of liking the rest of mankind. Does modern psychiatry bear me out?"

119

"Not in quite such over-simplified terms, of course, but much along the same lines."

"I'd expect that. Mumbo-jumbology must have its day. Anyway, it's reassuring to have some professional backing for one's views."

"Will you give Bianca a message from me?" I asked, breaking into James' new interest in popular psychiatry.

"Any excuse to talk to Bianca would be a pleasure," he said. "Or would you rather write?"

"This will need a note."

"I'll come and collect it."

I went to my room and scribbled a note to Bianca, telling her of Greenaway's death, asking her to keep the information to herself. We should have to postpone our journey to Rome until Saturday. I would come to her hotel at nine o'clock that evening, and hoped to dine with her.

James came in to pick up the note and to ask again whether he should stay, but I sent him on his way, and then sat down to my belated breakfast of cold coffee, rolls and apricot jam. Afterwards I shaved and dressed, and went down to the hotel manager's office behind the reception desk.

The manager and the plump clerk I had already met that morning were there with three other men, one in uniform.

The manager, grey-haired and about sixty, with a dark, cadaverous face, sunken eyes and a grey, wasted face, looked more like a neurasthenic don than an Italian hotelier. He quickly introduced me to the others: Signor Lucca, Doctor Godi, Lieutenant Caccia.

Lucca was, apparently, the pretore, or examining magistrate, from the Tribunale, a man of about thirty-seven or eight with smooth, thinning, black hair, Wellingtonian nose, and half-smiling, half-pouting lips. He shook hands limply. Godi, the police surgeon, tall, gangling, clean-shaven, with a high yellow dome of a head and iron-rimmed spectacles, bowed and took my hand with a grip like a stevedore's. Lieutenant Caccia of the Carabinieri was young, smart, keen-eyed, running to fat, his belly far too tightly indrawn by his belt.

"Doctor Godi has already conducted his examination, Doctor Frost," Lucca said at once in fluent but over-formal English. "We are grateful for your earlier attendance."

I nodded as he went on: "Did you know anything about the young man, Doctor Frost?"

"Very little, no more than one learns about strangers on a trip of this kind."

"I am told that you have kindly promised to help us in any way you can."

I nodded.

"I am returning to the Tribunale now. I wonder whether you would be kind enough to come there to see me in—let us say —an hour's time?"

"Of course."

"We have in Italy, I believe, different arrangements from your own for these unfortunate occurrences," he said.

"I did not know," I said, truthfully enough.

"Here everything relating to the enquiry is in the hands of a pretore. In this instance, myself. I shall hope to see you later."

I nodded. He bowed and left with Godi and the lieutenant.

26

So BEGAN a morning which remains in my mind as one of the bleakest and most wearisome of my life. The long hours were relieved only by flashes of interest in watching the Italian police and legal systems at work.

I had touched slightly upon their work during the last days of the war, after V.E. Day. Now they seemed more efficient, less vociferously anxious to prove something about themselves to themselves or to others. But it was still tiring.

I waited, smoking (rather nervously I was irritated to notice), in the hotel lounge for something over half an hour. Then Lieutenant Caccia returned and I went with him to the Municipio.

En route I began to question him. Perhaps his awareness that I was an English medical man made him explanatory, for he began to elaborate upon the superficial introduction to Italian legal procedure I had received from Lucca.

As far as my knowledge of the language allowed me to understand, I began to sense something of the importance of the pretore, whose presence earlier that morning had puzzled me. Signor Lucca, it appeared, would decide whether the case would be for the Pretura, the Tribunale, or the Corti di Assise. In this case, I gathered, it would probably mean either the pretore himself or the Tribunale: Greenaway's suicide was apparently straightforward and without complications.

"But who knows?" Caccia added guardedly.

And what was a Tribunale? I asked.

"The pretore, Signor Lucca, and three or four jurymen."

"People picked at random as in England?"

"Ah, no!" he said. "I have heard of that. No, signor. Here jurymen are officially appointed." He implied criticism of the haphazard English system. I groaned inwardly, foreseeing days of red tape. "And if Signor Lucca decides that it's all quite straightforward?"

"It rests with him. If he does, all is at an end. The case is closed when he says that it is closed."

"And meanwhile?"

"We shall need the pretore's official permission to remove the body."

"And then?"

"The official notice of death from the Uffizio Stato Civile-Mortus," he said portentously.

The Registrar of Deaths, I thought. "And then?" I pestered.

"Only the enquiry."

"By whom?"

"The pretore himself."

James's memory had served him well.

The pretore would first conduct an examination of relevant witnesses, the lieutenant went on.

"Where?"

"At the Tribunale in the Via Altinate."

I waited in the lieutenant's office whilst he made three telephone calls. Then his own telephone rang. "Si, Signor Lucca," he said quickly, almost standing to attention. Ringing off, he turned to me, alertness still puffing out his pigeon breast. "The pretore asks if you would be kind enough to go now to the Tribunale."

I was glad of the chance to escape into some kind of action. Caccia took me to the gate of the courtyard of the Municipio and directed me to the Tribunale. The walk took me through the Piazza Cavour. At one of the cafés there I ordered an espresso and, sitting in the sun, began to brood over the fates that kept me from Bianca.

Slowly I forced my mind back to the problem in hand and took out Greenaway's letter and read it through again, trying to memorize every detail. I had no wish to put a foot wrong with Lucca: it would look too bad for an English doctor to trip himself up by some foolish slip in playing an unsavoury double-game with the Italian legal system. Two more readings and I should know the letter by heart, I told myself, and called the waiter across, paid and went on, across the Via dei Zabarelli into the Via Altinate, beneath the Porta Altinate—a gateway of the ancient town wall, Caccia had said with pride—past the shop and arcades, almost past the Tribunale, a heavily impressive and forbidding building set at right-angles to the street. Outside, arguing in the sun, were the groups that seem to collect around all law courts. A similar group stood inside, within the great hall of the Tribunale. I gave my name to a smiling commissionaire, the only creature there who seemed remotely touched by the sunlight, shafting dustily through the high windows.

I was, apparently, expected, for the commissionaire led me immediately towards the wide staircase, thence to a wide gallery and along a cheerless stone corridor.

Why is it that such surroundings are so intimidating to us all, however law-abiding? The universal sense of guilt? Association of ideas? There but for the grace of God etc. . . ? My only recollection of that time is of resentful apprehension.

My smiling dragoman tapped one of the doors that spaced out the long corridor, announced my name and bowed me into a small high room. Lucca was seated at a desk. A male clerk, open shorthand notebook on his knees, was seated at the side of the desk. He was dismissed as I entered with pointed in-

123

structions ". . . ma ti darò un colpo di telefono", which I could just translate.

Did my apprehension derive from Lucca himself? I wondered as I sat down. But he was solicitous, almost beneficent. Yet elements in his face belied this urbane patina. The brown eyes might be merry: they could as easily be merciless. The full lips might smile and pout: I had no doubt that they could also snap. Yet these or similar contradictions are in all of us. Only in that purposeful high-bridged, enquiring nose were there no contradictions. No man need mistake its predatory instinct.

Lucca motioned me to a chair and said in his precise English, "Doctor Frost, it is possible that you are not acquainted with Roman law: with my position as pretore."

I shook my head. I might as well start from scratch.

He began to explain, repeating Lieutenant Caccia's explanations at greater length and to my greater understanding. Then he began to talk casually about the Anglo-Italian Palladian Society, asking about our trip, the composition of the party, the villas, the extent of the tour. Continuing his social enquiries, not altering his manner, he said, "You were first in the room of Greenaway, I understand, Doctor Frost."

"No, the maid had been there first."

"Ah, yes, of course. How did you know that?"

"I heard her cry out."

"You left your room to enquire into the reason for her cry?"

"No, I did not."

"Did you keep to your room for any particular reason?"

"None. I thought it was the business of the hotel."

"Yet you went out when the maid returned?"

"Yes."

"Why that time and not when you first heard the cry?"

"Because by that time I had more clothes on," I said, already irritated by his persistence.

"Ah, of course," he said slowly, his full lips smiling again. He paused before continuing. "How long did you estimate Greenaway to have been dead, Doctor Frost?"

"I made only the most superficial examination. To me he was, quite simply, dead."

"You would not care to hazard an estimate?"

"Not without a further examination."

"I understand." Another long pause. Then: "Had you met Mr Greenaway socially on this trip, Doctor Frost?"

"I had spoken to him."

"He had not consulted you in any way?"

Perhaps I hesitated for a moment. A flashed image of Sunday night, the hotel lounge, the waiting Greenaway came back to me. What time did night porters go off duty? Could Lucca already know from the night porter that Greenaway and I had gone out into the night?

"Not professionally," I thought it best to say.

"In what way, then, may I ask?"

"Romantically."

I was pleased with my reply, for it plainly puzzled Lucca. "Romantically" wasn't a word expected of an English doctor. For a split-second I had the initiative. "I do not understand," he said, and broke into Italian: "Se capisci italiano è la parola 'romanzescamente'?"

I remained resolutely English, unwishful to be put at yet greater disadvantage by becoming involved in another language. I repeated doggedly "Romantically".

"Go on," Lucca said, momentarily defeated.

"He was apparently attached to a young woman on the trip," I said. "He wasn't having much success. He spoke to me about her."

"Why should he select you, a stranger?"

"He had learned that I was a doctor."

"How had he learned that?"

"I am occasionally called 'Doctor'."

"Ah, of course. How foolish of me! And what was your view of Greenaway, Doctor Frost?"

"In what way?"

"Of his emotional state, shall we say? Or to use your own word, of his romantic situation?"

"I thought that he was a young man going through rather a difficult time."

"Did he seem to you unbalanced?"

"Certainly not unbalanced. Highly strung, perhaps. No more. Certainly not more than thousands who live around us."

"You would not have called him a suicidal type?"

"In my experience, those who talk suicide—the suicidal type, as you call them—rarely carry out their threats. The suicides I have known have been totally unexpected. As with Greenaway. Isn't that your experience?"

"My experience, Doctor Frost, is more concerned with ends than with beginnings," he said with a smile.

Our exchanges had gradually become more icy. And his English was improving as the interrogation continued. He was becoming less formal: he was remembering colloquialisms from earlier days. The war perhaps. He went on: "When did you last see Greenaway alive?"

"Last evening."

"At what time?"

"Soon after eight o'clock."

"What was his mood, would you say?"

"His usual mood."

"How would you describe that?"

Lucca sat back in his chair, chin on hands, gravely considering me across the desk, his brown eyes fixed unrelentingly upon my own. In disconcerting sympathy, as if to hear every word, he leaned forward.

"A swift change of mood from elation to despondency. Too swift a change," I said.

"A maniac-depressive, Doctor Frost?" Lucca said, to my surprise. "Or a schizothyme?"

"I would have to know far more of his history to give an opinion I should like quoted. To me he seemed to be at the parting of the ways. Success in his romance would have fortified him in the years that lay ahead. Failure caught him at a particularly unfortunate moment."

"Why a *particularly* unfortunate moment, Doctor Frost?"

It was a slip on my part. A foolish slip. "At the moment when the pendulum had swung right against him," I said, trying in verbosity to smooth away my error.

Lucca seemed prepared to accept my cliché.

"Greenaway was a scientist, I understand," he said, tangentially.

"So I gathered."

126

"A government scientist?"

I nodded.

"Did his career or any side of his scientific work enter into his sense of despair, would you say, Doctor Frost?"

"I wouldn't know."

"Did he leave you a communication of any kind?"

I shook my head.

Lucca said slowly: "The maid says that she gave you an envelope this morning. Apparently it had been pushed under your door during the night. An hotel envelope, she says. In fact, an envelope similar to the one left by Greenaway for myself—the magistrate."

"A message from a friend," I said, suddenly cold in the warm room. "Doubtless the same kind of envelope."

"Did the communication have any relevance to the matter of Greenaway?"

"Good heavens, no. It concerned a projected rendezvous."

"You wouldn't have it with you, by any chance?"

I shook my head.

"It wasn't in your room, Doctor Frost," he said slowly. "Not in your wastepaper basket. Nor on your breakfast tray."

I shrugged my shoulders. "It may be at the Police Head-quarters, perhaps in the street, perhaps at the café in the Piazza Cavour where I had coffee." I was tempted to go on, but thought that I had already said enough.

"May I ask the name of your friend?"

"Mr James Westlake."

"He would verify this, of course?"

"Of course."

"Ah!"

Again Lucca considered me as if weighing my worth as a man of truth or lies. Still watching me, he said slowly: "Doctor Frost, would it surprise you to know that Greenaway was a man under suspicion by your own security organizations?"

Did my face drain white or flush red? I wondered as I tried to accept the words in the puzzled manner of a man ignorant of such facts. "It would surprise me a great deal," I said, frowning.

"Nevertheless, it is true," Lucca said. "Yesterday we received, via Interpol, the international Police organization, of which you may have heard, a request to check the movements of Greenaway. You will understand now why my interest in his death is rather more inquisitive than it might otherwise have been."

Lucca's English was now quite fluent, even a trifle pompous. As he spoke, I wondered what my course should be. If I handed over Greenaway's final message to myself, would I not, then, be required to hand over that other envelope? The exigencies of the law in any country can be highly intimidating. And wouldn't I then be involved in treasonable activity? Certainly the papers would be photoprinted before being returned to London. I cursed the naïvety of the dead man, but my only solace to Lucca was the conventional wish that I could help him more.

He rose from his desk. "It is possible that I may wish to see you again, Doctor Frost. You understand, of course?"

"Not exactly, but I will do all I can to help you."

He nodded gravely and thanked me.

"There are certain formalities I should like to attend to," I pointed out. "For one thing, I feel responsible for seeing Greenaway to rest."

"But of course," he agreed. "Did you know that he was a Catholic?"

I shook my head.

"He was at pains to explain that in his last note," Lucca said, and then:

"You will also wish to communicate with his father."

I stepped delicately across that trap. "Is his father his next-of-kin?"

Lucca nodded, still watching me. "You will wish to take the address and English telephone number?" he said. He took out Greenaway's letter to the coroner from a dossier on his desk. I dutifully wrote down the details I already knew. "In Italy," Lucca began, "the parish priest is responsible for burials within his area. Even suicides. Unfortunately, there is no English church in Padua, but I have no doubt that one of our local priests will do all in his power to help. And Lieutenant Caccia will help."

He stood up. For the moment, it seemed, the day was done.

But not quite. As I leaned forward to raise myself from the chair he said, very quietly, "Doctor Frost, would you be prepared to show me the contents of your pockets?"

From the moment he had raised the question of the envelope in my room I had half-expected this question and had been racking my mind for adequate means of evasion or refusal. Yet no true reason existed. An uninvolved man would, in a foreign land, aid an official enquirer by all means in his power. But I was far from uninvolved and took what seemed my only course to react with a peppery bluff of insulted pride and pomposity.

"Certainly not!" I said, recovering from what I hoped was a successful charade of bewilderment. "My private papers! Indeed not."

"It is a pity," he said, considering me coldly. "It would make my task much simpler. And I would have thought you a man to react differently to my request."

"How, for heaven's sake?" I barked, continuing my bluster. Yet I felt sick in the stomach. At its best it was a poor show. Minute by minute, Greenaway's lies and now my own were leading me more deeply into complications.

He shrugged as if to go on were pointless. Then he said, "It would clear my mind of certain inevitable suspicions."

"I'm afraid I cannot help you in that. Am I to understand you also went through my clothes in my room?"

"You are to understand that," he said smoothly.

"I call that infernal cheek!"

"I call it an elementary enquiry," he said.

"I suppose you can have me searched now?" I said, challengingly, carrying my frail bluff to its limit.

"I could," he said. "Quite easily. But it is always difficult with the English and the Americans. They have different ideas of legal procedure. They also have active and sometimes bothersome consular officials. For the moment, as far as you are concerned, Doctor Frost, I must leave this matter. We shall meet again."

He opened the door for me and followed me out into the long corridor. We began to walk, side by side, towards the gallery above the stairs.

"What was the name of Greenaway's young lady?" he asked.

"Miss Elizabeth Castle."

"And she is today sightseeing?"

I nodded.

"And they will be back, when?"

"Between six and seven o'clock this evening."

He nodded, bowed and said good-bye. I took one step down and then turned. "When are you likely to wish to see me again, Signor Lucca?"

"Perhaps this evening. Perhaps tomorrow. Perhaps not at all. As a suicide it is all straightforward, Doctor Godi tells me. No complications. No suspicion of foul play. Greenaway's letter to the magistrate—myself—was most considerate and explanatory. Apart from the item of news I gave you—which you will wish to keep to yourself—nothing. Apart also from one or two reservations of your own. Apart from these considerations, nothing."

"I am sorry I have appeared unhelpful."

He put up his hand to stay my words. "Do not say that, Doctor Frost. You have been most helpful. But I have the feeling—'intuizione' do you call it?—that you are keeping something back."

I did not answer. Already in my brief experience of Lucca I had learned to be most suspicious of him when he was at his most confiding. "And you will admit that the information I gave you about Greenaway is disquieting," he added.

"My own feeling is that an answer is more likely to be found in England than here."

"That is a point of view, Doctor Frost, and you are entitled to it," he said smoothly, and bowed.

I left him and went slowly downstairs. In the hall, making my way round a gesticulating group, I looked back. Lucca was still at the head of the stairs, leaning on the marble balcony, gazing unseeingly down on me, seemingly lost in thought.

Disturbed, apprehensive and irritated by my own performance, I walked slowly back to Police Headquarters and made my way to Caccia's office. He was awaiting me. Lucca had already telephoned, and Caccia was keen to show how efficient the Italian police could be.

"If Signor Lucca—and he is pretore—suggests that we may go ahead, we may do so," he said portentously.

He already held the official notice of death. The burial could be fixed for Friday or Saturday. Saturday might be the more sensible day. Friday would certainly have suited my own plans better, but I thought it an unwise move at that stage to suggest the earlier day. I would leave things for the moment. To my own medical mind, Friday seemed, in any case, the more likely day.

"Where are the English buried?" I asked.

"In the Cimitero de Padovi—with the Italians," he said slyly.

I smiled thinly, and asked who would see the priest.

"I shall."

"And you will let me know?"

He nodded. I thanked him. Our politeness was of an unusually punctilious order. Presumably for my benefit he then rang the Jolanda and made arrangements with the manager of the hotel for Greenaway's body to be taken, within the hour, to the mortuary. As soon as possible, and by the tradesmen's entrance, he added, mordantly yet practically. He rang off and then, on an internal telephone, spoke to an assistant, giving instructions for the body to be collected. He was certainly efficient, whether for my benefit or the honour of the Carabinieri, I could not tell.

I asked him for directions to the Post Office. He took me to one of the gates of the courtyard and directed me towards the station and the Corso del Popolo.

I began to walk in the direction he had indicated, but, on second thoughts, decided to return to the Hotel Jolanda to make my telephone call to poor Greenaway's father. Waiting there would be less tiresome than in a post office. Ten minutes later, as I cooled my heels by the desk, I was told that there would be an hour's delay. The time was nearly midday, exactly the same as in England, I remembered, for Summer Time would govern English routine for another ten days or so. I gave instructions to keep the call in, and went wearily into the hotel lounge for a drink.

The day was warm and I was hot and still irritable. I ordered

131

a Cinzano which I thought I had earned and certainly needed. Withstanding Lucca's probing, however ineffectually, had been a nerve-racking exercise and I still smarted from the memory of my display, scowling afresh each time I recalled the impasse he had driven me into and the caricature I had been forced to become to work my way out of it. Grudgingly I gave Lucca full marks for his well-timed manœuvre and cursed Greenaway again for the trials he was posthumously causing me. I tried to tell myself that I had played a fairly reasonable hand, but I remained depressed. Blast poor Greenaway!

Somewhat defiantly, and perhaps foolishly, I took out his letter again. For the last time, I promised myself. I would memorize the contents and then burn it.

As I read the letter for the third time, I began to realize that its poignant words would help to explain more of Greenaway's disastrous life to his chief, Hankinson, and more convincingly than ten thousand words of mine. After all, the pathetic attempt at self-vindication was Greenaway's last offering to the world he had known. I ought to try to retain it and hand it on. In many ways it would be a bore, but I began to see the chore as a duty that ought to be done by one man for another. In any case, it could scarcely land me in more trouble than it had already threatened to land me, but if I had to see Lucca again I would make certain that James had temporary possession of papers and letter.

So, with overmuch reflecting, my dilemma grew.

Couldn't I at least address and post to myself in London this last letter from Greenaway? If it fell into other hands it might prove inconvenient but scarcely dangerous. Unless, of course, the other hands were those of Lucca or the bogus Franciscans. Then, in another moment, I knew I must keep it. Obstinacy, doggedness, mistrust of all foreign mail services, each played its part in the decision.

I put the letter back in my pocket, picked up the *Corriere d'Informazione* and tried my Italian translation. Finally, defeated by foreign journalese, I called for another Cinzano and went on waiting, bored and hot and miserable. At last, about half-past twelve, punch-drunk with boredom, I was paged for my call to Shropshire, England, went into one of the three telephone kiosks reserved for personal calls, to tell my mournful news.

From the time he has finished his duties as a house physician any doctor has had, too often, the duty of giving news of death to relatives. He has worked out his own formula for this melancholy duty, but no formula would have been equal to the task of explaining to the wavering voice at the far end of many lines that Peter Greenaway was dead.

"Peter! My son?" the voice said disbelievingly.

And so our scant allowance of time ticked away between the moments of dreadful silence and the halting call for further information. Then, at the end, the sad, faltering words: "No, I am afraid I cannot come out there. Where do you say? Padua? In Northern Italy? I was there once. A pleasant town. I remember the Giottos. No, I cannot come. My wife is too ill. I cannot leave her. My first duty is to her, and I have a lecture here on Saturday . . ." and so on and on, agonizingly, hopelessly. I promised to ring him as soon as I returned to London at the end of the following week. "You are very kind," he said when the Italian voice broke in to say the call was at an end. "Anything you can tell us will be of some comfort to my wife. Good-bye, good-bye."

Sick at heart, I went back to my drink. I must still pace out the unending hours before I could claim the comfort of Bianca. Already, after Lucca, the sun seemed dimmer, the hours ahead more ominous. And I could not shake off the mood of apprehension he had induced. I was a fool, I told myself again and again, to be thus overawed by officialdom. I seemed in danger of becoming wellnigh suffocated by the atmosphere that Greenaway's death had so unhealthily invoked.

To break gloom by action is always the only course. That I know, but too seldom act upon the knowledge. Men of action are born and rarely made. That morning, I remember forcing myself to get up and go out into the Via San Francesco. Once there, I walked quickly to the *Wagons Lits* office in the Piazza Cavour. The young booking-clerk, more like a film star than a transport minion, was helpful. He thought that there should be a reasonable chance of changing the couchette to Rome from Friday to Saturday night. One or two were usually available at this time of the year. If I could let him know my final decision by midday on Friday, all would be well. My medical experience still persuaded me that Friday would be the more likely day for the burial. I decided, therefore, after a moment's hesitation, to keep the Friday reservations.

Partly reassured, I went. To lunch at the hotel now seemed the most sensible course, in view of Lucca's possible wish to see me again that afternoon or evening.

I had retained the key to my room from the previous night and went straight up to the second floor by the lift. As soon as I entered the room I remembered Lucca's calm admission of his search: my two bags were set quietly side by side, that degree more geometrically precise than the maid ever left them. I crossed to the wardrobe. Two suits hung listlessly from their hangers. Well, his men had had little enough reward for their pains, I decided. Not even a copy of *Ulysses*. Until I had encountered Greenaway, I told myself savagely, my life had been innocent in the eyes of any nation's laws. Damn Greenaway! Damn Lucca!

The telephone rang.

"Reception, Signor. Doctor Frost?"

"Yes."

"Giovanni Criccoli is here and would like to talk to you."

"I don't know a Giovanni Criccoli. How do you spell it?"

He spelt out the name. Then silence. Then a different voice, Italian, speaking careful English "Doctor Frost? Good-afternoon. This is Giovanni Criccoli."

"Yes?"

"I would like to speak with you."

I was still too angry with Lucca and his lackeys to be civil to any Italian.

"What about?" I barked.

"Signor Greenaway."

That made me slightly more attentive but no whit less boorish. "What about him?" I said brusquely.

"It is a private matter."

"All right. I'll come down."

I went into the bathroom and washed my hands, scrubbing

134

the knuckles with a surgeon's vehemence, scarcely giving a thought to Criccoli, whoever he was. Journalist? Undertaker? Solicitor? Word of Greenaway's death had already had time to travel about the town.

I went down by the stairs, into the hotel foyer. Waiting by the reception desk were two Franciscan monks: the pair I had last seen waiting in the dusty road outside the Villa Anselmo.

27

FOR a split second I was tempted to return to my room or to pass them by and go into the street. They could not know me by sight, and the clerk behind the reception desk was pre-occupied in letter-sorting. And, already, my surprise was tainted by foreboding. I hate to admit it, even now, but there it is. Fear was growing within me like a malignant tumour.

The taller of the two men turned, saw me, and stepped forward. He was taller and bigger than I had judged from a distance. He must have been about six feet two and his shoulders were broad and square. His habit rested on him in the same light fashion that a dressing-robe rests on the shoulders of a boxer. He said, in thick-toned English, "I am Giovanni Criccoli. Brother Criccoli to some. May I introduce Ludovisi Marcello."

"Brother Marcello to some?" I asked, playing for time.

"To very few," Criccoli said with a ready smile.

"And to the others?"

"I have not learned."

The other man, the wizened one, was, strangely enough, slimmer and younger when seen close-to. He inclined his head, but remained silent. So did I.

"Shall we drink?" Criccoli asked, moving towards the hotel lounge. Meekly I followed, Marcello following.

"Acqua minerale for us," Criccoli said.

Suddenly I was less meek. I called the waiter and said, "Due acqua minerale." He stood there. I said testily, "Due. Due. No more."

135

Criccoli said. "You will not drink?"

"I am in a hurry. I have a lot to do today."

"It is understandable," he said, nodding. "You have not gone with your companions to Malcontenta or Rotonda. They are both places of great beauty. That is a pity."

"Would you like to come to the point and tell me your business?" I asked.

"Yes," he said. "I will come to the point. I understand Signor Greenaway died in the night."

"Yes, unfortunately."

"E' una cosa veramente triste," he said, but I remained stolidly uncomprehending and he continued in English: "I had some slight acquaintance with him. You, too, knew him undoubtedly?"

"I had met him. Why do you ask?"

"But now you are looking after his affairs?"

"I am looking after his burial. That is all. You said you were coming to the point?"

"Yes, Doctor Frost. The point is that Signor Greenaway had certain papers he had promised to let me have. I am wondering whether it would be possible for you to let me have them?"

Foreboding was consumed in fury. I blew up. Hunger and righteous anger helped. "What on earth do you mean?" I said, loud enough for three other occupants of the lounge, and a waiter, to look up, surprised from their midday torpor.

"I ask because I think it is probable that you have them."

"Look, Signor Criccoli or Brother Criccoli, or whatever you call yourself," I said, standing up. "This conversation is getting us nowhere. I know nothing about Greenaway's private affairs. His belongings are presumably now under lock and key and will be forwarded by the authorities to his parents after the pretore has decided what to do. That's all I know and, as far as I'm concerned, it's the lot. Now go!"

Criccoli did not get up. He sat back in his chair, and put the spatulate finger-tips of his huge hands together. The fingers were as stained as any chain-smoker's, I noticed. He seemed at ease. I wasn't. His dark brown eyes, under the heavy black eyebrows, considered me reflectively, perhaps wondering whether I were responsible enough to receive certain information. As if he had made a decision to take me into his confidence, Criccoli said slowly, "The papers I want are not in Greenaway's room. I went through his belongings, as you call them, yesterday and again this morning. Whilst you were at the Tribunale," he added. I was silent. He went on, almost contemptuously, "There is nothing there for me. Now I must look elsewhere. For certain reasons it seems to me that, logically, you are the next step."

"Perhaps you also examined my room, too?" I sneered.

"We also did that," he said easily. I resisted the temptation to laugh at the morning's inquisitive procession through my bedroom; resisted, too, the temptation to ask his reasons for making me his next step. I was too busy wishing I hadn't stood up so precipitately.

Momentarily, I think, Criccoli wavered before deciding to carry his bluff through to the end. He said, "You were with him in the piazza late on Tuesday night. You were, apparently, almost the first person to see him after his death. And you are a psychiatrist. Three years ago, in London, Greenaway was undergoing psychiatric treatment."

"Not with me!" I thought it safe to say.

"No, that is true."

Did I detect a momentary weakening in his bluff? I thought my best line now was once again to act the bewildered and pontifical Englishman abroad. I was having quite a morning in the rôle. I said, as loudly and stuffily as possible, "What extraordinary behaviour! I think perhaps I should tell the police. Or the magistrate."

"That, I think, would be inadvisable—for your own sake," Criccoli said quietly. "On the other hand you could. It would be interesting."

We were silent as the waiter brought a large bottle of mineral water to the table and poured two glasses. Criccoli and his partner drank deeply. Those heavy brown habits were undoubtedly hot on such a day.

Perhaps my modest act had come off better than I had dared to hope, for Criccoli said, almost pleading, "I am sorry, Doctor Frost. Won't you please sit down?"

I gladly sat down again, wondering whether the mollifying gesture would be in character with the man I was making myself out to be.

Criccoli went on, "The papers were important to me, Doctor Frost. Thus, perhaps my unconventional attempt to find them."

"And your unconventional attire for your unconventional behaviour?" I said, pointing to his habit.

"I was once a Brother in the Church," he said quietly.

"And now no longer?"

"No longer."

"Then why wear the uniform?"

He repeated the word appraisingly. "Uniform! Yes, indeed. Uniform it is. Yet it is, you will admit, the most anonymous of uniforms in Italy."

"As inconspicuous as a clergyman's in London," I said.

"More so. Shall we say, 'as inconspicuous as a bowler hat in London'?" he added, smiling.

"When were you last in London?" I could not forbear to ask.

"Last year."

"And your companion?"

He deliberately misunderstood my question.

"He, too, was once my brother in Christ," he said.

"And now?"

"My brother in a hope for this world in this lifetime," he said blandly.

I thought a few moments of digression might help to sort out Criccoli's intentions.

"I take it that, on a strict point of canonical law, you are not entitled to wear this uniform," I said.

"In my case it is a point that has never been resolved," he answered, suddenly quite serious. "I never officially left the Franciscan Order. There has been no official sundering of my relations with the Church." He smiled. His brown eyes were merry. He looked, for a moment, like a mediaeval friar in disputation. "Like many another member of the more militant Catholic orders, I worked with the Resistance throughout the war. I date my renegation from those days. Yet I did return to my vocation after the war for some years. Occasionally, unlike my more formal brethren, I even adopt more casual clothing. Tweeds, for instance. Or even a light-weight suit." He smiled. "Similar to your own, Doctor Frost, although, alas, not so well cut."

He spoke English well, with a touch of self-appreciating relish apt to afflict any talker enjoying the opportunity for practice in a foreign tongue. I wondered whether his silent partner understood any of the exchanges.

Meantime, I thought it best to continue with my line of the conventional English medico, humouring a mild eccentric. I said, "It is all rather beyond me. I am a doctor and prefer conventions."

"That is understandable," he agreed, taking another gulp of his acqua minerale. "Yet I have heard of unconventional surgeons."

"Possibly. I am a physician."

"Of course."

I felt the need for a cigarette and took out my case. They both accepted my offering eagerly. And still Marcello said no word.

"Does your Order permit smoking to its more conventional practitioners?" I asked.

I scarcely listened to his answer. A question was still wearing at my mind. Why had Criccoli so soon turned his attention to myself? How much or how little did he know or guess?

"The Franciscan Order is primarily a missionary force," he was saying: "It is also a more popular Order than others. I mean that it recruits from the people. We have, therefore, a less austere attitude towards what might be called more mortal frailties than the contemplative Orders, such as the Benedictines."

He continued to talk of the Franciscans, enjoying his monologue, watching the cigarette smoke rise before his eyes. It was all rather like listening to a Third Programme causerie, and the incongruity of my situation broke forcefully upon me. Criccoli gradually began to extract my grudging admiration. His voluble imperturbability was no more than a veneer. That was plain enough. He carried within himself a sense of authority, the air of a man who has tested himself and not failed in his own reckoning. It is a rare quality, but one easily recognized, I think, by others. The watchful brown eyes belied the heavy jowls and body. The down-turning underlip, from which the cigarette now drooped, gave his face a kind of brutish strength, although there was nothing brutish about the lively, questioning eyes. He looked like one of those self-indulgent but highly intelligent Irishmen one quickly learns not to underestimate in the Medical Schools. Irishmen from T.C.D., for instance, who frequently bely their rotund bodies by pugnacity on the football field or in the boxing ring.

"Have you any Irish blood?" I asked on the impulse.

"An Irish mother," he said simply. "From County Cork to Florence via domestic service with an English family. But I never knew her. She died before I came to my youth."

He leaned forward and stubbed out his cigarette in the ashtray on the low table and pulled himself up from the chair. His movements were far easier than I would have thought possible for so big and heavy a man. The younger man also stubbed out his cigarette and rose.

"It is sad that you have nothing for me," Criccoli said thoughtfully.

I was silent.

"We shall doubtless meet again," he said, bowing slightly.

Everyone that morning seemed certain of further meetings with me. I could have wished for some uncertainty.

"I do not think so," I said firmly.

"You are leaving Padua?"

"I was not thinking of that."

"Aha! Then we shall meet again."

The time to end mock-civility had come, I thought, and I said, even more emphatically, "I do not think so, and I trust not."

"Yet we shall," he repeated with certainty.

He bowed again and turned; his companion, too. They went out into the Via San Francesco without a backward glance.

I stood there for a moment, irritated, frustrated and more than a little disturbed. My hands were damp and I was no longer hungry. The events of the morning crowded in on me. First Greenaway, then Lucca, now Criccoli. The world was suddenly, for me, a dreary and dispiriting abode, particularly the world of Padua and the Hotel Jolanda. I needed desperately to quit the miasmic atmosphere for freer, cleaner air, and yearned desperately for the company of those who did not live out their lives in shadows and threats. I looked at the foyer clock. Just after half-past one. I fumbled in my pocket for the itinerary of the tour. The Anglo-Palladian Society, I read, was due to arrive at the Villa Rotonda at about three o'clock.

On a sudden decision I went out to the taxi-rank. Under the afternoon sun three taxis stood along the kerb, their radiators shimmering in the heat. Within, their drivers slept.

How swiftly one acquires the practice of suspicion! I crossed to the third taxi, a Lancia saloon, and tapped the windscreen. A tanned dark face, with a heavy stubble, lolled against the side-window. He came awake and pointed to the cars in front. I shook my head vehemently. He shrugged, sat up and lowered the window.

"How far and how much to Vicenza?" I asked.

"Ten thousand lira," he said after a minute of tooth-sucking calculation.

"Too much!"

"Nine thousand."

"Done."

To hell with my currency allowance, I thought, and told him to drive fast—but safely—out to the Villa Rotonda on the Vicenza road. I had never been more certain of the rightness of an impetuous gesture.

He swung his car out from the kerb, shrugging his incomprehensibility of the situation to his companions of the rank.

Beyond the town I tried to concentrate on the wide landscape of the Veneto, but my mind was too occupied with images of the morning. In a moment of apprehension I looked out from the rear window, but the straight road was a narrowing, dusty ribbon, empty of pursuers.

Yet I could not rid my mind of Criccoli.

I have often tried, since that day, to explain to myself the extraordinary sense of power that emanated from the man. Certain men give this impression by physical attributes: strong masculinity allied with outstanding self-assurance can go a long way towards enforcing the opinions of a man, if those opinions have any substance. Extreme competence and confidence, combined with adequate means of expression, will give a man authority in a specialist assembly. But what of those few men who are not especially personable and have no particular expertise? Rare politicians, perhaps, although I have known too many M.P.s as patients in my own country to have any profound conviction that men who normally advance themselves as the would-be arbiters of our social and economic destinies are any different from the rest of us. An occasional priest or preacher? I should want to know a good deal about their private lives as well as their public performances.

Criccoli's personality, however, I found immediately and unusually commanding, and I think this impression would have established itself in any gathering or set of circumstances. He was the kind of man I can easily imagine Paul of Tarsus to have been. A spleenish, authoritative man of action, quick to cynical humour, quick to biting anger, occasionally charitable, frequently capricious, but, above all, utterly single-minded. A controlled fanatic, in fact.

At that first meeting I sensed the urge to leadership, the natural authority that would have taken Criccoli out of the Church at an early stage in the war in order to be in a more active contact with his country's enemies: is it not another kind of fanatic who is first to rise against the established fanatic? The true democrat is slow to wrath and thus to rebel and likes to be fairly certain of the direction for his gradually aroused anger.

Had I come to know Criccoli better, I feel sure that I would have learned that his time with the partisans had been the happiest time of his life. If there are any qualities of leadership in a warrior-priest he starts with manifold advantages over a layman turned fighter. His cloth or habit gives incalculable authority and integrity to his purpose, and that purpose is adjudged to be of the highest quality until found hollow.

I could write at length on the subject of Criccoli. His personality was of deep interest to me, as it would have been to any practising psychiatrist. The renegade-fighter-priest is one of the archetypes of our times, but England, thankfully, has not latterly bred them.

Criccoli's authority was aided by his physical vitality. Sitting there in the low chair of the hotel lounge he had seemed too big for his chair. Even his smallest gestures were explosive. He lit a cigarette as if lighting the faggots round a pyre. He smoked the cigarette as if it were his first after long imprisonment. He crushed it out in the ashtray as if crushing a foul thing now expended. When he leaned forward to emphasize a point, his chest seemed to expand like a bellows and the veins in his neck stood out like cording. His hands moved with huge grace, as if he were weighing the worth of two boulders to cast at a target or an enemy.

He was like a mediaeval man, untrammelled by the conventions we have taken upon ourselves or allowed to be put upon us. He was larger than life-size. He would have been more at home in the courts of the Renaissance than in our own time, except, of course, in war. And perhaps that was his secret. He needed strife, combat, commotion. For him, even a cold war was a continuing form of disputation. He was the classic renegade type: the man who has lost his own faith and finds sadistic satisfaction in destroying the faith of others. I do not know. All I truly know is that he was the kind of man one remembers for the rest of one's days.

I speculated upon Criccoli's close watch on Greenaway. And how had he learned so quickly of his death? But that, I told myself, was more readily explicable in Italy than in almost any country in Europe outside the Iron Curtain. Criccoli would have his hotel contact. That would be easy enough in any city in the world, easier still in a small town. He would have helpers at every turn, all ready to submit their particles of knowledge, rumour and gossip. But where and how did I come into his calculations? I wondered where he had come from, what had given him his calls, first to Christ, then to Marx. I have listened to too many confessions to think that the call to Marxism comes as a clear-cut clarion. As many roads lead to Moscow as to Rome, and all are as deviously routed. But Criccoli's way I should never know, although both the man and his route intrigued me.

143

I wondered which member of the Anglo-Italian Palladian Society had been the contact between Greenaway and Criccoli. Greenaway had maintained that he had had no recollection of his contact from the night of the reception. Perhaps he had been lying. Yet I did not think so. That contact had certainly been another in a dreary chain that stretched from London to a room in Moscow. Someone in the coach was in touch with Criccoli. That was certain.

In memory I ranged over the faces of the Italian members I had seen, but all merged into a collective haze, except those of Revisi, Brunatelli, and, of course, Bianca. After I rejoined the coach I must examine my fellow-travellers more carefully, I told myself, and exercise any talent I might have for physiognomical surmise.

Swiftly, the driver put kilometre after kilometre between Padua and Vicenza. My attention began to wander. My mind, escaping from the baleful, compelling personality of Criccoli, or whatever his real name might be, began to revel in the prospect ahead. With this sense of freedom I grew hungry and asked my driver to stop at the next roadside trattoria so that we might have beer and sandwiches. How were we for time?

"Si! Si! Molto tempo!" he cried. Time, for him, was an abstraction, easily decimated or, at a pinch, utterly done away with.

So we stopped for ten minutes at a wayside café and then drove on faster still to Vicenza. Two enquiries, one in the town and one beyond, and we were outside the Villa Rotonda at ten-past three. The Anglo-Italian Palladian Society Coach had not yet arrived.

28

ROTONDA is probably the best known of all the domestic buildings of Palladio and one soon sees the reasons for its fame. Even my driver drew breath with admiration as we approached the hilltop villa on the outskirts of the town.

I asked him whether he could wait for an hour or so. Willingly, he said. Waiting there, within the car, we began to talk. I found the moments useful for practising my irresolute Italian.

The driver had heard of this famous villa but had never yet seen it. He was glad to be able to see it now. Yes, he had also heard something of Palladio. Wasn't he a builder of some kind? Near enough, I said, and wondered how much more than this a London taxi-driver would know of Wren. Why was Rotonda so famous? he asked. He could see it was beautiful, but was that the only reason? I began to explain, straining my rusty Italian to its limits. But he was patient and helpful and we nattered in the stuffy taxi until the coach arrived a quarter of an hour later. I thanked him for his long-suffering patience, requested him to wait, and got out to meet Bianca, James and Georgina.

James waved gaily from the window, and came quickly down the steps, first out after Revisi.

"This is a splendid surprise, old boy! How did you manage it?"

"Part efficiency. Part escapism. Where's Bianca?"

"Sitting with Georgina."

"And you with Miss Castle?"

"That's it. I'll put you in the picture straightaway. Before we started I told her Greenaway wouldn't be coming. She seemed almost relieved. Then the three of us lunched her at Vicenza and afterwards I took her for a walk in the garden and told her the truth."

The others were piling out. I turned and waved to Bianca and Georgina as they climbed down. James took my arm and firmly walked me away, forestalling my obvious intention of joining Bianca. I managed to turn and mime an explanation of my disappearance.

"How did she take it?" I said as we walked away from the coach, towards the high piers of the entrance gates.

"Extraordinarily well, considering how recently she'd seen him. Very shocked at first, of course, but I don't really think he'd made any deep impression on her."

"How much have you told her since?"

"Nothing. I just told her it was all in the hands of the local police. That's all."

"I wonder whether Greenaway mentioned her in his letter to the coroner? By the way, you wrote me a letter . . ." I said, and quickly told him of my interview with Lucca.

"That's all right, old boy, so long as I know. We'd better have the same story. I invited you to dine tonight in Venice. I wrote you because we usually get separated in the coach and you might have made other arrangements. O.K.?"

I nodded.

By now a keeper had come from the lodge and clanked open the high iron gates. We all began to climb the long slope to the pedimented portico, now beginning to loom above us like one of those dramatically improbable paintings by Pisani.

We trailed along in front of the straggling members. James said, "As a matter of fact, I've already warned Miss Castle that her name might have been mentioned in Greenaway's last letter to the coroner and that she ought to be prepared for some unwelcome publicity, both here and at home."

"And her reaction?"

"Astonishing. All she said was, 'Oh, do you mean the *Daily Mirror*—that kind of thing? Daddy won't like that!' Not a word about not liking it herself. Yet she's a well brought up girl, I'd say."

"The younger generation have different ideas about their private lives from old fuddy-duddies like us."

"So it seems."

"And what about Revisi?"

"I think we'd better tell him after this. Now tell me everything about your day, including your session with the magistrate fellow."

I told him as we climbed the final slope and reached the steps of the villa. By then we could see the side porticoes and some of the Rubina statues.

"We'll talk about this later," James said. "I don't like the sound of either Lucca or of Big Brother Criccoli."

We waited at the steps for Bianca and Georgina. I was amused to see that my taxi-driver had installed himself as a member of the visiting party, and was listening devoutly to

146

Brunatelli, now happy in the possession of an audience who showed no signs of restiveness or boredom. But of Signora Brunatelli there was no sign. Boredom, it seemed, had made her scarce.

So began an hour of enchantment within the Villa Rotonda, with its beautiful rooms, Maganza frescoes and fabulous circular sala with views from the four renowned porticoes over cypress trees towards the city and the hills.

I stood beneath one of the great pediments with Bianca.

"I have a taxi outside," I said quickly. "Why don't we drive to Venice and go again to the Pensione Greci?"

"Why not?" she asked, as delighted as a child offered an excursion beyond all expectation. For me, this delight in small things was part of her irresistible charm.

"Will it look very obvious leaving the crowd at this stage?" I asked.

She laughed. "Are you thinking of my reputation or your own, dear Rupert?"

"Of your own, of course. Perhaps we can slip away unnoticed. I'll tell James to tell Revisi."

I thought of Lucca's word that he might wish to see me again that evening, but his half-suggestion could not stand against my mood, and, in the company of Bianca, conventional dues lost all their urgency. Other factors also coloured my delight in this prospect of escape. I should not only not see Lucca again that day, I should be away from the unknown watcher in the coach and I should avoid Criccoli. And the thought of another night alone in the Hotel Jolanda was too depressing to contemplate for long. Yet, all the time, like a nagging whisper, the voice of my unstilled conscience told me that my most sensible course would be to return to London immediately. Yet, moment by moment, I became less capable of making that decision. I was, I knew, as weak as Greenaway had been. Already Bianca had become too near and dear for me. Yet, failing an immediate return to London, surely my soundest course would be to keep moving, or at least to cast away established routine? Criccoli had searched my possessions. He would know that if I still retained anything from Greenaway I would be carrying it with me. In those circumstances, wouldn't I be most vulnerable in my known sleeping quarters? By going to Venice I should be indulging both my native caution and my love. In such a manner I tried to placate my conscience. How convincing are the phrases of self-persuasion!

I left Bianca with a word and crossed the sala to James and Georgina, who were considering a trompe l'oeil fresco above one of the doors. I took James aside and told him of my plan for the evening.

"What more could a man want?" he said, laughing. "Circumspection and seduction! Only someone with Scots blood in his veins could work out such an unholy combination."

"What about Revisi?"

"I'll square him about Bianca's departure. By the way, I told him about Greenaway just now. Terribly upset. Proposed to cancel tomorrow's trip as a gesture."

"That's crazy."

"I thought so, too. I think I can persuade him to reconsider the idea. He probably thinks it's the proper course for dealing with the lugubrious English."

Bianca came across, and farewells were exchanged with James and Georgina. But we had timed our departure too tardily. Already Revisi was rounding up the reluctant members of the Society. We said farewell to our Italian hosts and went out, but we were already caught in the long straggle of departing sightseers. And Bianca's heels, as attenuated as pencils, slowed us down. Yet I was unperturbed, finding only delight in her preposterous tiptoe journey. My squeamish doubts concerning the suitability of her clothes had died. I was one of a countless host of those blinded by love. Long before we had reached the gates we had been overtaken by the more sturdily shod members of the group, including James and Georgina, but now I did not care.

My taxi-driver came up and thanked me for his unique experience. "The most beautiful palace in the world!" he said, and raised his eyes to heaven. He would bless my name for ever. What was my name? "Jones!" I said, and told him to wait.

As the gates of the villa closed behind us, and the party was about to embark once again upon the coach, Revisi held up his hand. First in English, then in Italian, he explained that he had just learned that Greenaway had died suddenly that morning and would be buried on Friday or Saturday. He had, at first, thought of cancelling the following day's tour, he said, but other, and, he had now no doubt, wiser counsels had prevailed. If anyone wished to attend the burial service, they would, of course, be welcome. There would be no visit on that day—probably Friday—in any case. A wreath would be sent by the Society.

There were murmurs of approval of his action, then subdued chattering as the party moved into the coach.

"Think of the number of airmail letters that'll be written tonight," James whispered as he followed the others into the coach. "But perhaps not by you. Can I ring you anywhere?"

"Nowhere."

"You won't attempt to come back to Padua tonight?"

"Not a chance."

"Good. Now forget Lucca and Crocodile, or whatever his blasted name is. I'll look after him if I see him around. Brown habit and stained fingers, you said? Possibly tweeds. Quick-change merchant, eh? Apart from the fact that it describes half the Italian male population, it's a pretty clear portrait!"

"He's bigger than most Italians."

"That's a great help," James said with heavy humour.

"But you saw him yourself at Anselmo."

"I was too busy enjoying myself," he said, waving gaily to Bianca.

I took Bianca by the hand and we moved up the lane towards the highway and the taxi. The hell with Signor Lucca and the gossip of the Anglo-Palladian Society! I thought in overpowering relief.

"But surely this is very expensive," Bianca said as she got into the taxi and settled back. "It can't be cheap." She laughed. "But it is very nice, Rupert."

"To Venice!" I said to the driver.

He was startled. "To Padua, Signor?"

"No, to Venice."

He shrugged and smiled. "Si, si, Signor." It was a good day's work for him, at least.

29

WE ARRIVED in Venice just before six o'clock, after a merry,
breathless journey. Despite the wearing and oppressive day I
felt exhilarated, freed of all burdens. Bianca had the gift to
exorcise all my demons of disquiet. Memories of Greenaway,
Lucca and Criccoli receded like unwholesome dreams.

We left our taxi-driver at the Piazzale Roma. By that time he
probably thought that he was in the commission of a pair of
genial goons, and would scarcely have been surprised, I think,
had we asked him to turn about and drive us south to Florence
or to Rome. He took his well-earned astronomical lire with a
series of nods, winks, bobs and curtsies.

We crossed the bridge and boarded a vaporetto to the San
Zaccharia quay. The magic of the Grand Canal possessed me
once again. The criss-cross passage was a time and mood for
magic. At the Zaccharia station we stepped ashore, and began
to hurry towards the alleyway that would take us past the
church towards our desire.

I think, in retrospect, that both of us half-feared that the spell
might be broken if our same room were not available. Lovers
have always been subject to these self-made superstitions. Fortunately, we were received by the flame-headed padrona with
a reassuring grin. "I promised that you would return!" she
called, coming down the stairs, after we had rung the cracked
bell on the rickety hall table. "Your room, too, is free."

I paid for the room. We should be leaving so early, I pointed
out. "Not earlier than I am about, Signor," she said, but
pocketed the money in her apron and gave us the key to our
room, for that, I know, is how we both considered it. Then
she left us to climb, unattended, to that blissful place.

We stayed there until nearly nine o'clock, and remembrance
of that time will always be with me. Even as I write these words
the hours return, engulfing me with the memory of their
tenderness and passion.

When, at last, we thought we ought to make a move, the
night had come and we were both desperately hungry. I
switched on the solitary bedside lamp and went to the window

to see, once more, how this corner of Venice looked in the night, lest I should not return for many years. I stood there, drinking in the fantasy and movement of the city, the canal below, the lights of the little shops reflected in the water, the gossipers and shoppers and neighbours, the leaning church tower almost at my elbow, the lagoon, which I could see from the window when I leaned far out. For me, then, despite my happiness, the scene was inexpressibly sad. But Venice, despite its legend as "the revel of the earth", is always touched with an invincible air of sadness. At least it is for me. And will be all my days.

When I turned, Bianca was lying, her arms behind her head, watching me. I crossed to the bed and stood, leaning over the thin iron rail, looking down on her body, more beautiful than any I had ever known or dreamed of knowing.

"You make me sad and happy at the same time," she said, smiling. "It is less trouble if a man makes you just one thing."

"You make me only happy."

"Always?"

"Always, although I sometimes think I foresee trouble ahead."

"What kind of trouble, Rupert?"

It was a time for boldness and I said, "Husband trouble. Country trouble. Can you be free? Will you want to be free? Will you live in England? I cannot practise as a doctor in Italy. Things like that."

"We have a saying in Rome that there are many bridges over the Tiber. If one is too busy, we say, one can try another. Let us try to do that."

She swung her long legs from the bed and crossed to my side. "You are a strange and funny man, Rupert," she said, putting her arms about my shoulders.

"Why strange?"

"Because I have met no one like you in my life before."

"I have met no one like you, yet now you seem a natural part of my life."

"You to me, too, Rupert," she said, holding my shoulders tightly. I recall the strength of her grip as if she held me in this room no more than a moment ago.

151

"Why am I funny then?" I asked.

"Because you are an innocent."

"Not always."

"No, not always, perhaps."

She kissed me and clung to me for several seconds. Then she said again, out of the blue, "Let us meet trouble when we come to it," and crossed to the farcical tin bidet in the corner of the room, took up the tall jug and splashed the cold, cold water into the bidet.

"Oh, Rupert!" she cried. "Women do much for men in this world, but never more than this. No water was ever colder."

I laughed, commiserating.

We dressed slowly, chattering and laughing. Then out into the Venetian night, along the canals, through to the Rialto where again we dined, listening to the sounds of the city all about us, caught in the spell of this unique place.

Afterwards we walked slowly back through the narrow lanes of the Merceria to St Mark's Square. There, Bianca had decided, we would have nightcaps of espressi and brandies and watch the promenading crowds.

As we came into the square, through that narrow improbable opening beneath the clock, the Municipal Orchestra was playing. A great crowd clustered about the circular rostrum under a ring of lights. Every visitor to Venice will remember what is, indeed, an unforgettable urban scene: the pattern of tables set out on the great square, the lights of the cafés and the crowds. Here, I always thought, was life in a great city as it should and could be lived. But first, perhaps, one must have water and bridges. And no cars. And a reliable climate.

The orchestra was playing *The Thieving Magpie* overture, and the whole square seemed to have caught the racing gaiety of the melody. Scores of shoes beat time on the mosaic paving: hundreds of fingers tapped out the rhythm on the table-tops.

"Let us listen to the band first, then have our coffee," Bianca said.

We crossed to the crowd and stood at its periphery, taking in the music and the joyful night. Gradually, in the manner of all onlookers, we began to move in towards the centre of the crowd as the overture raced to its final bars. Then followed a crescendo of applause for the native conductor and composer. Clapping and "Bravos" echoed between the walls of the square. New, stencilled legends were slipped into the announcement board: SYMPHONIC POEM: DON JUAN: RICHARD STRAUSS.

"I think this will be better appreciated sitting down," I said.

Bianca took my arm. "How clever, Rupert, to know what music to stand up for and what to sit down for."

I laughed and confessed my simple formula. "Stand up, or, better still, dance for merry music: sit down for sad. Don Juan is sad."

"I think it's even more clever to know that Don Juan is sad."

We had almost reached the edge of the crowd, moving out towards the café, when I saw a solitary Franciscan silhouetted within the brightly lit arcades of the Procuratie Vecchie, the long northern façade of the square. He was moving away from us, towards the narrowing end of the piazza, carefully surveying the late-night crowds at the tables. I stood still, placing one hand on Bianca's.

"Che c'è?" she asked, aware of my tension.

"Nothing. Or it may be nothing."

For a moment I chided myself. I seemed to be investing all monastic figures with the attributes of Criccoli or Marcello. Franciscans are, as Criccoli had said, as ubiquitous in any Italian city as bowler hats in London. I had seen perhaps a dozen that day. Yet had I not looked a second furtive time on each occasion? I reminded myself. I was getting jittery. That was the simple, unpalatable truth.

Then the Franciscan came from the shadows of the arcade into the bright lights of the café once again and I knew I was right. Despite the fact that he was moving away from us, this was Marcello.

As he scanned the crowds I could see the sharp, mean profile I had seen that morning. As he moved on and was lost to sight behind the pillar, I could see the same drooping figure I had watched leaving the Hotel Jolanda; the figure of a long-time student, unwillingly coerced into exercise. Yet now he seemed to be moving purposefully enough, slowly disappearing within the arcade, reappearing on the step above the tables. Then moving on.

153

I still held Bianca's hand. She was silent.

Almost in a reflex action, I edged away from that side of the crowd towards the New House of the Procurators. Still within the shelter of the crowd, I looked out and saw, far off, over towards the north-eastern corner of the square what I had half-expected, half-feared to see: the more massive Criccoli moving slowly in and out of the shadows and blazing lights of the arcades of Scamozzi's later building.

Panic was bringing visions, I told myself. Yet, even as I looked again, I saw Criccoli come once more into the light and gaze intently across the tables on his side of the square, thence across the square to Marcello. Then again into the shadows in his steady quest.

I stood irresolute, thinking of the envelopes within my pocket, cursing myself for a fool. Why had I not entrusted them to the post to England? Only my foolish obstinacy had prevented me from the logical step. Again Bianca said, "Is anything the matter, Rupert?"

"It is possible," I said, and then, after a long minute of hesitation: "Bianca, at a certain moment I want you to come quickly with me. When I say 'Now'. It will be necessary to be quick. As soon as we leave the shelter of this crowd slip out of your shoes. Give them to me and run with me."

She laughed, unperturbed by the idiocy of my request.

"To be in stockings will not turn me into a runner, Rupert. But anything you say I will do. As I will always do," she added, gripping my hand.

I watched Criccoli's slow passage towards the Campanile at the end of the Nuova Arcade. But why should he retrace his steps? I asked myself.

Panic too quickly takes one into its grip and will not let go. Supposing Criccoli, after reaching the end of the arcade, waited there for an hour or more? Or went off towards the Molo and waited there? We might meet him at any point *en route* to the Pensione Greci. He could take one of a dozen courses. His was the initiative. He might even know we were at the Greci.

A hundred thoughts bemused my mind. Presumably the contact on the coach had taken the number of my taxi, and met the driver on his return to Padua. He would have been easy

154

enough to trace in a place the size of Padua. Inconsequentially, I wondered how Criccoli and Marcello had got to Venice. By car or train? And had they other helpers? Apparently not, at present.

Criccoli reached the end of the arcade and paused within the shadow of the Campanile. He stood there for a moment and then began to cross the square diagonally, coming towards the crowd around the bandstand.

"The Franciscan is coming this way," Bianca whispered.

Why shouldn't I go out and meet Criccoli face to face? I asked myself furiously. Yet in my bones I knew that would be no more than a gesture of folly. But why? Why? Why? I begged of myself in that same second.

"As he gets close to this crowd we will walk out from it towards the tables," I hissed, defying my neighbours.

"Can I keep my shoes on?" Bianca giggled.

"For the moment."

Mercifully, the vast crowd ranged as far as the outer line of the tables. With reasonable luck, we could pick our way towards the arcades, taking what cover we could from the comparative shelter of the crowd. Tensely, I watched Criccoli's slow approach. He stared about him as he walked. The plaintive music of *Don Juan* moved within the square, a melodious dirge. Then, as Bianca whispered that the Franciscan was almost up to the crowd on the far side, Criccoli reached the crowd on the nearest side and was immediately lost to sight. From now on, all was luck and guesswork. I took a gambler's chance and stood on tip-toe. I could see the top of Criccoli's head, the tonsure taking the bright lights like an upturned bowl. Then I saw Marcello. The pair plainly had a plan, for each began to pace around the ragged edge in an anti-clockwise direction, Criccoli coming from the Campanile corner, moving south.

Again, in a fleeting, inconsequential way I wondered why they should be here. Had one of them seen us earlier and then lost us? But it was time for action, and, at the moment that I judged Criccoli to be almost level with us in a line to the edge of the crowd, I uttered a mumbled apology to my tight-packed neighbours and suddenly bent down to my shoes, forcing

155

myself against their hips and thighs. Bianca, playing up, said loudly in Italian:

"Ah, poor dear, your pain again! Excuse. Excuse." She bent towards me, whispering, "This is fascinating, Rupert. Will you explain one day?"

In resentful compassion our closer neighbours moved a few vital inches away, but the mass, unaware, remained unmoved. Silently I counted "One—two—three—four—five" and then stood up, said aloud, "Now!" and began to move against the crowd, muttering apologies, pushing a boorish way out to the thinner edges. Others were also beginning to move away, perhaps because of the austerity of Strauss after the gaiety of Rossini. We were in a gradually stirring, restive crowd within a crowd.

I shoved and pushed and was pushed and shoved in return. Bianca clung to my coat. As we reached the edge of the crowd I put my arm about her and walked slowly towards the Clock Tower, aiming to reach the arcade just beyond the far line of tables, trying even harder to make us seem like any other pair of lovers caught into the sentimentality of a Venetian holiday.

We reached the arcade. Folly or not, I had to look back, to know for certain whether we had escaped. I saw no sign of either Franciscan. Bianca stood by my side. Then I saw Marcello slowly completing his circuit around the crowd's wide edge, near the point where we had broken from it. Then he was joined by Criccoli, who had also come full circle. They stood talking for a moment, doubtless concerting another sweep in their eerie quest in which somehow, somewhere, I knew I figured.

"Take a good look at both of them and give them a miss in future," I told Bianca as we sheltered within the shadow of a pillar.

She looked out and carefully studied the two men.

"Have you ever seen them before?" I asked.

"I do not know many priests," she said, laughing.

"Would you know them again?"

"I think so. The big one certainly."

"Good. Now let us go."

"But look, Rupert!" she said suddenly. "Now there are

156

others." I looked and to my surprise saw two men in dark suits join the friars. They were fairly young men, not more than thirty, and looked like typical Italian working men; dockers, porters or the like, although one wore a battered straw hat. They both looked powerfully built men, even at this distance, and not likely to ask questions. I did not like any part of these new developments, and I took Bianca by the arm and drew her away. We went through into the Merceria before striking right. Losing and finding our way, we made a slow return to the Pensione Greci.

"To dodge those friars in that manner looks as if you were trying to escape from your conscience, Rupert," Bianca said at one point, smiling, teasing.

I shook my head. "In a way, I suppose I'm trying to give a man his conscience back."

"Is that a riddle or the beginning of a story?"

"The end of one story and the beginning of another, I'm afraid."

"You speak too many riddles for me, Rupert."

"And for me, too."

"Why are you afraid? And what are you afraid of?"

"Do I seem afraid?"

"If I run away from something, I tell myself I am afraid of it," she said with simple logic. "What do you fear, Rupert?"

"Mostly we make our own fears," I said. "But I am not so sure I've made this one."

"Were you—are you—afraid of the Franciscans?"

"I think I am."

"Why?"

"I can't tell. I only met them this morning for the first time."

"Is that why you fear them now?"

"Not exactly *fear*," I said. The Italian word, I suddenly remembered, was almost the same. "Apprensione."

"Ah!" she said. "Will you put apprehension aside when we are in our room?"

"More easily there than anywhere in the world."

"I will do what I can to help," she said, laughing. She asked no more questions.

"We missed our coffee and brandy in the square." I pointed out as we passed a small sidewalk café. "We can stop here."

"I think you would rather go on."

I took her hand again and we went on, more deeply into the lanes and bridges of Venice that lie between the Palazzo Trevisan and the Rio dei Greci.

Not until we were once again within the confines of our room did I begin to put apprehension aside. Not until we were once again lost in each other were all thoughts of the complications, in which I had been so unwittingly involved by Greenaway, driven from my mind.

30

EARLY on Thursday morning I awoke to find that the bleakness that had afflicted me throughout the previous day had lifted. In thankfulness, I turned to Bianca, the cause of this transformation; but she was sleeping as if with a thousand years of life ahead.

I lay for a long time watching her, captivated by the beauty that had helped to remake my life, but sadness suddenly clouded my happiness to an unbearable degree and I looked away, impatient for movement and the day to begin.

My watch marked six o'clock as I slipped out of bed, crossed to the window and stared down once more upon this corner of Venice, now slowly awakening. Men in denims and sandals walked slowly towards the Schiavoni quays; black-robed older women ambled towards the shops: a few energetic gondoliers were even poling their pleasure and commercial craft towards the lagoon. And, already, a strengthening sun lay heavily upon the city.

Within the room, I heard the creaking of the ancient bed as Bianca stirred and came awake. I turned to watch her. Puzzled, she looked around the room, seeking explanation. Then, seeing me, she smiled in relief and called out, begging me to return to bed, for we should have to leave soon enough. Meantime, at least, we could be together.

I could have stayed by the window for a long time, lost in masochistic pleasure, keeping from Bianca, watching her emerge from the bedclothes. But the breeze moved into the room, and, suddenly chilled, I was with her again.

We had established a timetable that would get us back to Padua in time for our commitments. Once there, I knew too well, my unwanted chores would reimpose themselves.

First, I would have to ring Lucca. Then probably call on him. Then consult Lieutenant Caccia. Then consult the parish priest.

Only after that dreary round could I begin to plan a reunion with Bianca. These points I explained as we sank once again into the creaking bed. These points Bianca saw clearly enough, but she was moved to fierce hatred of the hours that would keep us apart. I shared her protests. In such poignancy is love provoked and rediscovered, but that was scant comfort to us then.

I left Bianca at her hotel just before nine o'clock and went on by taxi to the Jolanda. By that time the unoffending hotel was utterly repellant to me. Even the foyer was invested with memories of my own searched luggage and clothes, and I detested the innocent management with unreasoning fury.

But why should I stay there a moment longer? I suddenly asked myself, as I entered the hall and took my key from the desk-clerk. Why should I condemn myself to two more nights in Padua when Venice provided more entertainment, and—I scarcely dared admit to myself—more cover from Criccoli, despite his searching of the previous night? The contrast between the bustling efficiency of the Jolanda and the run-down Pensione Greci was suddenly wholly in favour of the Greci. Then why not stay there until we left for Rome?

In sudden decision I crossed to the telephone kiosk and asked for the Hotel Grande Italia, and spoke to Bianca almost immediately.

"If I can't meet you later today," I explained, "let us meet at our new home this evening. Sometime after four o'clock." I was ashamed to find that I took care not to mention the Greci by name. How quickly fear and suspicion possess the mind!

159

Then I went up to see James. He was in his shirt-sleeves, finishing breakfast. Had he seen Lucca? I asked after our exchange of felicities.

"Not a whisper," he said, somewhat to my surprise.

"No Franciscans either?"

"None."

That surprised me less, and I told James something of our strange game of blind man's buff in St Mark's Square. He listened and nodded. His own replies had induced a sense of anti-climax. The homing traveller does not expect to find that life has proceeded so smoothly in his absence, but James, unaware of my reactions, asked gaily whether I should be returning to the Anglo-Italian fold for that day's sightseeing.

"I must ring Lucca first," I said, and crossed to the bedside telephone and asked for the Tribunale.

After long delays and requests from minions that I should wait a moment, I was through to the pretore.

"I am relieved to hear from you," he said. "I rang you three times last evening, the third time very late. You were very late returning from Venice."

"I thought only three people knew I was in Venice," I said.

"Perhaps I was an accidental fourth."

"And now?"

"I should be grateful to see you this morning. Perhaps in an hour's time?"

"I shall be there."

"What more does he want?" James asked, as I rang off.

"Only the letter and the papers I got from Greenaway—just like everybody else in this blasted town."

"Why not let me carry them today?"

I shook my head. Then I said, "Yes, this morning might be a good idea. I'll take them back later." I took them from my pocket and handed them across.

He was surprised.

"I should have posted them to London, I suppose," I mumbled.

"In a way, but I see your point," he said. "I'd think seriously myself before letting them go."

I thanked him for his understanding of my own obstinacy.

160

"Will you try to catch us up again later today?" he asked.

"I don't know. My currency allowance won't stand any more cross-country taxi drives, although I've got this extra money of Greenaway's."

"You can have some of mine—willingly."

I waved his offer aside. I was too dispirited by the prospect of my meeting with Lucca to plan very far ahead.

"Why don't Georgina and I stay behind? Bianca, too?" James broke in. "Why don't we have a day off?—or at least the afternoon—by ourselves in the country? Or we could all go to Venice."

Optimism returned, slowly ousting apprehension.

"But aren't you seeing today's villa?" I asked. "And isn't that rather interesting?"

"I can live for quite a time without another villa or another day in the coach. I'd far rather have an unplanned day in the Veneto or on the Lido."

I was delighted. "If you're prepared to gamble that Lucca will have finished with me by midday, there's nothing I'd like better. But what will you do meantime?"

"I haven't seen the Giotto frescoes in the Scrovegni. I haven't done any shopping. I haven't really had one quiet morning with Georgina. Where shall we meet, and when?"

"The station. One o'clock. Then straight to Venice."

"Ah! Action!" he cried, delighted. "The name of action. I'll go and stop Bianca and Georgina embedding themselves in the coach."

He put on his jacket and went. I walked along to my room. All was as neat as a set for an amateur theatrical performance, and I hated the whole place.

31

A MOOD of controlled elation upheld me through the first part of that day. From early morning I had foreseen a day of gloom. Instead I had been offered a prospect of pleasure, scarcely to be dimmed by Lucca himself.

Yet even Lucca was different that day.

He received me again in his high small room. Wary of his technique, I waited for him to speak, but he seemed in no mood to play the inquisitor and began by tapping the closed dossier on his desk and coming briefly to the point.

"Doctor Frost, it is my official duty, as pretore, to recommend a course of action in such a case as the one we have been discussing, the unfortunate affair of Mr Greenaway. I have made all relevant enquiries and I propose to take no further action. I thought you would be interested to know that."

I sat silent, surprised by this unexpected opening and apparent conclusion to the meeting.

"Do you have to put in a verdict as we do in England?" I asked, after a pause.

"My view—and the medical view—is that Greenaway killed himself whilst his mind was disturbed. Would you not agree?"

I nodded.

"I am not altogether sure that his mind was disturbed in the conventional sense," Lucca said reflectively. "For example, he left me, as coroner, sufficient money to cover his funeral expenses. I find that he cashed sufficient travellers' cheques at the hotel desk at ten o'clock that evening. Such consideration is rare. Do you not agree?"

"Very rare."

"Such consideration also suggests a certain lucidity of mind?"

Again I agreed.

"Not all the money he cashed has been left with me," Lucca said, watching me carefully. "He cashed one hundred and fifty thousand lira, of which he left me sixty thousand. Would you have any ideas concerning the destiny of the remainder of the money?"

"None at all." I was so much more confident that day, knowing that James had the Greenaway papers. I felt prepared for anything that Lucca could throw at me.

"A pity. It is one of many small mysteries in a larger mystery."

I did not take up his observation, and he went on: "You will

162

know by now that I have made no enquiries of your friend, Mr Westlake."

He was still smiling but watchful.

I nodded.

"From other enquiries I find that Mr Westlake had no acquaintance with Greenaway. As for that matter of the hotel envelope, I knew I should have no more from Westlake than corroboration of your own story. No occasion arose, therefore, to call him to this office."

"And Miss Castle?" I thought it prudent to ask.

"I saw Miss Castle last evening and my opinion agrees with your own. I found her an attractive young woman, typically English, I would say, both in her looks and in her reaction to the tragedy."

Curiosity overrode caution, and I asked the question he probably awaited.

"Why so typically English in her reactions?"

"A certain hardness of heart," he said casually, and then: "A certain lack of imagination concerning the condition of mankind."

"She is young and pretty," I said, partly in her defence, partly to provoke him to further words.

"Yet even the young occasionally have hearts," he said. "At least they have in this country."

"By 'mankind' do you mean 'men'? or the human condition generally?" I asked, shrugging away his other comments.

"Men," he said simply.

"In a nation as dominated by males as England, Miss Castle's attitude is possibly inevitable. But it is probably no more than a superficial impression."

He pouted disbelievingly. "Wherever I find it, I deprecate it."

He seemed to be settling down for a morning's disputation, a session for polishing up his English, but I was still suspicious of his mood and his felicities. Lucca was too direct a man for such digressions. Then, too, as I was well aware, my own alertness could easily die in this atmosphere of bonhomie.

"Would you not agree?" he asked.

"Not quite," I said. "I am not altogether in favour of the undisputed dominion of men. It is an English philosophy, I

163

have always thought, largely inculcated at our boarding schools. I was at a day school. And I have owed too much to women in my life."

"Englishwomen, of course?" he asked genially.

"Of course."

"Avete avuto molte avventure con donne italiane?" he said suddenly, still probing my knowledge of his language, but again I was dull and he said, "You have had little experience of Italian women?"

I wondered how much he knew, whether he was still probing.

"Very little."

"It is always an enlightening experience for an Englishman to find himself in the company of a woman who considers herself not unequal to men," he said, watching me, awaiting my reaction.

"I have known such Englishwomen," I said, almost adding that I had married one, but caution restrained me.

I was increasingly curious concerning the trend of his conversation, wondering where his apparent digression was to lead. That it had direction, I had no doubt. But, to my surprise, Lucca said, very quietly, neither changing his voice nor his apparent mood: "Doctor Frost, I think I should warn you that you may be in some danger."

I was so bewildered by this smooth but startling *volte face* from social enquiry to sudden warning that I probably played the part I might have tried to affect, stammering, "What on earth . . . ?"

Again he tapped the dossier, almost fretfully.

"Doctor Frost," he began gravely, "permit me to be very frank with you. Then I shall ask you to be frank with me. As far as I am concerned, the case of Greenaway is finished. That he committed suicide, Doctor Godi has no doubt. Therefore, I have no doubt. Tomorrow Greenaway will be buried. But as far as others are concerned, he is still very much alive. I have come to believe that you may be involved in this affair, perhaps innocently, perhaps less innocently, but still misguidedly. If so, I implore you to consider most carefully what you do. Even your very next step. Ask my help and I shall do all in my power to help you."

As if deciding to take me into his confidence, he added: "I have received from Interpol this morning a further report on Greenaway. It is thought that he might well have been intending not to return to England."

"Another Pontecorvo, in fact?" I asked.

He nodded.

"Not from what I gathered," I said, in threadbare justice to Greenaway.

"Then it is possible that he was here to pass on information."

"That I would not know," I lied.

"Well, there it is," he said.

We sat there, our eyes trickily involved, for several long seconds. Then, giving up, he shrugged his shoulders and opened his hands in mock-despair.

"At this moment," he said, "I am powerless. I have done all that I am required to do officially. I cannot force you to be helped. I can only give you a warning that I think you should ask for help if you feel you may possibly, even remotely, need help. I may, of course, be talking to you in riddles. I hope I am. You may think I am mad. Even that would be reassuring."

He smiled as thinly as his pouting lips permitted.

"You are talking to me in riddles," I said. "But I have no doubt that they are well-intentioned, and for that I am grateful—as anyone would be."

Again he shrugged. To the best of my niggardly histrionic power I tried to retain an expression of complete bewilderment. Once Lucca had the papers, I asked myself again, wouldn't I become, in the moment of giving, a party to the passing on of official secrets?

It was a dilemma with a number of attendant subtleties I was not prepared to explore at that moment. I knew that I would keep to the course I had decided upon, including the impossible reservation that I wanted both to return to London and proceed to Rome.

"I puzzle you, Doctor Frost?" Lucca said.

"To say the least."

"Then I am glad," he said. "Forget all that I have said. If you are truly puzzled, I am truly relieved."

My conscience was momentarily touched by his apparent sincerity and my certain duplicity, but sometimes a man must go on. And I had to go on. That I knew. Perhaps Lucca knew it, too, for he suddenly stood up from his desk and the interview was plainly at an end. I also stood up, saying, as casually as possible, "Will you be needing me any more, Signor Lucca?"

"Not unless you think you need me."

He seemed unable to make a break with his earlier suspicions. A heavy sense of responsibility for my well-being seemed to rest upon him. He could not shrug it off. Was it concern for me, himself, his job or his country? I wondered as I bowed and said, "An improbability, I think, but thank you."

As we stood by the door, I asked whether the final arrangements for Greenaway's funeral had been made. Lucca turned back to the dossier on his desk and opened its stiff covers. The service would be held on Friday, the following day, at two o'clock in the afternoon, he said, reading. I had a moment of relief remembering my sleeper reservations to Rome for Friday night. I should now, at least, be spared the trouble of trying to transfer them to Saturday night. Meanwhile, Lucca was explaining that Signor Revisi had been informed about the service. So, too, had the British Consul in Venice. Any other details could be learned from Lieutenant Caccia.

He turned, opened the door and ushered me from the room. As we walked along the echoing corridor he said, "I have implied to the Church authorities that Greenaway's death was perhaps accidental. The Church is always anxious to give the benefit of the doubt. He will thus be buried as a believer," he added with a thin smile.

"A touch Greenaway would have appreciated," I said.

Then we were at the stairhead and he put out his hand.

"At the risk of being a bore, Doctor Frost, I will say a final word. If by any mischance you are caught up in events which are new to you, I beg of you to think twice before going on. The men Greenaway had become involved with are quite merciless. If you are in their way, you will be ruthlessly put aside. If necessary you could even be—as the Americans say— rubbed out." As he turned he said, "You did not suggest that

Miss Castle might have had the rest of the money Greenaway cashed.

"Why should I?"

"It would have been a natural suggestion—or even question."

"Also impertinent."

"Ah!" he said and smiled and walked away.

His warning, uttered so quietly and casually within the great hall of the Tribunale, had a profoundly disturbing effect upon me. I was suddenly chilled and dejected, for I knew that I had been speaking to a man who was speaking of a world he knew authoritatively. And I knew too well that it was a world of which I knew only by newspaper headlines. I am not writing in the light of later events. My mood of that moment returns even as I write. A mood of utter dejection, frustration and self-anger possessed me as I went heavily down by the wide staircase.

I remember my surprise at finding the sun still shining in the Via Altinate. I had expected to meet a grey and overcast world. I began to walk slowly towards the Piazza Garibaldi. As I crossed the Piazza Cavour I saw a familiar Franciscan habit on the opposite side of the square. I stepped into the shade of the canopied area of the café at the corner of the piazza, and waited until I saw Marcello disappear into the narrow street leading towards the University. I found, as I began to walk again, that my hands and brow were damp with sweat and my legs trembling. I despised myself for such weakness. I sat down at a side-walk café and ordered an espresso and a brandy. The café commanded a view of the square, and I had some shelter within the shade of the table canopy. Why shouldn't I see Marcello? I asked myself fiercely. Padua was a small town, well known as a centre of Franciscan learning and activity. Didn't the fact that Marcello was wandering about the street in this manner suggest undue panic on the part of Lucca and, through him, myself? But that didn't dispel my sense of foreboding. I was caught up in circumstances I did not fully comprehend, and, like most men of peace sensing far-off hints of violence, I was more than a little perturbed. I sat there for several minutes, until, again calm, I paid for my drinks and crossed quickly to the bookshop that faces the Piazza Cavour.

Touched by the prospect of my imminent reunion with Bianca, and determined to put aside Lucca's doleful warnings, I browsed amongst the novels, searching for a book for Bianca, one eye on the door. But my Italian was too poor for the task. I turned to the shelves containing the architectural books. There I found the one-volume reprint of Palladio's *Quattro Libri del l'Architettura*, known, I daresay, to all architectural students but new to me. I bought the book and arranged for it to be sent to Bianca at the Hotel Italia Grande. A far better souvenir of our time together than any novel, I persuaded myself, as I scribbled a note to be sent with the book.

32

JAMES was already in the station booking-hall when I arrived by taxi from a rank near the bookshop. I was ten minutes early, but he'd only just arrived, he said.

"I've got the tickets," he added. "There's a train at one-thirten. We ought to be able to catch it if our women don't let us down."

I glanced from the high windows into the wide and dusty station forecourt. No movement. No taxi. Just one waiting bus with three sleepy occupants and a dozing driver at the wheel.

"Busy morning?" James asked, as we stood within the shade of the high, cool hall.

"Not too bad."

"How was Lucca?"

"Very civil."

"Let you off with a caution?"

"Just that, in fact."

"It's still a holiday, then?"

"More or less."

"Well, isn't one suicide a reasonable substitute for a queue of would-be suicides?"

168

I smiled, but didn't rise to his raillery.

"Well, isn't that a fair description of your day?" he persisted.

"Fair to middling."

I was still nervous and kept glancing through the windows to the far corner of the courtyard, towards the Corso del Popolo, where the taxis swung round boldly into the station yard.

"Why so jumpy?" James asked.

"No particular reason."

"I don't see any monkish types."

"No, thank God, but where the hell are Georgina and Bianca?"

"We had to rescue Bianca from one just now," James said casually. Too casually, for I asked dully, "One what?"

"One of your brown-frocked bloody friars," James said, watching me carefully. "The small mean-looking one."

"What on earth d'you mean?" I asked. The words echoed in the large hall.

"Up by the Piazza Cavour," James said calmly. "Some damned sneak-thief pinched Bianca's handbag. We were having coffee in one of those places by the Piazza Cavour and saw the whole thing happen. Not quite the snatch, but the general shambles afterwards. The priest was one of the first on the scene. He seemed to be taking command of things, but I wandered across and took over. Bianca was a bit shaken, but there was nothing valuable in the bag, I gather. Georgina took her back to her hotel. I came on in case you were fretting—as you would have been by now, I've no doubt."

"As I am!"

"As you are indeed!"

"Genuine bag-snatching or the Greenaway game?" I asked.

"Your guess is as good as mine," James said. "Bianca doesn't look exactly poverty-stricken at any time in those clothes. And those heels of hers would guarantee no more than a token pursuit."

"Very funny!"

He smiled fleetingly and took my arm.

"Anyway, they'll both be here in a minute, so relax, old boy," he said, ignoring my brusque mood.

169

"How was Bianca?"

"More furious than shaken. Absolutely livid. Wonderful chance to see the Italian female temperament at full blast."

"It *must* be that bloody Criccoli."

"It could be, I suppose. Especially the nearness of the other chap. Too much of a coincidence. What's his name by the way?"

"Marcello. When did all this happen?"

"Half an hour ago."

"I must have missed it by minutes."

"It only took a minute. Now do relax. They'll be here in a second."

I nodded and tried to relax.

"I suppose there was nothing of importance to you in the handbag," James said quietly.

"Nothing. If you've still got the papers, that is," I said irritably.

"I've still got the papers," he said patiently and held up his hand in peace. "I'd return them to you now if we weren't so much in the public eye."

"What else could Bianca have?" I asked.

"God knows. I just wondered."

"D'you think I'm mad?"

"Not more than most of us."

Again we were silent: a thunderous silence on my part, gentle and puzzled on James's, but he was not to be gainsaid, and came boring in again: "At the risk of being impertinent, Rupert, are you quite certain that Bianca's everything she looks and says she is?"

"For God's sake . . ." I began, but again he put a restraining hand upon my arm.

"Now, take it easy, Rupert. Relax. Just look at it from my point of view. You've been carrying some extremely valuable papers around with you by all accounts, and, at the same time you've been floating around with an unknown Italian popsy, probably pursued by some other Italians interested in the same papers. If I were in the same position, wouldn't you be a trifle anxious for my safety?"

"Perhaps," I said grudgingly.

"You're absolutely sure of Bianca?"

"Utterly."

"There's no possible chance that she could be mixed up in it?"

"How, for God's sake?"

"Well, these characters have odd ways of imposing their wishes. Blackmail, and so forth."

"Then why pinch her bag?"

"Why not if it makes a good smokescreen? Georgina and myself conveniently nearby and all that."

"Smokescreen for what?"

"For you, perhaps."

"Nonsense."

"Probably. When did you last look at the Greenaway papers?"

"When I gave them to you, of course."

"You couldn't be certain, here and now, that other papers might have been substituted?"

"I haven't looked. And I wouldn't know, in any case. The envelope was sealed when I had it. Substituted by whom?"

He shrugged. I remembered Bianca's sleeping face, and almost exploded with hatred of James's logical, persistent mind.

"We slept in the same room, but I'd go to the gallows swearing by Bianca."

"So be it," he said. "You're the one concerned."

"But not the only one!" I had the remnants of decency to add.

By then I was shaken and trembling with fury. Fortunately I suddenly remembered that the sight of Marcello, after my meeting with Lucca, had driven all thoughts of Caccia from my mind. I muttered a garbled excuse to James and went across to the telephone and rang the Municipio. Yes, all was in order, Lieutenant Caccia said, agreeably enough. The funeral was fixed for two o'clock on the following afternoon at the Cimitiero. That was all. Mourners would make their own arrangements for transport, of course. The cemetery was about four kilometres beyond the town.

I thanked him and returned to James just as Georgina and Bianca came through the glass doors of the booking hall.

171

Bianca seemed very pale, I thought. She came towards me and took my hand.

"Oh, Rupert, how good to see you!" she cried. In that instant, nothing that James could have said or implied could have undermined my belief in Bianca.

We made our way to the platform. The train from Milan was due in three minutes. On time it arrived to take us from Padua, a beautiful city perhaps but a city that was rapidly becoming, for me, a place of pleasure tinged with nightmares. As we clambered on board James said, very quietly, "I'm sorry about just now, old boy."

With the arrival of Bianca, anger and bitterness had left me and I said, "Forget it," and sincerely meant my words.

"My immediate intention," he said.

Within the train he was in his merriest mood, as if in sudden relief from a growing tension. As we were drawing into the station at Venice he handed me the Greenaway envelopes. He smiled as he did so. Bianca and Georgina were looking from the windows at the Venetian scene, which seemed to draw even the train into its thronging, bustling life.

33

IN REACTION from the events of the morning, I think we were all in a mood for escape, and that day, or the remainder of the day, was the perfect answer to our mood.

In the train I had moments of foreboding when I recalled Criccoli and Marcello and the previous night in Venice. Venice is a city of some size, but the area usually chosen by sightseers is apt to be concentrated and available for careful inspection. I could not hope for similar good fortune in again evading them. After all, I told myself, hadn't we missed their attentions by a mere fifty feet the night before?

Fortunately, James, with his own clear-cut plans for the day, drove out these morbid reflections.

"What about a trip to one of the islands?" he asked, asserting rather than requesting.

172

"Would Chioggia be too far?" Georgina asked, taking out a small red-covered *Carnet di Venezia* from her handbag and rapidly turning over the pages. "There's a boat at three o'clock."

"Too far," James said decisively. "The journey takes a couple of hours, and we'd have no time there at all."

"But why not?" Bianca said. "The journey is beautiful. Right down through the lagoon. What time do we have to be back?"

"No time at all," I said. "Let's forget time, anyway."

"Hear! Hear!" said James.

"The vaporetto leaves Chioggia at six, arrives Venice at eight," Georgina read from the guide.

"Then why not go?" Bianca said for all of us.

"Good!" James said. "I'd like it, too. No walking about. No villas. Just sitting on board a steamer holding hands."

I was relieved to think that we might be away from Venice for so long, for I had been gloomily contemplating a time spent in St Mark's Square, sitting in the sun, a cynosure awaiting Criccoli's pleasure. I hated myself for my fear, but there it was, nagging, senseless, yet ineradicable.

We took the vaporetto from the station to the Molo and lunched by the quayside, looking across to San Giorgio. Our meal was as gay as our journey had been, and the chianti helped in dispelling memories of Criccoli and Marcello. And Lucca.

Afterwards, we walked along the Schiavoni quays to the steamer berth. The sun was hot, the sky cloudless and our mood carefree. I was with Bianca, and that was enough.

The passage to the fishing-port of Chioggia, through the southern half of the Venetian lagoon, is one of the most beguiling journeys in European waters. Even the islets of San Servolo, La Grazia and San Clemente, with their sombre buildings for consumptives and lunatics, seem to have a part to play in the journey, reminding the traveller of the transience of his pleasure, adjuring him to seize the moment. Then the islands are left astern and the traveller can relax utterly.

We sat, as two pairs, opposite each other on the upper deck. Despite the splendour of the afternoon, the gaiety of the

173

lagoon and the novelty of the scenes about us, I dozed, my head slipping gradually upon Bianca's shoulder.

I lost consciousness in a mood of self-pity, not an uncommon occurrence for those beset by anxieties. I was a fool to fear Criccoli, I told myself again and again within this confusion of thought, yet there it was, as obvious as the sun. When I thought of the hours that remained before I could leave Northern Italy for Rome, I was as nervous as a child. If only my puritanical conscience had not insisted upon my attendance at Greenaway's funeral, I could have been four hundred miles away. It was all a foolish, pompous and unnecessary gesture, I told myself. A dead man is a dead man. That was the logical view. And, in the same moment, I told myself again that to attend the service was the least I could do for the memory of Greenaway and his parents.

In an odd, twisted way, the burial was beginning to take on a kind of symbolical significance. If I could get beyond that ceremony, I kept telling myself, I should be safe. I should have my time in Rome with Bianca. I would take Bianca back to England. I would deliver the papers to Professor Hankinson. All would be well. Like an inveterate gambler, I had inextricably linked my future with a symbol; in this case, my days in Rome. That I knew. In Rome I should be free of these fears of Criccoli.

In Rome, too, I could venture my love for Bianca to the limit, I told myself, for I now knew beyond all doubt that I loved her without the slightest reservation. I had no wish to change her. She had made me live again. She had become for me the symbol of a new life, escape from the living dreariness of the past months, escape from myself. In Rome I should make the greatest gamble of my life and ask her to become my wife and come with me to England. Only Greenaway's burial intervened between intention and action. These were my last waking thoughts, and I doubtless carried them deeply into my sleep, for I awoke to find my head on Bianca's breast and her hand resting lightly on my brow.

"Where are the others?" I asked, coming fitfully awake, fighting for consciousness against the afternoon's heat.

"Promenading."

"Where are we?"

"We have just left Palestrina."

"Where's that?"

"Just there," she said, waving astern. "We shall be at Chioggia in half an hour. Go to sleep again."

"Have I been quiet?"

"A little restless."

"No snoring?"

"Not once. But you are worried about something, Rupert. You stirred and sighed. What is it?"

"A little worry, but it is less when I wake and find you here."

"Can I help?"

"You help just by being here. You help more than you can ever know."

"That I love to hear, but what is the worry?"

"It is really nothing," I said. "Tell me, what did you lose from your bag?"

"A little money, a pair of ear-rings, my lipstick, powder and some cigarettes. A note from you, two other letters. That is all.

"Much money?"

"Six thousand lire. No more."

"What was the thief like?"

"A small man, young, dressed in black. One of five hundred Padovans I could have passed this morning."

"And the friar?"

"One of the two we saw last night."

I was silent.

"Will you tell me the trouble between the Franciscans and yourself?" she asked, very quietly.

"Yes, I will. Today or tomorrow. Tomorrow when we leave Padua."

"When shall we leave Padua? How shall we leave Padua? I cannot wait."

"I had booked to leave by rail tomorrow night, but I've been thinking that we could go with the others by the coach to Vicenza and travel to Rome overnight from there. I could probably change the tickets."

"Could we fly?"

"We can enquire. Then we could be in Rome on Friday

175

night perhaps. But we shall certainly be there on Saturday morning."

"That will be good."

"And alone," I said.

"For how long, Rupert?"

"At least a week. How long can you stay in Rome?"

"For at least a week," she said, smiling.

"And then?"

"We shall see, shan't we?"

"What shall we see?" I asked.

"If we like one another when we have no Anglo-Italian Palladian Society to keep us busy."

"Nonsense."

She laughed.

I raised myself from my place of solace as James and Georgina returned, hand in hand: it was an afternoon for such sentimentalities.

Away to the right was the Murazzi, Georgina said, reading from her guide-book.

"And what the hell is the Murazzi?" James asked.

"The great sea-wall built in the middle of the eighteenth century on either side of the Porto di Chioggia," Georgina read obediently.

"I wish I could have a few of the same chaps to keep my sheep walls in repair," James said, historical romance standing no chance against his earthbound practicality.

"Sheep! Sheep! Sheep!" Georgina cried. "And here we are in the fabulous lagoon of Venezia."

James grinned, and kissed her boldly.

A few minutes later we were within the harbour and alongside. We wandered ashore in the golden glow of the late afternoon sun, crossing the Piazzetto Vigo, with its column carrying the lion of St Mark, making our chattering way to the tree-shaded piazza.

We had an hour and a half ashore. In that time we explored the seaport with that feverish excitement that besets all travellers deposited in a place to which they have no certainty of returning. The intimidating town hall, the Campanile, the Cathedral were all taken in on our whirlwind tour. Only at the end, as we sank back in our seats on board the steamer, did I realize how successfully our wanderings and sight-seeing had exorcised my qualms and fears. Temporarily, at least.

Through the dusk, we returned to Venice. The lagoon, with its criss-crossing vaporetti and motoscaffi, their lights appearing as darkness grew, had that poignancy held by all sea scenes at nightfall. We were silent as we moved through this busy, magical world.

We dined within the canopies of the quayside restaurant by the Rialto. We had all enjoyed our day, and were now possessed by that genial laziness that sees the world through a rosy haze. Even I was lulled into a softening belief that the future would assuredly fit into the pattern I intended.

Georgina was especially gay that evening, teasing James as if he were her long-time lover. Their relationship had changed. Where, before, he had gently baited her as if she were a wayward, well-loved child, now he was content to be her victim. She dealt with him in a tenderly merciless manner as if he presented a continuous challenge to her femininity. And she could not have found, in the wide world, a more willing foil for her quips.

I wondered whether they had become lovers in recent days or nights, or had taken up a love once put aside. Or whether she could not bear to contemplate a future life without him. Or finally, more simply, whether he still resisted her allure, and deep down (or perhaps not so deep) this fact provoked her. I had seen before how his genial detachment towards women could madden them. I had seen it at work in this very city at the war's end. Yet it was clear (perhaps less clear to a woman) that he was devoted to Georgina, her willing slave. But "slave" was scarcely the right word. He held always within himself an integrity, or possibly obstinacy (it is often difficult, even for the so-called expert, to tell where the lesser trait becomes the nobler) and if that had been aroused he would remain aloof.

At one point Georgina said, "Why should we rejoin the Palladian boys and girls, James? Why shouldn't we go off to Rome—like Bianca and Rupert?"

177

"Probably because Bianca and Rupert want to be alone," he said, deliberately obtuse.

"Don't be silly, James. You know exactly what I mean. Of course we shouldn't intrude on them, but why don't we play hookey every day—just like this?"

"Truancy is only exciting by contrast with duty," he said grandly, infuriatingly.

She fumed with exasperation, but then said, over-patiently, "Well, then, in my case, two weeks' truancy against fifty weeks of duty. I know your life with Mrs Harker is fifty weeks of playing hookey and this is *your* fortnight's duty."

James smiled. "You're speaking of a housekeeper I love and need."

"I sometimes think you do, too."

"Where would you like to play truant?" James asked, unperturbed.

"Portofino. Naples. Even Rome. I'd give Rupert and Bianca a written guarantee not to run into them."

"But you must come to Rome," Bianca said. "Rome is a big place. And friends meet when they wish to, do they not?"

"We may do that," James said reflectively, and I well remember the smiling certainty of his words. "Sometime at the end of next week perhaps."

By the time we had finished our meal and discussed the manifold approaches to playing hookey, the restaurant clock stood at eleven and our waiter was beginning to fret. We paid our bill and left, walking slowly to the Rialto vaporetti quay, a few yards away, James and Georgina to return to the Santa Lucia railway station, thence to Padua, Bianca and myself in the opposite direction, towards San Zaccharia.

We stood talking together at the quayside, and arranged to meet again at the Cemetery outside Padua just before two o'clock the following afternoon. Georgina and Bianca began to talk about Rome and clothes.

James took my arm and took me a yard or so away.

"Revisi proposes to take the Society out to the service *en bloc*, in the coach, then drive on to Vicenza for the next part of the trip. You remember the arrangement?"

"Vaguely. I suppose you've booked your hotel in Vicenza."

"I have," he said. "Or, at least, Georgina did. We're there for three days if you want me. Have you booked anything in Rome?"

"I've rather left the hotel to Bianca. She's got one or two old favourites."

"So you don't know the name of it yet?"

"Not yet."

"You'd better let me have it tomorrow."

I nodded. "I suppose Revisi knows I'm coming to the service."

"I didn't tell him. I've left him to assume you are. Don't you think the less anyone knows about your movements the better?"

"Probably, although Criccoli may well know I'm booked on the sleeper if he's made any enquiries."

We began to pace to and fro along the quayside.

"I doubt it. He probably thinks you're coming with us to Vicenza," James said, determined to be optimistic. "What time does your train go from Padua tomorrow night?"

"Twenty-to-one."

"How d'you propose to fill in time between the burial service and your train departure?"

"I hadn't thought."

"Where does the train leave from?"

"Here. We could come back and join it here, I suppose. I hadn't thought of that possibility. I'd assumed we'd join it at Padua."

"It might be better. Once Criccoli discovers you're not on the coach trip to Vicenza he's going to make some very pointed enquiries."

"He'll find out about the sleeper bookings then if not before. I dare say his spy system's pretty well organized in these parts, and he'll have several hours in which to make his enquiries."

"Don't sound so gloomy. He's left you alone so far."

"I haven't given him much chance to do otherwise, have I? I've been moving around quite a bit. I haven't spent an hour in the hotel since I saw him there. I've given him no chance. Deliberately. I believe it was me he was looking for in this very place last night. And that business of Bianca's bag today rather clinches it as far as I'm concerned."

"You're probably right," he said, serious for once. "Well, what are you waiting for? Why don't you go back to London tomorrow?"

"Because I can't. Why should I let all this and Greenaway ruin what I see as my chance for the future?"

"I see all that," he said gravely. "I see the other side, too. This thing with Bianca, then, is as serious as all that?"

"Absolutely."

"You'd marry her?"

"I shall marry her."

"Well, well. She'll certainly add a touch of colour to the Wimpole Street scene."

"You don't approve?"

"Approve. You make me sound like a bishop. I think she's terrific."

"What about your comments earlier today?"

"Just looking after your welfare, old boy."

"You'll probably have to be best man—or at least a witness."

"I'd be delighted to be either. A touch of envy will doubtless creep in, but you'll forgive that?" He took my arm as we walked.

"Then you quite like Bianca?" I asked in mock surprise.

"Like her! Who wouldn't? It's just that you're sometimes a bit of an innocent outside your consulting-room and I was a bit concerned."

I was doubly relieved. Although James had shown an outward pleasure in Bianca's company, he could, I knew from long experience, most skilfully hide any reservations he might retain. Live and let live had always been a guiding principle in his human relationships. But I also knew him well enough to recognize his sincere opinions, and I was absurdly delighted to hear his unequivocal words. The course I was set upon placed me sufficiently at the mercy of my own conscience to be reassured by words of support—or what I could interpret as support.

The lights of a vaporetto were approaching from the station on the opposite bank of the Canal. It was time for farewells.

"Why don't I pay your bill at the hotel tomorrow and

collect your bag?" James said as we turned towards Bianca and Georgina, now chattering as gaily as lifetime friends. "You won't need to come back to the hotel then. I know you don't like the place any more, and it might even help to confuse the enemy. You can take your case off the coach at the cemetery and transfer it to your taxi."

"It's an idea," I said, for I had been dreading the return to the hotel.

"Good. Take a taxi from the station, collect Bianca's stuff and meet the coach at the Piazza Cavour at half-past one."

"Or at the cemetery."

"Better still. Do that!" James said with all his usual understanding.

He had met half-way my overwhelming wish to avoid all contact with the members of the Anglo-Italian Palladian Society. Somewhere, carefully sheltered within that coach, was an informer upon my Italian way of life, and if I could fox him (or her), so much the better.

We said our last good-nights. Our two vaporetti had arrived almost simultaneously. The boat for San Zaccharia stood away from the landing stage until the other had embarked its passengers. Then, as the vaporetto carrying James and Georgina moved away, I had a moment's vacillation, called, "James! Leave my bag at the hotel. I'll collect it."

"As you wish," he called across the dark waters.

34

WE WALKED slowly back to the Pensione Greci. There we left a note asking for coffee and croissants at eight o'clock, before climbing once more to our home from home.

Perhaps because I had slept in the sun that afternoon I was wakeful in the Pensione Greci that night. For a long time after lovemaking we lay together in silence, occasionally caressing or kissing, lost in the aftermath of passion, watching, entranced, the play of moonlight on the white walls of the room.

181

My own thoughts were a tumultuous medley. James's words at the quayside had heartened me. We are all childishly wistful for reassurance. I brooded over his words, harbouring them to strengthen me in my purpose. My real trouble was, I saw clearly enough, that a year of continence, despair and apathy had made me a willing victim to my present circumstances. I had latently been ready for such a relationship, part romantic, part worldly, wholly satisfying to my pride and wishful thinking. For the first time in many months I had held a woman's body in my arms and lost myself and my anxieties in her beauty. Once again I had heard my own remarks causing a woman to laugh and turn to me in shared delight. I was caught in the most enclosing and beguiling of all meshes, sympathy and sex.

All this was new and intoxicating. Against it I would raise no defences, nor wished to. I must go on. So, in this self-hypnotic mood, I asked the question that had been chiselling at my mind for what seemed a lifetime. "Bianca, will you tell me the truth about yourself?"

She lay on her back, considering the ceiling. Then she asked, very quietly, "Do you know the truth about yourself, Rupert?"

"What I take to be the truth."

"When people have brought you their problems, have they always told you the truth?"

"That is my task: to help them to get at the truth."

"Is it ever simple?"

"Never."

"Is the truth about you simple?"

"I doubt it."

She raised herself on one arm. In the moonlight I could see that she was smiling.

"Can you tell me six simple things about yourself, Rupert. Let me begin for you. You are a widowed Englishman and a doctor. Those two facts you have told me and I believe them to be true. But after that?"

"I am not only a widowed Englishman," I said, "but a bewildered Englishman—in love with an unknown Italian woman."

"Why bewildered and why unknown?"

182

"Bewildered because the way ahead sometimes seems difficult. Unknown because, quite simply, I don't know anything about you."

"You know a great deal," she said, laughing.

Then I went on with a rush, "Don't you see, Bianca? I love you. I want to marry you. I want you to come and live in England."

"And then?" she asked quietly.

"That is enough for the moment."

"Is it?" she asked gently, as if I were an impetuous youth. I did not know. Did I, like more youthful lovers, think that the mere statement of love drove out difficulties?

"No more?" she asked as I remained silent.

"No more. But isn't that enough? Beyond that the future is too hazy. All I know is that I want that future with you."

She lay down again. Then she put out her hand to find my own. We were silent for a long time before she said: "Do you want me to start from the beginning or from the end and go back?"

"Just to start."

After a deep sigh, as if she had decided upon an unpredictable course, she said, "I told you that I grew up in Rome?"

I nodded.

"I grew up in the tenements behind the Tiber. I was one of a family of eight. We lived in two rooms. We were lucky. Others lived eight in one room. At fifteen I escaped. I became a messenger girl in a magazine office. Then I learned to type in the evenings. Then I learned shorthand. What natural talent is to a boy, these things are to a girl. Then, in the war, I worked for the Government. I became a secretary. Then I thought I was in love and I married. An airman. A boy of twenty, and he was killed within six months. It is the story of a million other women in the world. Then after the war I worked for the Americans. Then, because things were difficult, I began to live with an American major. It is a way of life in wartime and afterwards. You know that. He was married. Then he went back to New York and another took his place. Yet another was unmarried and wanted to marry me, but by then I was not the marrying kind."

183

"And your family?"

"I helped them. Now they live in the suburbs of Rome. All good Italian girls help their families—especially if they are not good girls," she said, gaiety suddenly returning.

"And then?"

"By then, Rupert, I am perhaps a professional mistress."

"There were many others?"

"Two others."

"And now?"

"Now is no different, Rupert. I am the friend of a Neapolitan shipowner. He is rich and I am comfortable. He is married and has four children, he is a good Catholic who does not believe in divorce."

"How old?"

"Fifty-three or fifty-four. He does not talk about *his* birthdays. Only mine."

"How long have you known him?"

"I met him five years ago."

"And do you love him?"

"I like him. He is kind and generous."

"And he loves you?"

"I do not think so. He is a sensualist. He likes my body. That is all, I think. He is not greatly interested in my mind. His own mind is for his business. He is very like my first American, who was a stockbroker in New York. He thought women should be interested in stocks and shares. He did not know that I thought men should be interested in books because I like reading. Neither does my friend in Naples. Men are like that."

"Where is he now?"

"In America. In New York. He is there for a month. And I am here."

I was deeply shaken by her confession, which was so utterly unexpected. I had imagined, until then, that she had been, as she had first implied three days before, the estranged wife of a successful business man, much about her own age. I had pictured them drifting apart; Bianca, bored perhaps by material success and childlessness, he irritated by a sense of

184

ultimate inadequacy. A mirror, in fact, of half the world's urban marriages. Now, face to face with a different and more complex situation, I was at once appalled, and yet, in a dreadful, sickening fashion, unnerved and excited. I suppose that similar admissions by women have appalled and aroused men in similar fashion in the long, involved history of the sexes. Throughout my professional life I have accepted these paradoxes as part of the mental patterns of my patients. I have seen how much extremes are so easily (I almost write "naturally") involved within one mind.

There, in that Venetian bedroom, I began to sense, within my own more conventional mind, the fascination of these polarities. Even as I lay there by Bianca's side, I began to experience a new thrust of desire. The rescuer and the sensualist conjoined? The dominant male? The lure of an unknown world? And yet might not Bianca's set-up in Naples be as mundane and respectable as a similar set-up in Liverpool? I asked myself, twisting the dagger. And then, again, do any of these things matter? Wasn't the simple fact that I loved Bianca and thought that she loved me enough? Yet even then, enthralled as I was, I could see that her words had made the way ahead a great deal trickier.

"Why did you say you were married when I first met you?" I asked.

"It makes things easier."

"How, for heaven's sake?"

"Because, for one thing, one is asked fewer questions. One is granted more respect. One is left alone."

I was fleetingly touched by her reference to "respect", but I said, ruefully, "I haven't left you alone."

She laughed and took my hand again.

"Nor I you, Rupert."

"And this is the whole truth?"

"There are always so many truths, Rupert, but I think this is the most part of the whole truth."

"Tell me more if there is more to tell."

"All of what I told you is true," she said, a faint note of protest appearing.

"Yet tell me the rest."

185

"Isn't it better to leave ourselves just as we are?" she pleaded.

"Nothing in the world stays as it is."

"Rome is always the same," she said smiling.

"Don't tease," I said. "Tell me."

What folly drives us all on to such limits of explanation? Then I knew, or thought I knew. I thought I must know all I could about Bianca because I saw my life continuing with her, and it seemed to me essential that each should know everything about the other. Now I am not so sure. I had known everything about Helen—or thought I knew. But circumstances alter truths as well as cases. And we are always far short of knowledge, however far we go. All my medical experience had shown me that. But the demand of the moment drives out a lifetime's experience. We think we must know. And so we go on, delving and delving.

I turned to find that Bianca was still watching me, considering me with an altogether unaccustomed gravity.

"No, Rupert, there is no more. There must be no more. You have seen that mine is a very simple, old-fashioned story. You asked me to tell it and there it is. To go on is to go round and round."

That was the truth. "And what of the future?" I asked.

"I did not think about the future until I met you, Rupert. I thought my life would go on like this for five years . . . ten years. Beyond that no woman thinks. That is why I have told you of my past."

"Is your present relationship exciting?" I asked.

She laughed aloud, partly in relief, I think. Relief that I had relaxed my questioning, relief in being able to talk of her present life.

"Oh, Rupert. If only you knew. I am as respectable as the wife of my baker. Perhaps more so. This . . ."—her arm moved in the moonlight to take in the room and ourselves—"this is the wickedest thing I have ever done in my life. For the first time in ten years I have been free—to do exactly what I wished." I took her in my arms. Questions died in tenderness and love.

186

35

WE SLEPT until the late morning, for we had no necessity to catch the early train. An arrival in Padua at half-past one would suit us well enough, I said, as we lazily awoke.

I remember that morning in Venice as a time of relaxed enchantment. Now there were no reservations. Shadows and secrets might remain, but they were the smaller infinities that are never unravelled or resolved. It was enough that now I knew the main pattern of Bianca's life. With that pattern I must deal and make my terms, and, I hoped, my peace.

Our red-headed, scarecrow padrona brought us breakfast, telling us that the day beyond the window was heaven-sent. We could have lots more coffee if we wished, she added, but would we take it in the hall or courtyard? The steps were many and no bell worked. With a wide cracked grin and a genial wave she left us.

We breakfasted in bed, talking and laughing. The serious mood of midnight had gone and we were lost in pleasure until at last I thought it imperative to rise and shave. Otherwise midday would be upon us.

As I shaved, I persuaded myself that this could be a routine as easily established in Wimpole Street as Venice. The sun might not shine as bravely or as regularly, and the architecture around us might not have the same variety, but we should have the warmth of central heating, theatres and restaurants, rooms of greater comfort—and ourselves. So my mind moved in images of self-persuasion.

The only interruption to these thoughts was the all-besetting problem of escape from Criccoli, for in that light I now began to view the next twenty-four hours. I had already convinced myself that once in Rome I should be safe. How strongly the gambler persists in all men! I had made Rome a symbol of escape from Criccoli's oppressive spirit and the symbol gave me some kind of comfort.

Time and again, since those days, I have tried to recall what qualities in Criccoli gave me this sense of apprehension, and convinced me that I must elude him. Even as I write the word "elude" I realize that I am still refusing to accept his full impact upon my mind. In truth, I had only the desire to run from him. It is not a word an Englishman likes to use concerning his reactions to another man's personality and that man a foreigner. Yet there it is. I am not wise after the event. I recall only too well my innermost feelings at that time. Meanwhile, my mind was preoccupied by the smaller problems within the main problem of getting to Rome. Above all, I wanted the least visible means of transport I could find.

Looking back to that morning, I find that my vacillation was probably due to my awareness that my reservations on the overnight train from Padua to Rome gave me what the army is pleased to call an area of manœuvrability. If Criccoli had already learned of those bookings he would undoubtedly reckon upon the certainty of my travelling by that train. On the other hand, he might not know of the reservations. In that case, he would reckon upon my travelling by coach with the main party. After all, I had discussed my possible changes of plan only with James, Georgina and Bianca. My accidental foresight had, at least, provided me with the possibilities for alternative action or, in my case, alas, possible inaction.

As if to deny my own vacillation I made the sudden, almost defiant, resolve to fly, if we could get the bookings, from Venice to Rome that evening, or, failing that, the following morning. I would try to cancel the sleepers when in Padua. Or even let them stand. Confusion of Criccoli was surely worth a modest investment or loss. On a sudden moment of resolution I decided to go immediately to the Alitalia office. I began to see myself as a man of decision and wondered why the plan had not occurred to me before.

But first, the Alitalia office, I told myself firmly, knotting my tie.

"Will you tell the padrona we may be back again tonight?" I asked Bianca as we went down by the beautiful ruined staircase.

"We shall?" Bianca said, astonished. "But what of our trip to Rome?"

"I want to see if we can go another way."

"By vaporetto, gondola or Lambretta?" she laughed, as we

188

crossed to the rickety desk. I took up the telephone directory and checked on the Alitalia office: in or near St Mark's Square, apparently. Bianca rang the handbell for the padrona, who appeared, unexpectedly carrying three bottles of chianti. Bianca explained the possibility of our return. "But of course!" the red-head cried. "It is your room for tonight. I shall not let it."

I paid for the previous night and the night ahead, the padrona vociferously deprecating the gesture but delightedly pocketing the lire in her vast apron.

"She seems devoted to you," I said to Bianca, as we walked towards the Schiavoni quay.

"We give an air of respectability to her establishment," Bianca said, smiling. "It is not every tumble-down pensione in Venice that numbers an English doctor amongst its clientele. And a doctor who pays in advance. But tell me your new plan, Rupert? To stay here? Go by sleeper? Or travel by helicopter to the Colosseum?"

"To go by air."

"Oh! I was right! How nice! I see you are an artist in travel, Rupert. A man of temperament and mood." She laughed and hugged my arm. I, too, was elated by my new resolve, and began to walk too fast for Bianca's pencil heels. She slowed me down, laughing. Yet I was impatient to get to the Alitalia office. With the pendulum swing of my temperament I was already dubious of my chances. But it was an effort worth making, I assured myself firmly. Anything to leave Criccoli far behind.

I left Bianca at Florian's and went on across the piazza. The small office was elusive, tucked away in a corner beyond St Mark's Square, despite the telephone directory. Inside the office, the usual air-booking mêlée was on: everyone loud with pleading and bullying determination to travel at their self-appointed hours. The clerks were standing up manfully to their gruelling inquisitions. Of all transport officials, air travel booking-clerks seem to me to have the most depressing time. I have always thought they should work two hour shifts followed by one hour's recuperation.

At last it was my turn, but I was unlucky. "It is hopeless for this afternoon's flight," the clerk said, consulting his booking-sheets. "I have one vacancy for the early-morning flight tomorrow and another for the afternoon flight."

"Any chance of cancellations?"

"In Venice there is always chance of cancellations," he said, smiling. "It is a city of movement and changes of mind."

I said I would have preferred two bookings on the early-morning flight, but would take the two separate bookings. Should I return that evening to see whether a late cancellation might have been made?

"It isn't likely, but if one falls through I will keep it for you until half-past six. Have you any hotel I can ring?"

"None, alas."

"I will keep them on your word."

Slightly daunted but more than a little relieved, I returned to Florian's to find that Bianca had disappeared. I had a moment of panic and began to stare wildly towards the far corners of the piazza. Then, to my relief, I saw her gloves and sun-glasses resting on a copy of that morning's *Corriere d'Informazione* on a nearby table. I sat down to await her return, shaken by my perturbation. A pointer to the state of my nerves or of my increasing dependence upon Bianca's companionship? I wondered, beckoning the waiter. Had madame ordered? I asked. He nodded. Coffee, he said, but she had gone inside to telephone.

Waiting there, I gradually became prey to all the cumulative suspicions prompted by James's words. Why had Bianca needed to telephone? And to whom? And why at this precise moment? Why immediately after I had told her I had changed our route to Rome? Why? Why? Why?

I hated myself for these suspicions as they moved within my mind like an army of maggots. Yet I could not kill them. There, in the sunlight, in the great piazza, I was as suddenly at their mercy as a chained prisoner in a dark cell.

Then Bianca reappeared, and as I saw her cross towards the table my doubts once more began to die. Yet not completely, and for that I hated myself.

"I am so sorry, Rupert," Bianca said, sitting down. "I rang my apartment in Naples. I risked a long-distance call and

190

was lucky. I wanted to know if there were any messages for me. My daily woman comes at eleven and I thought I might catch her."

"And were there any messages?"

"Two cables from Detroit."

"Cables demanding answers?"

"Only one."

"A long answer?"

She put her hand on my arm. "A short answer, Rupert. I was asked if I would like to fly to New York last night for a holiday. And last night, as you know, I was otherwise engaged."

"And what did you reply?" I asked, monstrously.

"That I had been in the country for a few days," she replied patiently.

"Which is true," I said, and wondered in that same split-second whether I might one day get such cabled answers to my own entreaties. As suspicion receded, jealousy took over. And, as with all these things, it was my own mind that I damaged. The waiter brought our coffee, momentarily staying my enquiries. I looked around. Minute by minute, crowds were beginning to move into the square to take their morning coffees or ice-creams. The sun rested like a blessing upon our heads. Only forty-eight hours before and the way ahead had seemed so simple. Now my mind was partitioned by a multitude of problems, all complex, poisoned by suspicions and doubts. I wondered where, along the way, the simple view had faded.

Bianca poured coffee. Setting my cup before me, she said, "Rupert, you are in a black mood. You are even jealous."

"That is true," I admitted, smiling at last, perhaps ruefully. "But isn't your friend jealous sometimes?"

"All men are jealous," she said. "So life has taught me. Yet you have no need to be."

"I have. You seem to be escaping from me. That is enough to make me jealous—and frantic."

"I am here and you are there," she said. "We are in each other's minds for as long as we shall live."

"I don't want you just in my mind. I want you in my home as well."

"I am here to be taken."

"Then what are we waiting for?"

"For our time in Rome together. For our minds to be certain. Even for my visa," she added with a smile. And then, more gently, "I also have a life to leave, Rupert. All my life till now. You will return to the life you know, but I have a mother and friends to whom I must say good-bye. I have a home I must sell or give away. I have an apartment I must let. And should I not explain everything to my friend? He has been kind to me for almost five years. You would not have me run away, would you?"

"Sometimes to run away is sanity!" I said dully, cornered, thinking perhaps of my own flight from Criccoli.

"I think that is true. I would run from Vesuvius. But not from this. How could I, Rupert?"

I put a hand upon her own. "Perhaps you are wiser."

"Women have to be wiser sometimes," she said, smiling. "Gli uomini sono sempre così intelligenti." I smiled, too, translating for myself: *Men are always so intelligent.*

Even in gentleness her banter persisted and I smiled at last without reserve. Then we both laughed and were almost at peace again although there had been no war, only perhaps a rumour of war.

"When does your friend return?" I asked.

"In a week's time."

"For how long did he want you to go to New York?"

"For three days."

"He is very rich," I said.

She nodded. I was again in inner gloom. Between thoughts of Criccoli and Bianca's protector my mind was becoming wholly possessed by darkness and frustration, I thought. All that had seemed so near had moved a million years away.

I sat in silence. Bianca let me be for a time and then quietly began to talk of Venice. Gradually I came alive again, delighting in her beauty, her gaiety, soothed by her patience, only too willing to prolong our time here and put off the need for action. But at last I said that we must leave if we were to get to Padua and the burial service, yet even as I paid the bill, another course with possibilities for confusing Criccoli crossed my mind. How full of brain-waves I was that Friday morning!

192

"Why don't I take you to Padua, collect your baggage, then send you back here by train whilst I'll go on to the burial?" I said. "I could rush back here as soon as possible by taxi or train? What about that as a plan?"

"As you wish, Rupert. I am no good with plans."

"It's crazy for you to come to the Greenaway service," I went on. "Burials are gloomy enough for those who must go— or think they must."

"I will do exactly as you say, Rupert."

"Now and always?"

"Now and almost always. To be certain is to be dull."

"That you could never be," I said with fervour.

"Ah!" she said. "I have moods, too."

"Only gay and gentle moods."

"When I am well fed and well loved I am like a house cat, Rupert. I purr when I am caressed. But when I am angry I have claws."

"I haven't seen even the tips of claws."

"Never with you, Rupert. You would be hurt long before claws were ever needed."

So we talked, half-bantering, half-evading the things that must be talked about sooner or later.

We lunched at the station buffet and then travelled by the one o'clock train to Padua. We were quiet during the journey. Once again, approaching the ancient city, I was possessed by inexpressible foreboding.

I tried to cast out this uneasiness in action. From the station yard we went by taxi to the Hotel Grande and then back to the station. A train to Venice was due within ten minutes. I stayed with Bianca until the train arrived. Then, more regretfully than I thought I should ever say good-bye to any woman, I kissed her and waved farewell. Her company was becoming as necessary to me as a tranquillizing drug to the anguished.

In the taxi I once again fell to brooding upon the complications that Greenaway's death and Bianca's life had brought to my own way of life. Yet I realized that my apathy of a month before had gone. I was now alive to my finger-tips. I might detest all that Criccoli represented, but he had certainly made my mind work energetically. My brain was less like an abacus

193

than it had been for more months than I cared to number. And Bianca had transformed my entire life. I knew that I was enwrapt, even besotted by her beauty, but she had done more than make me again aware of physical desire. She had quickened my arid emotional life, caused me to love and hate again. Her ways, her words, her curious worldly wisdom had all helped to make what promised to be a new life for myself. I stretched my legs in the taxi and said aloud, "To hell with Criccoli!"

The Paduan cemetery, a few miles beyond the town, is as ghoulish as any cemetery in that beautiful land, and I was moved to wonder why a nation with so many splendid memorials to its long history and great men should specialize in these dreadful relics for the recent dead.

The taxi took the ramshackle Padua-Vicenza road at speed, leaving a crew of cursing surveyors in a cloud of dust. I hoped that their pot-hole measurements might mean that amongst others, mourners, too, would soon be spared the horrors of this approach.

Opposite an iron foundry and a marble works we turned into a drive with gravel paths on either side. Ahead was an architectural melange of pale pink main block, black-and-white tower and yellowing arches and pilasters. The general effect was like a series of schoolboy's ties hung out to dry. Beyond were cloisters in striped yellow bands. These buildings were enclosed within the eternal Italian setting of cypress trees and yews.

The coach was already there, drawn up by the chapel, with members of the Anglo-Palladian Society standing around in a stiff, forlorn group of pathetic doggedness. Signor Revisi was talking to two priests in black cassocks. Gloom clung to the group like a sepulchral smog.

I asked the taxi-driver to wait, partly because I hadn't yet decided whether to return to Venice by train or taxi, partly to confuse the unknown informer within the coach, if relaying news of my movements were still part of his (or her) essential duties.

James and Georgina stepped out from the crowd and came across. "Where is Bianca?" Georgina commanded at once.

194

"In Venice."

"A pity. I need a sympathetic companion on this kind of outing."

"Gloomier even than I'd anticipated," James said. "It's even silenced Georgina."

"I suppose it has its own gloomy fascination," Georgina said. "I've never been to a Catholic burial service before."

"I'm prepared to have all depressing experiences by proxy," James said firmly.

"All men are mental escapees!" Georgina decided, and James agreed wholeheartedly.

I recall the service as vividly as if it had been this afternoon. I tried to think compassionately of Greenaway, but I knew that sudden death had saved him from a death drawn out through many years. And with these thoughts were mingled fears for my own skin. I could not believe that Criccoli or Marcello would not be present. And I could not believe in the service itself. Death seemed (and seems) too serious a matter for so mechanical a ritual against a background of such vulgar and ostentatious display as the family vaults I had glimpsed beyond the chapel. In death, as well as in life, it seemed, privilege could buy a front seat. Only in the serried patches of earth beyond the marble tombs, where old bent women in voluminous black dresses tended graves of unknown Emilios and Giuliettas, was death the great leveller. Elsewhere death had been put firmly in its place by wealth. My wandering thoughts were recalled by the sonorous intonation of the priest. The conventional burial service, even for unconventional death, droned on interminably.

As if from a distance, I heard the door of the chapel open, and knew that this was the sound I had been waiting for. Frowning faces turned to still the intruder, but they saw, as I saw, a Franciscan friar making the sign of the cross. I knew too well the figure in the shadows of the great door. Criccoli had come as I had known he would come.

He moved slowly from the door towards the group of mourners. James, who had turned towards the door with me, grew taut and took my elbow in a fierce grip. But I was intrigued by the thought that the religious service seemed reduced to its man-made patterns by the mockery of this renegade. The priest at the altar might have his own sincere beliefs. So had Criccoli. The rest of us were flounderers in half-beliefs and non-beliefs. Meanwhile, the Latin phrases held me prisoner in their mournful rhythm.

Then the chapel service was at an end and we all began to leave the echoing building in a shuffling, self-conscious group, slowly following the pall-bearers along a gravelled path to the grave.

I tried to make a mental note of the position of the grave relative to the chapel and tower. The Reverend Greenaway might still wish to visit this last resting-place of his son, improbable as the prospect might seem at that moment.

I am hazy about the rest of the service. At last all was over and the grave-diggers had begun their doleful chores. A few minutes later we were returning slowly along the paths towards the coach, towards my immediate decision: to Venice by taxi or by train.

"Does Revisi think Bianca and myself are travelling in the coach or under our own steam?" I asked James.

"God knows. He hasn't asked. When I joined the coach I told him we were meeting you here this afternoon. That's all. You saw your bloody Capuchin, I suppose?"

I nodded and went on to outline my changed plans and my reasons for keeping the reservations for the overnight couchette standing in my name at Padua station.

"Deception at such a price must make your Scottish forebears wince," James said, "but it's a good idea. At the moment, then, as far as Criccoli knows, you could be travelling from Padua or travelling with us to Vicenza. Would he know that you might be travelling from Venice? Presumably nobody knows about your proposed flight."

"Nobody except the booking-clerk—and Bianca!" I added pointedly.

He did not take up my point, and I regretted my words. After his generous words of the previous night the remark was mean, but I had not time to retract or explain, for, as we approached the coach, Criccoli stepped across our path, almost as if he had appeared from behind a tombstone.

196

"May I speak to you, Doctor Frost?" he asked.

"Not a chance!" I said.

"Nevertheless, I must," he said.

He fell into step with James and myself. "Doctor Frost, I must ask you for the last time, to let me have the papers Greenaway was carrying for me."

"You must be mad!"

"I am as serious as I have ever been," he said gravely. "It is imperative that I have those papers. I believe you have them and I shall make it my business to get them. This is not an empty warning. This is your last opportunity to carry out Greenaway's wishes."

I was astonished both by his intrusion into my talk with James and by the unabashed ferocity of his words. Not so James. Into the intense unreality of this atmosphere, he introduced a typical near-farcical touch.

"We haven't been introduced," he said evenly, "but I couldn't help overhearing your remarks to my friend. My name is Westlake. Don't you think Doctor Frost would have sent those papers you're speaking of to England by registered letter if they'd been so valuable?"

James was plainly in a mood for argument and provocation. The *enfant terrible* impulse was at work again, but I now believe that he made an appalling mistake in speaking. I can see only too clearly that his comment made quite clear his knowledge of the papers, also that the idea of sending them back by mail had been considered and had probably been rejected. His words also brought him into the picture. Perhaps that had been Criccoli's deliberate intention: to confirm or destroy at one stroke a suspicion of James's part in these activities. To a man of Criccoli's training in dialectical subtleties James's words must have been straightway apparent. Criccoli was trained in disentangling the inferences and confessions embedded in half-statements.

Even as I heard James's words, I was slightly taken back, although I knew the quirks of his mind, his delight in baiting. I put a restraining hand on his arm. That gesture, too, I now believe to have been a grave error of judgment, for it confirmed that I had taken James into my confidence.

"I am not here for argument or entertainment," Criccoli said brusquely. "It is out of character for any Englishman to trust any papers of value to foreign mails. Your remarks confirm me in that belief. Unless those papers are left with the porter at the Jolanda Hotel in a sealed envelope before ten o'clock tonight I can no longer be responsible for your safety."

"Are you responsible for his safety now?" James asked quizzically.

"Strangely enough, I am," Criccoli said, brushing the attempt at jocularity aside. "Until this moment I have been reasonably certain that Doctor Frost would not be foolish enough to retain the papers. I have been able to restrain my colleagues. We do not invite trouble. Like most of my kind I prefer peace."

"On your own terms?" James sneered.

"On our own terms."

I wish I could convey some of the eeriness of this episode and its background: the sun, the crocodile of Anglo-Palladian mourners straggling along the gravel path, Criccoli at my right hand, half-turning to us both, James at my left, two Italian women and an English architect five yards behind, Georgina and an older woman five yards ahead. With these words Criccoli raised his arm in some kind of gesture of farewell or finality and stepped aside into the arcade we were passing.

"I hope I didn't speak out of turn," James said.

"Of course not," I insisted, yet I had a heavy heart.

"I'm afraid I did. I was foolish. Damned foolish. Put it down to the after-effects of the lunch-time chianti and the sight of his pugnacious face."

"I rather like his face," I said.

"Humanism can be taken too far."

We stopped by the coach, away from the rest of the group.

"D'you think his reference to ten o'clock tonight suggests that he knows you're not going with us to Vicenza?" James asked.

"It rather looks like it."

"What will you do now?"

"I'll collect my bag now and go on to Venice."

198

"How?"

"By train, I think."

Georgina joined us.

"Why not keep this taxi and take him on?" James said.

"I had considered it, but I don't think I will."

"Is it a question of lire?"

"Not really."

"How are you for money?"

"Quite well placed."

"When shall I see you again?"

"I shall be back in London in a week from now. Tomorrow week, Saturday."

"So shall we."

"Then bring Georgina to lunch at Wimpole Street on Sunday."

"I'd love that!" Georgina said. James nodded agreement.

Georgina smiled, "Shall we have Bianca as hostess?" she asked slyly.

"I doubt it, but not long afterwards, I hope."

"James told me of your plan. I hope I shall be asked to be a witness too."

"The only two I want," I said, adding that I hoped Peggy and Joan would also be present as additional, albeit unqualified, witnesses. Revisi called.

"We must go now," James said. "This really is the parting of the ways. Which is your hotel, by the way?"

I had noted the address on an envelope and took it from my inside pocket. At the same time I felt for Greenaway's two envelopes. They were still there. Criccoli, apparently, didn't add sleight of hand to his accomplishments. James copied the address, *Albergo Tolfa, Via Liguria, Roma*.

"Good," he said, returning the envelope. "And I hope it's cool, quiet and comfortable."

We shook hands.

"I don't like this one little bit," Georgina said. "But it has been a wonderful week." She reached up, took my head between her hands and kissed me on the cheek. "Give my love to Bianca, and I hope all your problems—if you have any—will work out."

"Our hotel is a place called the Villa Rosa, Vicenza," James said. "I gather it's some kind of upstage pensione. If you want any help or money, you'll find us there for the next three days. Before half-past eight in the mornings, after seven in the evenings."

He followed Georgina into the coach, Revisi saw them in and turned to me, "Shall we see you in Vicenza, Doctor Frost?"

"It is doubtful."

"That is very sad," he said. "Must you return to England?"

"I think I shall."

He shook his head gloomily. "Vicenza, you know, is the essential memorial to Palladio, and we have an interesting itinerary there."

He took me warmly by the hand, bowed, climbed into the coach. The door closed. The great Fiat coach backed, swung round and moved slowly out to the main road.

My world was suddenly emptied of friendship and warmth. I felt cold and forsaken in the hot afternoon. I walked slowly across the gravel path towards the taxi. As I walked, I looked back. Criccoli was walking from the arcade towards the thousands of tombs as if he were returning to look for something forgotten on Greenaway's grave. He turned and saw me. As if surprised, he stopped and then began to wave and then to beckon. To my lasting shame I turned and began to run towards the taxi. Thirty yards. No more. Yet I ran. I can still remember my overwhelming self-disgust as I sank back in the taxi and said, "Albergo Jolanda." I was only gradually realizing how much I had owed to James, his gaiety and uncondemning friendship. Were despair and cowardice the only qualities I could now put in their place?

At the hotel I went straight to the desk, asked for my bill, then for a porter, and, with him, went swiftly to my room. Everything about the hotel was touched by an oppressive air. I hastily packed my shirts, ties and two suits, still on their hangers in the wardrobe.

My bill, modest enough, was awaiting me. I paid and went. Never have I been so relieved to leave any place of temporary residence! So with Padua itself, I am afraid. A beautiful city, I have no doubt, but, in my memories, a place of undying fear and apprehension.

Fortunately, the train service between Padua and Venice is frequent and I had no more than ten minutes to wait. I used the time, striding up and down the platform like a man in a cell. With the fervour of a gambler, I wanted action, or at least movement.

36

I SAT in my compartment in the train reviewing my meeting with Criccoli, trying to sort out what he had meant.

Had he meant that he might resort to force? It seems to me preposterous that I should ever have thought otherwise. He had made himself clear enough. But the English, backed by centuries of respect for civil rights, are always loth to think that others are prepared for violence at an early stage in any clash. Nevertheless, I reassured myself, each minute put a mile between myself and Criccoli, and my proposed flight would increase that distance by four hundred miles.

By the time I reached the Santa Lucia station in Venice, I was half-way towards a new sense of security.

By then it was about four-thirty. I took a vaporetto to the Molo, left my bags at a quayside restaurant and walked round to the Alitalia office. Around me, afternoon Venice was coming to life. To my surprise and delight the booking-clerk said he could now offer me two seats on the morning flight.

"Venice is not good for early risers," he said smiling. "Especially those on holiday. Early-morning cancellations are quite popular."

That the two seats were available seemed to symbolize, for me, complete escape from Criccoli. I pocketed the tickets and walked back along the piazza like a schoolboy on the first day of holidays. I collected my bags from the restaurant and quickly arranged with a quayside porter to carry them as far as the Pensione Greci.

I think he found the canvas bags a relief from the huge trunks which the Venetian quayside porters are frequently bidden to manhandle, for he stepped out at a pace in keeping with my own light-hearted mood. We talked of Venice, of England, of the weather, and at our parting were as gracious as two ancient Venetian courtiers.

These felicities, my good fortune with the air tickets and the sun-dappled waters had wholly changed my mood. I was one of Georgina's mental escapees, I told myself, with all an escapee's passionate delight in freedom.

Bianca was in bed, asleep. She awoke, immediately, but lazily. "I am so sorry, Rupert," she said, sitting up. "I should have been sitting by the window, combing my hair. Just like in the story-books. But give an Italian woman the chance for a siesta and there is no argument. Are you tired?"

"I was, but not now."

"Was it sad in Padua?"

"Sad and desperately boring, I'm afraid."

"And how were Georgina and James?"

"Well, and sent you their love. Georgina needed your company as I do, too."

"Then come and join me here."

We stayed in our room until eight o'clock, lost in a delight made more intense by the prospect of the days and nights in Rome and the knowledge that now we should not be parted for our journey.

I experienced that evening, I remember, a sense of freedom I had not known since my first meeting with Criccoli four days before. All my plans would fall into place, I decided, with the elated conviction of a manic depressive. The doubts and distresses of the previous night and that morning had gone. I would look only to the future. Positive action, that was the key. Didn't all successful men of action practise just that?

After all, I declared as we dressed, this was an occasion for rejoicing. Our time for introduction was over. Now we would get to know each other.

Bianca, standing by the window towelling herself after the cold, cold water, laughed aloud. "Oh, Rupert, you are so funny. Most of my friends would say that in our time for introduction, as you call it, we have got to know each other very well indeed."

"Physically, yes, but each other?"

"I sometimes think that all we know of another is through the body."

"Modern psychiatry half bears you out."

"It is nice of modern psychiatry to be so old-fashioned," Bianca said, smiling. "And what does modern psychiatry say is the other half?"

"That we shall discover in Rome."

"You almost make me frightened, Rupert," she said. "You make it sound like an examination. And worst of all a viva voce. I was no good at those examinations when I was trying to be a secretary in Rome long ago."

"Nonsense," I said. "A lifetime of learning, all to be discovered in a week, the magical monotony of love all to be learned in seven days."

"Won't you mind that?"

"It is what I want above all things."

She stood for a moment before the window, facing me, her long legs apart, towelling her back.

"For me, too, Rupert, it is all that I want. But I have never had it. You have. For me I have seen the end of each friendship in each beginning. Even of my marriage."

"But not in ours?" I half-pleaded, half-asserted in my new-found freedom from apprehension.

"That is what I try to think."

Then she was suddenly gay. "What will you have for dinner, Rupert? Not scampi again, surely?"

37

WE DINED in the Danieli, in that high restaurant above the lagoon, drinking a good deal of chianti with our scampi.

Afterwards we walked slowly back to the Pensione Greci for our last night in Venice, a night in which all my agony of the past two years seemed to be exorcised in tenderness and understanding.

We awoke early, for we had to be at the Lido airfield by seven-forty for an eight o'clock departure. Our padrona was already awake and about and insisted upon providing us with hot coffee, croissants and butter, which we ate standing by the hall desk. She stood with us, drinking her own black brew in great noisy gulps. In high humour she promised us a certain return to Venice. She was psychic, she added, and could see all such things crystal-clear.

At last I took up our bags to go. We parted in the courtyard with cries of reunion in that very house within a year. "It is in the stars!" the padrona called, standing on the steps, her hands gripping her bristle broom as if she were an amazon of the barricades.

These contributions to our well-being I took as further omens of good fortune. Walking towards the San Zaccharia quay I felt that we were walking light-heartedly out of a time of shadows into clear air and sunshine.

My mood was enhanced by the approach of a porter *en route* to his morning duties on the quays. He swiftly sold me his services. At the quay we were soon caught up by the arrival of the airport launch, then by our last sight of the great waterway slowly burgeoning into its perennial summer bustle. The motor-boat moved swiftly towards the Lido.

The flight was smooth and uneventful and we were in Rome soon after ten o'clock.

38

THE first hours of our time in Rome were among the happiest of my life.

For one thing, the Hotel Tolfa was all that any hotel ought to be for such an escape: a small, old-fashioned hotel not more than two or three hundred yards from the Via Veneto. Even the reception desk had its unique quality, for it was more like a counter in a countryside post office than the hub of a contemporary hotel. This impression was heightened by an elaborate telephone switchboard at one end of the counter, out of all proportion to the size of the hotel.

The desk-clerk was of a piece with this *fin de siècle* property. With drooping white moustaches and bony chin he seemed more like a retired Italian cavalry officer than hotel servant. The maids we encountered were equally *en place*: they might have been maids once upon a time: now they were square-built decorous grandmothers.

The dining-room on the mezzanine floor, which I glimpsed as we rose in the ancient lift, seemed rather like the old Café Royal with its white napery and red-gold walls. In fact, the whole place had an air of red-plush comfort more evocative of Old Regent Street or Jermyn Street than modern Rome.

The lift attendant had put Bianca's bags into our small double room and vanished before I had put my own bags down. That, too, was scarcely contemporary practice, I thought.

And there we were. In the Rome we had been promising to each other for what seemed a decade. We embraced and laughed, caught into that elation in which lovers so swiftly involve each other. Here, at last, I thought, was one dream come true. Why shouldn't other dreams come true?

We would go straight to Dhony's, I decided. There we could be seated in the midst of Roman life, to me more lively and entertaining than the life of Paris, London or New York, for I find Romans, of all communities *en masse,* the most sympathetic. They seem, to my eyes, less preoccupied with ambition, greed and money-making. The simple pleasure of simply being alive seems sufficient for them. I may well be wrong. Roman history certainly gives my views no substance. But each man makes his own terms with any city.

We lunched merrily but lightly, for we had decided not to return to our room for the siesta, but to explore Rome. Bianca had not visited the city for several months and wished to wander, to watch, above all to have no plans.

The sun was so hot that our explorations were conducted mainly by fiacre. For Bianca this was the most beguiling of all forms of transport, and long before the end of the afternoon I was prepared to agree with her. To jog through the streets of Rome in an open carriage on a hot afternoon is to perceive the motor car as the most misguided of all mankind's inventions. The clip-clop of hooves and the slowly passing scene combined with the memory of the Hotel Tolfa, to give me a sensation that I was an Edwardian visitor from half a century before.

"You should have a parasol," I said at one point to Bianca.

"But I love the sun!" she cried out, shocked by the idea. That was the difference, of course. Sitting there in her pale grey linen suit she seemed to absorb the sun. The women before World War One, of course, had been absorbed, poor things, by underskirts and petticoats.

Where would I like to go first? Bianca asked.

I chose immediately to go to the Pantheon. From its portico to its open canopy of light, the building has always seemed to me the perfect architectural form.

Hand in hand we explored, entranced by the play of light within the great circular building filtering from the open cupola.

"James says we live by contrast," I said, as we came out. "Where shall we go now for perfect contrast? I chose the Pantheon. Now you choose."

"The Villa Borghese."

"The interior or the gardens?"

"Oh, but the gardens! I have seen enough of the interiors of villas for many months to come."

"But the picture gallery is world-famous."

"Then let the gardens be famous just for us."

And there, in the shaded gardens, so near and yet so far from the city, we spent the afternoon, sometimes watching the Saturday afternoon world of Rome, sometimes wandering in the wide parkland, two more visitors beguiled by the Eternal City.

Yet I think that despair first inescapably possessed me in those same hours of sunshine. We were having tea in the villa and, like a man hypnotized by a fear he cannot control, I returned to the subject that was threatening to dominate my waking life, asking Bianca more about her life in Naples. How did she spend the summer months?

This year she had been mostly in Capri, she said.

"By yourself?"

"Partly by myself," she said, steadily considering me as she spoke. "Partly with a woman friend. Partly with my friend."

"Where do you stay?"

"In a small hotel."

"Luxurious?"

She nodded, smiling.

"Does he take his family there?"

She shook her head. "They have a villa to the south of Naples," she said. "Neapolitans do not love Capri as the English and the Germans do."

"You enjoyed your time there?"

"I am a lazy creature, Rupert," she said, slowly repeating her confession in Italian, "Sono una ragazza molto pigra," and then, "I love the sun and the sea and doing nothing."

Each word chilled the warm afternoon air for me, yet I went on as we always go on.

"How can you bear the thought of leaving such things?" I asked.

"Only for other things," she answered, smiling gravely.

"And will you?"

"Will you ask me?"

Twenty-four hours before I had known my answer, but, as each hour passed, my resolution faltered. I am a man of caution. We cannot escape our genes or the environment of our early years. I had been made by the caution of Scottish forebears and the respectability of the London middle classes. Horror of avoidable indiscretion was part of my very being. Against those influences I was fighting, I can now see, for what I thought was my hope for the future.

Only overweening masculine self-confidence can take a man on in such circumstances, and mine, never strong, was wilting almost imperceptibly perhaps, but slowly, slowly. A man knows. The kind of confidence I needed, I told myself miserably, was possessed by men of thirty or thereabouts, assured, unattached, with a long record of success with women, at long last willingly in the mood for changing a way of life and settling down. I was and had none of these things. I had known

207

but one woman intimately all my life. I was middle-aged. I was already settled in my ways. As I looked across the table at Bianca I seemed to see her beauty through an impenetrable haze. Moment by moment, the uneventful ease and comfort of her life seemed to take her unattainably away.

I think Bianca sensed these things, for she began to talk of her life in Naples, implying that her days there were somewhat less than luxurious, but I saw, as I had not seen before, that there were great areas of unknown land to be crossed during the coming days in Rome. Could they ever be crossed? I wondered and began to doubt. Looking up, I saw that she was considering me with tender and reflective eyes.

"You have doubts, Rupert?" she said.

"Only of myself."

"Then I put them there?"

I denied the truth of her words vehemently. Perhaps I protested overmuch.

"What has put the doubts there, then?"

"A sense of the little I can offer you. An honest man's greatest handicap in lovemaking."

"But you offer me everything," she said. "I am happier than I have ever been in all my life. You make me feel good."

"Respectably 'good'?"

"No, no," she laughed, and then, "Yes, that, too, but you have made me come alive."

"Yet what of your life in Naples?"

"What of that?"

"You will miss it."

"Some of it. But I will have other things."

A flat in Wimpole Street? I thought. Two young step-daughters? Hours of loneliness in London? Less comfort? Less sun? Few friends? Yet it was a decision made daily by many thousands of women. But was that true? Were thousands of still-young Neapolitan beauties, mistresses of rich men, asked to translate themselves to London at the besotted request of middle-aged medicos? I asked myself bitterly.

There was no answer then. Only the days ahead would show, I told myself. Perhaps Bianca agreed, for she argued no more.

We walked slowly back towards the hotel, hand in hand. I think that, in some ways, this was the saddest short journey I have ever made. Despite the sunshine of the world about me I was sad, as we all must be when caught into moments of measurable happiness, and that afternoon I thought I could see a limit set already upon my own. And I was very tired.

We slept until nearly eight o'clock, lost in the half-light of the sunshine glinting through the shutters. Slowly we awoke and began those most felicitous of all travellers' joys: the leisurely preparation for the evening ahead. A long soaking bath, meditative moments of shaving, considering a mirror-image far less careworn than I had seen reflected for too many months, then changing into fresh linen and a dark suit which miraculously had lost its travelling creases. Then we were ready. Bianca hatless and in a close-fitting black dress, carrying a soft grey fur stole.

39

YET, as I have said, that night our mood did seem to change again. Perhaps Bianca had a greater power to control my moods than I suspected. Yet I have always considered myself (and been considered, I believe) a man of fairly equable temperament, self-contained to a degree, but I was certainly susceptible to Bianca's power of exorcising momentary despair or gloom. That I had already discovered.

We dined at Alfredo's and our mood seemed as carefree as any holiday mood should be. I remember only gaiety. But somewhere in my memory there is a stabbing faraway recollection that we were both determinedly over-anxious to avoid reference to the lives each of us had lived before our meeting.

At one point, Bianca seemed already forgetful of her fateful words of half a dozen hours before. "Will you come back to Italy?" she asked, giving words to my silence.

"If you invite me."

"Then I invite you now."

"Will you always be as free?"

209

"If you tell me I must be free."

Once more I took the step to make my happiness, as I thought lifelong and immeasurable: "Will you come to England, then?"

"If you invite me."

"I invite you now."

"Are you so sure, Rupert? Is it considered not a bad thing for a doctor to invite a strange woman to his house?"

"You are not a stranger and not a patient."

"Perhaps I have been your patient, Rupert. Without your knowledge you have made my life more happy than it has ever been. Do you know that? And isn't that what is called a cure?"

I laughed aloud, but as always when I laughed with Bianca, sadness took my laughter from me. She took my hand across the table. We were seated behind a row of small cypress bushes in tubs behind a low fence. From time to time, like a man with a tic, I peered over the tops of the bushes. I wondered what I expected to see. A Franciscan monk? I did not know, but Bianca noticed my glances.

"You are nervous about something, Rupert," she said. "What is it?"

"Nothing," I said, and then, "Curiosity probably. Rome after ten years."

"It is not the look of the curious man but of a nervous man. And you are not a nervous man. You are behaving like someone who thinks he is being followed. I am the one who should be worried about that."

"And aren't you?"

"Not one tiny bit."

Gradually, Bianca's laughter and the security of the restaurant caused me to relax. Bianca talked gaily of Rome, of Naples, of the crowds. Gradually, the oppressiveness of Criccoli's personality lessened. The hell with Criccoli! I thought as I poured myself a third glass of chianti. We sat over coffee for a long time.

"Have you plans for our next week?" I asked.

"No fixed plans."

"Any plans."

"To sleep, to make love, to eat, to walk, to go to Naples,

210

perhaps to Florence. No more than that. Should there be more than that?"

"It seems a full programme to me."

"Then we will not go to Naples or to Florence. We will stay here."

"I should like to go to Naples."

"Then we will go to Naples."

"Are you always so accommodating, Bianca?"

"Accommodating? What exactly is that?"

"Agreeable ... easy ... compatible."

"If I am happy. Of course."

"What makes you unhappy?"

"How do we know these things? Physical things chiefly, I think. I know the world thinks Italian men are all wonderful lovers, but not all of them are so. Something like that begins and the rest follows, don't you think? You must know all about these things, Rupert."

"Not all about. Something about."

"Well, then, there it is. This is one of those things that if you know something about, you know all about, don't you think so, Rupert?"

I half-nodded, smiling at the simplicity of her logic.

"One day I shall tell you more," she said. "Perhaps next week. A lifetime can be lived in a week, can it not?"

"It can when one is young," I said. "Now I am not so sure. I remember the seaside holidays of my youth. How interminable they seemed."

I began to ask about her childhood in Rome. She talked easily of her life in one of those high tenements I had often seen in the alleyways leading away from the Tiber bridges.

"I grew up in the war," she said simply. "None of us believed in Mussolini's empire. I was sixteen when the war started."

"Wasn't it a brave new world?"

"We all knew it was too threadbare."

"Didn't you belong to any of his youth movements?"

"I was too fond of boys, Rupert," she said, smiling.

"And didn't they belong to movements?"

"On the evenings I didn't see them perhaps."

"What was your father's work?"

211

"He died when I was five: my mother worked in a laundry."

"How much schooling did you have?"

"Until I was fifteen. If you are bright in Italy you can go on. I could have gone on until I was eighteen and then the university perhaps."

"And you didn't want to?"

"I wasn't clever enough at any one thing. I wasn't really clever at all. And I wanted my mother to spend less time ironing strangers' pants."

"Did you love your husband?"

"Probably. Now I scarcely remember him. I take out his photograph and it is the picture of someone I knew in another life. Do you think the young know anything about love, Rupert?"

"They have their own kind of love. Selfish, demanding, possessive."

"If that is young love, Rupert, then most people never grow up."

"Most people don't. But one doesn't have to be a psychiatrist to know that."

"How different is older love, then? Or the love of older people?" she asked.

"Sensuality becomes a substitute for sexuality," I said.

She was puzzled, and when I did not continue, she said, surprised, "Nothing else?" looking at me with astonished eyes.

"Nothing else," I said gently. "In one case in a million, tenderness comes. But not often. More often it is tolerance, which is all right, but a poor substitute for tenderness. One I always think of as negative: the other as positive. Do you follow me, Bianca?"

"I think so," she said. "Do you think we are in love?"

"I know I am in love," I said, very seriously.

"Are you possessive and jealous about me then, Rupert?"

"Of course."

"How nice," she said. "And demanding? And selfish?"

"Of course."

She smiled. "And tender?"

"Very tender."

"Then you are both young and old, and that I think is true."

"But don't you find me demanding, possessive?" I demanded. Again she placed her hand upon my own.

"I hadn't really noticed. I like it all the way it is, whatever it is. You *are* tender too. Perhaps that is what makes you such a strange man, Rupert."

I paid the bill and we turned once more towards the Porta Pinciana. Then, in the same moment, we turned and walked towards the hotel. Bianca took my arm and slowly, gaily we returned to the hotel. We had the week before us.

Of our return to the Hotel Tolfa I have the clearest and dearest memories. There, between the moment of entering the room and sleep, was only the magical world we made for ourselves.

40

SOMETIME in the night the bedside telephone rang. I groped awake and finally got the thing off its hook and said, still scarcely conscious, "Yes, what is it?"

A voice, almost as weary as my own, said, "Doctor Frost? Is that Doctor Frost?"

I said, "Yes, who is it?" and a voice said, "It is a long-distance call from Vicenza for Doctor Frost. Is Doctor Frost there?"

"This is Doctor Frost."

Another voice, more peremptory, said, "Is Doctor Frost speaking?" and immediately a voice I recognized said, "Rupert, listen, this is Georgina. Can you hear me?"

"Yes. Yes," I said. now wideawake. "What is it? What's the time?"

"Rupert, listen, it's nearly five o'clock and I'm speaking from the hospital in Vicenza. I'm here with James, but he's in a very bad way." Her breathless, inimitable voice broke in the poignant manner I remembered so well.

"Can he talk?" I asked.

Her voice was strained and broken. I thought I heard sobs

as she said, "Rupert, he can't talk. The doctors aren't even certain that he'll live."

I think I said, "Tell me everything, for God's sake, Georgina," but one never recalls the exact phrases. I remember switching on the bedside lamp and noting the time by my wrist-watch. A quarter-past five. That moment in time I shall remember forever. The light. Georgina's heartbroken voice. My own chilled and sickened stomach. Bianca coming suddenly awake, saying, "Rupert, what is it?"

But Georgina was speaking again. "I'll try to tell you as briefly as I can, Rupert." She sighed, took a deep breath and began: "Last night, whilst we were having dinner in the hotel, James was paged. He went out to the hall. Someone he thought was Revisi was on the telephone and said he had some booklets about the villas we had seen to send on to you. Could he have your address? Were you in England? James said you were in Rome, but he hadn't got your address there and then, but he'd let him have it later. He came back to the table and then began to wonder whether it was Revisi who'd rung. He also suddenly got bothered about the address which he'd left in his other jacket in his room. I was certain I remembered the address, but he wanted the piece of paper itself. Then Revisi came into the dining-room and James tackled him, asking whether he'd rung. Revisi was surprised and said no, he'd only just come in from a party. James then went upstairs. I don't know much about the rest. It seems he must have interrupted somebody in his room going through his things. I don't know. Twenty minutes or so later I began to wonder what had happened to him, went up to his room, got no answer, got really worried and tackled the hotel people. By the time they'd got the pass key and opened up I suppose half an hour had gone. I shall curse myself for that the rest of my life. James was lying . . . oh, Rupert, it was terrible. Poor, darling James . . ."

She stumbled into silence as I said, "Tell me, Georgina."

She said at last, "Oh, Rupert, I've never seen so much blood. I can't go on. The doctors say it's . . . Rupert, I can't go on."

"You must," I said.

"Rupert, Rupert, I can't."

"Please, Georgina."

214

But it was no good. Only her sobs answered me.

"Can I speak to one of the doctors?" I pleaded. "Please, Georgina."

"What is it, Rupert?" Bianca asked. She was sitting up in bed, her large eyes fearful and querying.

"Something serious has happened to James."

"How serious?"

"I shall know soon."

A voice said, "Doctor Bernardo Dolci here speaks. That is Doctor Frost of London, speaking in Rome?"

"Yes."

A telephone operator's voice interrupted, but Dolci brushed the interruption aside and we continued. "Mr Westlake is your near friend?" he asked formally, and then: "il vostro amico molto intimo e vicino?"

"Yes, yes," I said.

"Mr Westlake is in serious condition, Doctor Frost. He was stabbed twice and I am afraid the right lung is pierced. Unfortunately he was not at first discovered. Mr Westlake has lost much blood. A blood transfusion has been made, but his condition is very grave.

"Will he live?"

"As you know, Doctor Frost, that is always a difficult question to answer. It is doubtful. Has he a wife or children or parents who should be with him at this time?"

"Nobody known to me. Mrs Sandford knows more about these things than I do."

"Very well, doctor."

"Can I telephone the hospital?"

"When you wish. I will leave the message that you are to be told what you wish to know."

"Can I speak to Mrs Sandford again?"

"Certainly."

Georgina spoke again. "I'm sorry I cracked, Rupert. What does all this mean, Rupert? Is this to do with this priest business?"

"I think it probably is."

"That means you can't come here?"

"Not at the moment, I think."

"That means you're in danger, too?"

"Perhaps."

Her voice rose shrilly to its giddy pitch and then broke poignantly again. "Oh, Rupert, can't you go to the police? They are here. I've seen them. They seem very helpful and efficient."

"I shall see. I may have to go straight back to London. I will ring you tonight from here or from London. You'll be at the same hotel?"

"Yes, yes, Rupert. The Rosa. Oh, Rupert, do take care. Please."

"I'll ring. How are you for money?"

"Quite all right. Please do ring, Rupert. You will, won't you?"

"Of course. One last thing, Georgina. Were you there when James spoke to Revisi?"

"Yes. At least I was only a few feet away."

"Did Revisi seem genuinely surprised to hear his name had been used?"

"Yes, he did, Rupert. I'd swear."

"And do you know how many attackers there were, according to the police?"

"Yes, Rupert. I heard them discussing it, and they have talked to me. One man apparently. They seem to think he panicked after a short struggle. They think he had his knife out prising open the wardrobe door. But they say, too, that he had obviously used a knife before. Oh, Rupert, do be careful."

Again the telephone operator interrupted. Sadly I said farewell to Georgina and put the receiver back in its old-fashioned cradle.

Almost mechanically I got up and crossed to the window, drew the curtains and looked down into the street, partly to sort out my shattered thoughts, partly, I suppose, as a reflex action to all that I had just heard of James's attacker.

I then realized that I was cold and trembling violently. I left the window, draped my dressing-gown over my shoulders and sat down in the armchair and tried to think sensibly about the immediate future.

216

The most unnerving fact was that for the first time in my life I was utterly afraid. I had known fear often enough during the war, especially during the battles after Naples, but then we had all lived in a dual climate of fear and hope, but, above all, we were together as comrades. And comradeship subdues, or, at least, helps to control fear. Now, despite Bianca, I was alone. That was only too glaringly obvious to me. The episode had suddenly acquired a grim certainty. I knew that I was the one, the only one, involved.

For a moment I was impotently furious with myself for having behaved so farcically out-of-character. This was the sorry state that sensuality and latter-day romance had led me to. Worse still, my own selfishness was directly responsible for this tragedy to James. Had I gone straight back to London in the first place, none of these things could have happened. I was sick with fear and angry with regrets. And against that union of despair no man has strength. I suppose, too, that the miserable, dispiriting and unhealthy life I had been leading in the preceding months had lowered my vitality to a point that a week of sun and tenderness could not repair.

I looked up to see Bianca watching me. "Tell me everything from the beginning," she said gently.

I told her the story as briefly as I could. At the end she said simply, "And now you are in danger?"

"So it seems," I said dully. My will to action had gone.

"Then you must go back to London."

"So it seems."

"Now?"

"As soon as possible."

"And you must not stay here."

That thought had already occurred to me. If James's attacker had now got my address in Rome—which presumably he had —then my own position was desperately vulnerable. Surely Criccoli would have contacts in Rome. Or would he come to Rome himself? Grudgingly I agreed with Bianca that I should try to leave the hotel as soon as possible. Already it might be too late. I went to the window again, but the world outside was still empty of kerbside watchers. Or so it seemed.

"You must leave now, Rupert," Bianca insisted again.

"Perhaps you are right," I said, still sitting on the edge of the bed.

"I know I am. What is the time, Rupert?"

"Just after five o'clock."

"Where will you go?"

"Where, indeed? An all-night café. A station? Aren't those the places one goes to when on the run?" (And isn't that where those on the run are always picked up? an echo murmured.)

"And then, Rupert? What will you do later?"

"I shall try to get a plane sometime this morning."

With those words I moved into a kind of trance of movement. I stood up, crossed to the bathroom, unscrewed my safety razor, fitted a new blade and began to shave.

Bianca, sitting up in bed, laughed tenderly. "Only an Englishman would shave at this moment, Rupert?" she called quietly from the bed.

"It's silly, I know," I admitted, "but I'd always rather meet an emergency looking presentable—even when I feel like death. But there are other things we must discuss now—quickly. Please come in here."

Even in that moment of stress I was disturbed and excited to see the flash of her body as she got out of bed and wrapped herself in her yellow dressing-gown. She came and sat on the edge of the bath.

"Bianca," I said, "if I come back for you will you be here—in Rome?"

"When will you come back?"

"Tomorrow afternoon, or Tuesday morning."

"I think so, Rupert."

"Why are you not sure?"

"I had wanted this week to find out many things."

"Don't we know all that we need to know?"

"I don't know, Rupert." She looked as if she would begin to cry at any moment. I was shocked to find her so near tears. I had always thought of her near laughter.

"Do you love me, Bianca?" I asked quickly.

"More than anyone in my life before, Rupert. That is true."

"Isn't that enough?"

"I do not know, Rupert. I do not know if I can make you a

218

good wife. I am not sure that my life has been a good beginning for the kind of life I would have to lead with you. I do not know England. And I told you yesterday, I cannot come now."

"When could you come? Two weeks, three weeks?"

I finished shaving. Bianca stood up, put her arms about my neck, and kissed me. "These things I must try to find out, Rupert. Leave me with them and then come back for me."

"Then you would have to go back to Naples?"

"Yes, Rupert, I must."

"Would you come to London after that?"

"I think so. If you still want me. If you will come back for me."

"Your friend will try to persuade you to stay."

"Probably."

I drove the masochistic dagger in and twisted it.

"He will be very persuasive. He will tell you how much he needs you. He will do all in his power to keep you in Naples."

"Isn't that understandable, Rupert? Anyone would do these things."

"He may succeed in his persuasions?"

"I do not think so, and you should not think so."

We moved back into the bedroom. I began to dress, talking rapidly as I tugged on my shirt and knotted my tie.

"When do you think I should come back, then? When will you know for certain?"

"In two weeks, three weeks. Come to Rome again. And then to Naples. Please, Rupert. I want you to meet my friends."

"And your especial friend, too?" I half-sneered.

"But why not, Rupert?" she pleaded. "He has been good to me. He knows I have never loved him. Now I love you. We have nothing to be ashamed of. I loved you straightaway at seeing you. He has no hold over me. If I am strong enough to leave him, you should be strong enough to meet him."

"Bianca, I'm sorry," I said. "I'm confused and rude."

"No, you are not, Rupert dear. It is understandable. But I am worried. What will you do now? And shall we meet somewhere before you leave Rome?"

"I shall get to the BEA office as soon as it opens and try to get a seat for today's flight. Then I shall ring you."

I had finished dressing. My bags were packed. I was ready to go.

Now that the moment for departure was at hand I felt a dullard, a man defeated before he started. Men of action may possibly be born. I think they are. But there is also a technique to be learned. As a psychiatrist evolves his own technique, so must the man of action. I imagine that there were typical Rommel and Montgomery moves in the war as there are doubtless typical take-over moves in the City. For that moment of crisis in my life I had no technique, as I was quickly realizing. Years of the clinic and consulting-room are no preparation for action and movement.

Even to get out of the hotel presented a new problem to me. I had always left any hotel by the front door. Yet it seemed to me far wiser, in those circumstances, to leave by any other door. And should I pay the bill or leave the money with Bianca? Should I take the man at the desk partly into confidence or should I try to find a back door myself?

Even the knowledge of the attack on James could not change my nature. I would find myself floundering around in the lower regions of the hotel. I said as much to Bianca. She smiled. Then she said, "Don't look so sad, Rupert. You always make me want to weep when you look like that. Perhaps I can help. But will you think I have passed my lifetime leaving hotels by back doors?"

"Don't joke, Bianca!" I begged. "All I think about you, you know."

"I wonder," she said quietly as she picked up the telephone and said sharply, "Is that the night-porter? Will you please come to room four hundred and seven straightaway?"

I heard the grated answer "Si, signora," as the telephone clicked dead.

Bianca reached for her handbag, but I forestalled her.

"How much?" I asked.

"Two thousand lire."

I took out the notes.

"And for the room?" I said. "Perhaps you had better settle."

"It would probably be easier."

I put out more notes.

220

We both listened to the lift as it wheezed its way up the shaft, then to the subdued clash of the glass and wooden doors, and waited for the tap on our door.

"Entrate!" Bianca called.

A broad, black-haired youngish man came warily into the room, tense and suspicious. Bianca plunged in: "For the good name of myself and this hotel it is necessary for my friend here, an English doctor, to leave this hotel unseen by anyone." She handed the notes across with a splendidly regal gesture. "You have a tradesman's entrance?"

"Si, Signora," he said in relief. This was obviously a lot easier than dealing with the kind of crisis in Room 407 he had probably foreseen.

"Have you seen any watchers of this hotel?" Bianca asked.

"There are only the all-night taxis, Signora."

"Do you know the taxis that usually wait?"

"Si, Signora."

"Go to the window and see if you see a taxi that you do not recognize."

He crossed to the window and looked down to the street.

"There are two taxis, Signora. I know both drivers well."

"Good. Please leave the room and wait for the doctor outside."

"Si, Signora."

The porter left the room. Bianca turned to me and took me in her arms. "Good-bye, my dearest Rupert. Let us meet once more before you go if that is possible. Will you promise?"

"Of course. I will ring you here at about half-past nine. Have your breakfast in the room here."

"I shall not leave. Now go quickly!" At last her imperious mien broke and she began to cry.

"Good-bye, Bianca, darling. I shall see you soon."

I took up my bags, shut the door quietly, and went out to the lift. My eyes were filled with tears.

41

THE night-porter was waiting and took me down in the lift without a word.

At the ground floor he locked back the lift doors very deliberately and then turned right, away from the foyer. I followed him down a flight of stairs, along a short passage, then down another short flight of stairs and along another passage. But why downhill all the time? I wondered, following. As he went ahead, he flicked on the electric lights, small unshaded bulbs casting garish patches of bright light and deep shadows along the white-washed, damp-stained walls. Hundreds of bottles of chianti were stacked in recesses in one wall, I noticed as I followed like a hunch-back along the narrow arched cellar way. In another recess, half a dozen broken gilt chairs rested against each other like broken-down royalty.

We came to a small iron door. The porter opened this with a big key which he took from a hook at the side of the door. He stepped into the street, looked around and then ushered me out into the thin grey morning light. Only then did he speak. His face relented from its surliness for a moment. He grunted "Via Veneto" and pointed to the right, to a high steep-rising flight of two or three hundred stone steps, almost facing me.

I realized then, of course, that the Via Veneto and its surrounding network of streets are built on one of the Roman hills, and remembered how I had noticed that morning that the Hotel Tolfa was built on a steep slope, along one of the side streets that fall away so sharply from the summit. The picturesque but wearisome flight of steps facing me was probably my only way to avoid a long detour, I decided as the iron door clanged shut at my shoulder. I was on my own in the dawn. The walls of the hotel and its neighbours rose above me like the sides of great cliffs.

I crossed the narrow street and began to climb the steps, thankful that my canvas cases were lightly loaded, conscious, too, of that sense of conspicuous inanity likely to afflict anyone wandering in the streets in the early hours of the morning.

Without a doubt, I looked like a crook or a commercial traveller down on his luck or his uppers.

Half-way up the steep flight I paused for breath and reflection: it was time to ask myself where I was proposing to go and what I proposed to do when I got there. I sat down on the steps and looked around in the hope of spotting the window of Room 407, but already the Hotel Tolfa was one of hundreds of anonymous roof tops in the Roman skyline.

Where, in any case, was the BEA office? I suddenly wondered and cursed myself for a fool in not having noted the address before I had left the hotel. True men of action never overlooked these essential details. Then I remembered that during the flight to Milan a week before I had taken a couple of the Flight Guides that are given away by the Corporation. I had thought that Peggy and Joan might find them helpful in their geographical studies or plans for future holidays.

I zipped open my smaller bag and dug into the flap in the canvas lid and took out one of the booklets of contour maps indicating the international routes across the nations of Europe. On the inside back cover I found what I wanted: a list of BEA offices overseas, and the address of the Rome office: *Via Nationale 6a at the Hotel Quirinale.*

Suddenly the bizarrerie of my position struck me. How should I explain my presence on the steps if a member of the Carabinieri should see me there? As if to answer my fears a man appeared on the topmost step and began slowly to descend. I saw him first as a menacing silhouette above me, slowly nearing. I began to count each step in his interminable descent. Twenty . . . twenty-one . . . twenty-two . . . and so on. Then he passed me with no more than a glance of mild curiosity. A waiter from or on his way to work? A railwayman? A postman in plain clothes?

I hastily zipped the bag shut and continued my ascent. At least I had one piece of necessary information.

I came out just above the street where the Via San Isodoro joins the Via Veneto. Two taxis were on a cab rank opposite. I crossed to find the drivers playing cards in the back of the second taxi.

"Where can I get coffee now?" I asked in Italian through the window.

"Probably at the station," one said, taking out a large half-hunter from a woollen waistcoat.

"Will you take me there?"

"Will you wait, Signor, until we have finished this hand?"

I said, "Of course" and climbed into the front taxi.

They finished five minutes later. My driver thanked me for my consideration, adding that he had won thirty lire and that he was now very willingly at my service.

Seated in the taxi, I had decided that if Criccoli and any of his colleagues were *en route* to Rome from Vicenza they would doubtless arrive at the station. Presumably that would have been their only means of transport. I was on the point of re-directing the driver when I decided that I could, at least, check on the expected time of arrival of any overnight train from Vicenza to Rome.

I paid off my taxi almost unwillingly. Hatred of my solitary state was beginning to possess me. I furtively crossed the pavement to the doubtful shelter of that fabulous stone and glass building, the finest railway station in Europe. Fleetingly I noted its aspects of grandeur.

Inside the station I made enquiries about the arrival of an overnight train from Vicenza. Yes, there was such a train, due in at 7.23 on Sunday mornings, at Bay 5, I learned at last. By then the time was just after six o'clock. The restaurant was already open and I took one of the chairs set inside the great expanse overlooking the entrance bays to the platforms and ordered coffee and toast. I took out Friday's unread copy of *The Times*, which I had bought on Via Veneto the previous day, and tried to read, but it was no good. At any moment I expected to look up to find Criccoli standing before me and to hear his implacable greeting: "Doctor Frost?"

I would have to sit it out and wait and watch. Meanwhile, I drank two more cups of coffee and ate more toast. Soon after seven o'clock I paid my bill, deposited my bags in the luggage office and took up a position by one of the great pillars, well suited to my unwelcome but, as I saw it, necessary task of watching the arrivals at Bay 5. I might yet learn something to my shrunken advantage.

By then the vast station was beginning to be crowded with thousands of Romans off for the day to the coast and the countryside. Sweethearts and family parties bustled across the wide approaches, all quite silently, thanks to the unusual construction of the flooring, which rendered the multitude of footsteps quite inaudible. At first, the experience of *listening* to these silent footfalls is quite eerie: but soon the listener is thankful to the unknown architect.

The train from Vicenza was on time: a crowded explosive arrival. One moment the platform was a sedate, concrete stretch, almost empty of human beings, the next smothered with bawling, calling, laughing, wailing humanity. My protective pillar was well away from Bay 5, but near enough to give me a fairly clear view of the crowds along the platform, now sorting themselves out.

With an unexpected sense of acceptance and inevitability I watched Criccoli and Marcello advance along the platform. They looked as purposeful as any two Franciscans in the whole of Rome, a thoroughly reliable pair of proselytizers off for their next soul-saving assignment, I thought mirthlessly, and wondered whether missionizing friars get assignments or preferments?

They gave up their tickets at the barrier and were accosted immediately by two men in black suits who had been awaiting them. There was a moment of all-round introductions.

Both laymen were around thirty, I judged: one thickset, bull-necked, short-legged, powerful-looking, the other younger, much slimmer, fairly tall for an Italian, alert, even nervously tense. Neither wore a hat. Both had black hair, the younger man's cut *en brosse,* the other man's thin and weak, looking, from a distance, more like a sprinkling of iron filings than hair on his tanned scalp. I could not place them as the men I had seen with Criccoli in the piazza at Venice two nights before—or was it three? I wondered—but I could not be certain. Yet these men had been awaiting Criccoli in Rome. Presumably they were Romans, deputed to aid him.

Criccoli did the talking, towering over the other three and

plainly dominating their plans. He continued to talk quickly after the group had been joined by another man from the train, a short, plump young man in a brown suit and dirty misshapen panama hat, looking uncommonly like a Sicilian peasant adrift in the big city. I would have gambled that he had been one of the men I had seen in Venice. They made an odd group, I thought, but only to northern eyes: in Rome it would be a commonplace scene.

They moved, as a group, across to the station buffet, just as my three cups of coffee suddenly threatened to catch up with me, and I had need to begin the interminable continental search for a lavatory. The restaurant would have facilities, I knew, but that was out: Criccoli and his group were there. I asked a porter. Fortunately for me the lavatories were on the side of the station where I stood in cross-legged agony. I joined the crowds and made my way underground towards relief. Even more efficient men of action, I reassured myself, have frequently found themselves at the mercy of their bowels and bladders. Hadn't Wellington and Churchill made pertinent comments on taking every chance of relief?

Within five minutes, however, I was far less certain of the wisdom of these renowned men of action, for, as I was leaving the wash-room, one of the two dark-suited men was buttoning his trousers at one of the pissoirs. Our eyes met, his blank, mine fearful. He continued unconcernedly with his chore as I steeled myself to leave and climb the stone steps without a backward glance. Just another minor shock in what was already beginning to prove an oppressive morning, I told myself as I turned and hurried from the station, cursing myself for a fool and my bladder for its natural limitations. How easily Criccoli might have been the one I had encountered! Presumably friars also had occasion to use these predominantly secular institutions.

Outside, in the great forecourt, the crowds were thinner and the sun stronger. Already the stupor of a sunny Sabbath morning rested heavily upon the city.

I crossed the crowded trolley-bus terminus and then struck right towards the Piazza del Cinquecento. I would have more toast and coffee at one of the cafés there, I decided, and give

226

Criccoli and the others the best part of an hour before returning to collect my bag.

As I walked I had a moment's panic, thinking that perhaps the BEA Rome office might be closed all day on Sundays, but I put that doleful thought aside: no great airline would be likely to conduct operations on such a leisurely routine. I took a seat in one of the restaurants overlooking the piazza. The position was prominent, but it offered the advantages of a huge pillar at my back and a clear view across the piazza to the station.

My watch said eight-thirty. I had less time than I thought. At ten to nine I paid my bill, went down into the square, hailed a taxi and drove across to the station. *En route* I asked the driver in my painful Italian if he would be willing to collect my bag from the luggage office. I had a splitting headache, I said.

"But of course, Signor," he said. "I also know a pharmacia open on Sundays."

"No, thank you. I have to go straight to BEA at the Hotel Quirinale."

He collected the bag whilst I wedged myself well down inside the taxi. Roman taxis have too much glass for shelter and I took out my copy of *The Times* and enveloped myself within the newsprint. The driver returned, expostulating, What crowds! What madness! Who would go to the country in a stuffy train? Was it worth it? Still shaking his head, he climbed once more into his seat, and continued to keep my Italian exercised as far as the Hotel Quirinale.

I have never felt more fearful of the outcome of any interview than asking about the possibilities of a flight to London that very day. I was so sick at the probability of failure that I could not think about an alternative route. I had persuaded myself that the chances of a seat must be reasonably good, but I realized that the winter timetables were probably already in operation. Yet didn't planes from the Far East and Africa put down at Ciampino? If my luck were out I should have to go by train. I must leave that day whatever the route. The tragedy of James and the memory of the five men at the station enforced that decision.

I was at the BEA office at 0905 hours by air-route timekeeping, but already three other travellers or would-be travellers were before me. I sat down, stood up, paced the blue linoleum floors, stood on one leg, crossed both legs, calming my nerves only in a mockery of movement. The query of a young American girl returning to London was settled by the booking-clerk. Then I had to listen to a voluble middle-aged Italian woman asking about an improbable journey, three weeks ahead, to Sheffield. Then to a precise, donnish, grey-haired Briton checking on flight times for the following Thursday. Why must you check at this ungodly hour on this so-called godly day, you asinine oaf? I silently screamed. Then it was my turn and I heard myself croaking out my query.

"A flight for today? To London?" the clerk repeated, doubtless in a delaying ploy which would enable him to sort out his reply or brush-off. For me it was a maddening *non sequitur,* but I stilled the raw edges of my nerves and nodded.

"Not by BEA," he said, glancing cursorily at his passenger lists. "We might have a seat available by BOAC, leaving at eighteen-twenty-five hours this evening."

"Nothing sooner? I am a doctor and it is urgent."

He remained impassive, apparently unmoved by a line he must have heard a thousand times before.

Again he consulted his booking sheets, slowly shook his head, and then took up a telephone. I was keeping nobody waiting. I momentarily relaxed. He seemed, at least, prepared to enquire. Hope stirred in my mind, bringing me alive again, as he spoke briefly into the mouthpiece, a fast, technical incomprehensible gabble in Italian, beginning, "C'è un dottore londinese che dice di dover tornare in Inghilterra oggi . . ." He replaced the receiver slowly and deliberately and took up his ball-point pen again.

"Yes," he said blandly. "There is a seat on BEA flight one-three-one leaving Ciampino at fourteen-thirty hours. Please be here at thirteen-thirty." He had the nerve of all booking-office clerks, explaining that the hopeless situation of a moment before has now been transformed.

"Can I give my baggage in now?"

"That counter there."

"Can I travel direct to the airport?"

228

"Of course, but please be certain to be there not later than fourteen hundred hours."

I took my bags across and for a long moment was tempted to take out the two envelopes I carried in my pocket and put them in one of the canvas bags. Wouldn't that solve everything? I thought. Couldn't I then go out into the streets of Rome and to hell with Criccoli? Couldn't I then stay on in Rome with Bianca? But I realized the hopelessness of the hope even as I dreamed. The envelopes wouldn't get farther than the Ciampino Airport if I weren't there to take them on their homeward journey. Security officials would soon be examining the contents of the bags if nobody turned up to claim them. It was a foolish thought, anyway. If I stayed in Rome, I should soon be in the same agony as James.

I let the bags go without regret. Already I felt unencumbered and almost on my way, but my elation was fleeting. I was as suddenly weary. Four hours of nervous wakefulness were hitting back. I went through into the Hotel Quirinale and rang the Hotel Tolfa and asked for Room 407. Bianca answered immediately. I took the risk that someone might overhear. I was on my way and I had to talk.

"Rupert, how wonderful to hear you! How are you?"

"Quite safe. And you?"

"All right, but so worried about you. You have had no trouble?"

"None."

"Where are you now?"

"Somewhere fairly comfortable and not too far away."

"Have you seen anything of those dreadful men?"

"Yes, at the station."

"How many of them?"

"Five."

"Oh, Rupert, please be careful. One of them telephoned here and asked for you. He said he was a friend of Mr Westlake's, but I am certain it was one of those men."

"What time was that?"

"About an hour ago."

"What did you say?"

"At first, I thought I would say a mistake had been made.

229

But then I said Doctor Frost had gone out to buy a newspaper and would be back later, but could I give him any message? I thought that best. Did I do right, Rupert?"

"Quite right. Far better to try to confuse. And then?"

"He said no, it would do later. I asked his name, but he said it did not matter and that you would know him."

"An English voice, or Italian?"

"An Italian voice speaking good English."

"Where shall we meet?"

"Is that wise, Rupert?"

"We must meet. Leave your bags in the room and pick them up later. Leave the hotel by the way I left. The same porter won't be on duty. Ask another to show you out. You'll only have to look helpless for a moment. It's easy for you. Say where?"

"Anywhere!"

"Somewhere safe and open."

She was silent for a moment.

"How much time will you have, Rupert?"

"Until one o'clock, or later. We can take a taxi to the airport. I thought we would lunch early and then go out to Ciampino together."

"Let us meet at St Peter's and then decide where to go."

"When?"

"What is the time now?"

"Ten to ten."

"And I am still in bed, Rupert. I fell asleep for a time. I am sorry."

"Have you had breakfast?"

"Not yet. Nor have I had my bath."

I laughed. "How long will you want, then?"

"Half an hour. No more, Rupert."

"Eleven o'clock then."

"That will be lots of time. St Peter's then. At the foot of the steps. We can't miss each other there, can we?"

"You remember what I said about leaving the hotel?"

"Yes, Rupert. Good-bye. I must rush."

I returned to the hotel foyer and dozed in an armchair for half an hour.

Some time before eleven o'clock I made my effort, arose and went outside into the Via Nazionale to get a taxi to St Peter's. The streets were still quiet. The sun was stronger still.

42

I WAS early at St Peter's and paid off my taxi at the far end of the Via della Conciliazione, so that I might approach the cathedral slowly. I could thus take in its magnificence if not its so-called beauty, to which I have always been invincibly immune.

I regretted my decision from the moment I had left the taxi. The sun was merciless. Heat rose from the stones like a haze from an oven-plate. And far more people were already crowding the square than I had foreseen. Stolid groups moved like pockets of ants across the piazza.

I was hot and tired and yearned for Bianca. Even the prospect of walking towards St Peter's, across the piazza, under the fierce sun, was too daunting, and I crossed to the right, towards the great sweep of the Bernini colonnade, to my eyes the most beautiful element in the visual impact that St Peter's makes upon the visitor.

I stepped over the low chain which guards the entrance to each arm of the colonnade and was at once enclosed within the restful shadows. For me, at that moment, this was the most beneficent place in Rome. To walk on such a day between the great columns, set four aside and each about five feet in diameter and probably fifty or sixty feet high, was comparable to sauntering between an avenue of giant evergreens. Even the small, square cobblestones were a relief to the feet after the large flagstones beyond. This delight in the shade, and the sense of retreat from the tumult of Rome, was heightened as I traversed the slowly curving colonnade by the sight of a youth hosing down the cobblestones.

I sat on the low podium of one of the inner columns and let my head rest gently against the great stone pillar and stared up to the shadowy roof of the colonnade with its enormous

231

lanterns. Within his vast yet simple plan, Bernini had also had time and imagination to think of these intriguing decorative details. This, surely, was the essence of genius, I thought, as weariness gradually took possession of me. I must have dozed.

When I awoke, a few minutes later, the piazza was even more crowded and the sunlight more intense. I was, momentarily, a privileged spectator, looking into a sun-baked arena from a shaded terrace. I would go out into the arena, I decided, meet Bianca and bring her straight back into the shade of the colonnade. There we could discuss plans for my journey to London and an immediate return to Rome.

I moved out from the shade of the colonnade and began to walk towards the wide steps leading up to the Cathedral. I could not see Bianca.

By then the crowds were increasing at an alarming rate. Innumerable excursionists were across my path, making progress a matter of lively dodging and side-stepping. They seemed to carry with them an air of collective gaiety, as if they were there for some festive and important occasion. I would have liked to have escaped these crowds and the sun and returned to the comfort of the colonnade, but I was already beginning to be seriously worried by the absence of Bianca. Half-past eleven and still no sign of her.

I paused by the great statue, one of the pair I had by-passed on two earlier visits to St Peter's: its partner in the great Bernini plan for the piazza was perhaps eighty yards away. I turned and went back. The statue offered some slight shade and a view over the whole piazza. An inscription on the base of the statue recorded that the bearded ancient, holding a sword and reading from a manuscript, had been raised in honour of Pope Pius IX. At any other time I should have been sceptical of his pose with pen and sword, but I was, by then, far too desperately worried.

Wearily and fretfully, I sat on a low iron rail around the plinth of the statue, and looked down towards the Via della Conciliazione. I felt certain Bianca would come from that direction. After all, it was the main approach to the piazza.

My spirits had scarcely ever been lower. In those moments I think I was more depressed than I had been at any time since

Helen's death. Alternating bouts of elation and tension during the past few days had probably strung my nerves to snapping-point. Love for Bianca, fear and hatred of Criccoli, concern for James, the longing to see Peggy and Joan again, suddenly welled up in a great wearying moment of self-pity and despair. I closed my eyes and possibly dozed again for a few minutes. I think I did. I was tired enough, God knows.

By the time I opened my eyes again the piazza was transformed. Startled, I scrambled quickly to my feet, scarcely believing the sight before me. A few minutes before, there had been crowds, but now these crowds were being swept aside or rather gathered into a great regimented concourse, quite unlike a normal sightseeing crowd. Long, marching columns and processions were coming from every corner of the square, and an even greater procession was advancing towards the piazza along the Via della Conciliazione. At their head a brass band was playing stirring march music. Poor devils! I thought, sharing a commiserating moment for the musicians. Who would blow a cornet or beat a drum on such a day! I seemed to recognize a Sousa fragment carried faintly on the air.

The crowd had assembled—and was assembling—with the frightening speed of a great crowd at a cup-tie. To look down on them, as I could from this slight rise, was like watching a monstrous dark blanket being knitted under one's eyes. And still they came! From the great gates, filtering in through the colonnades, fanning out, merging with the nearer crowds. Crowds upon crowds.

By then I was nearly distraught; in fact, near panic. Not only did I despair of meeting with Bianca, but by then I had realized that my chances of getting out of such a crush in time for my departure from the airport were vanishing fast, if, indeed, they had not already gone for good.

Already the crowds were hemming me in around the iron rail of the statue. I began to shoulder my way out of the crush towards the Cathedral in the forlorn hope of seeing whether Bianca had managed to reach the steps, but thousands were already gathered there, and the movement of the crowds was forcing those on the lower steps slowly upwards and onwards towards the distant porch of the Cathedral.

233

I said, in Italian, to a man who was also shouldering his way steadfastly towards the steps, "What is this gathering?"

He turned to me, his eyes wide-open with surprise. "It is the Convention of the Catholic Trade Unionists," he said pridefully. "The Convention begins tomorrow. The Pope is to bless the Convention and its Leaders."

Together we went on, inch by inch, side by side, puffing out remarks as we half-stumbled, half-shuffled forward like a pair of prisoners in a chain gang.

"And how long will the ceremony last?" I gasped.

"Not long," he said. "Half an hour perhaps. Not longer. The Pope is a busy man."

"And then can I get out?"

"Ha! Ha!" he laughed. "That is a different matter. As you see, the crowds are in a holiday mood. Crowds beget crowds. It is best to go with the crowds, I assure you!"

The Italians with their long history of pageantry can organize a procession and gathering with a timing and discipline unmatched throughout the world. The numerous groups and units were being marshalled into position with precision and authority by the mounted and foot police of the Vatican. Nobody was being allowed too near the Cathedral porch. The police seemed unhurried and in complete control.

Then suddenly, well away to the left, I saw Bianca.

She was standing, on the steps, as we had arranged, but many steps above our promised meeting-place. She was plainly being pressed forward and upwards by the crowds. Even as I watched she was still being swept slowly but irrevocably on.

Despite their vastness, the crowds were fairly quiet, impressed into silence, perhaps, by the solemnity of the background, perhaps by the discipline of their group leaders and the police. I put aside any remnants of English self-consciousness and called loudly, "Bianca! Bianca!" and waved furiously.

She saw me and managed to wave back before being lost to my sight again as the crowd swept slowly on. But I now knew where to look and, as she reappeared, as if above a foreshore breaker, I waved and called again. And still I edged on, sweating it out inch by inch. By then I thought I had lost my

234

unknown companion, but to my surprise he reappeared on my other side. Had he burrowed or leapfrogged his way? I wondered as we went on.

It would be better to stand still, he said, and I nodded. If only I could.

Slowly we came to the first of the steps. I stumbled. He took my arm and I righted myself. In company, we began to tread upwards like a pair of blind men, feeling our way ahead with our feet, trying to judge the width of each step, taking all on faith.

Gradually we were ground to a halt. The pressure around us enclosed us like a mighty clasp. We had come to the end of our particular pilgrimage, at least for the moment.

"Where does the Pope appear?" I asked my puffing companion.

"Above the great doorway."

"Have you been to one of these conventions before?"

"Last year I was also here and it was a great occasion. As it is today."

Fortunately, I could still see Bianca, now also halted, halfway up the steps. She was perhaps thirty yards off and somewhat above me, for she was on the fifth or sixth step and we were at the very foot of the slow rise.

Bianca looked around, surveying the crowd, I thought, and then, suddenly, in a voice shrilling out above the crowd's vast murmur, she called in English, "Rupert, Rupert! Those men! I was followed. I thought I had lost them. They are here! There!"

She pointed away from herself, down, away from St Peter's and the Vatican City.

I waved some kind of recognition to her warning and then stood there like a moron, trying to get my confusion and fear under control and into some kind of order.

I was taller than most of those around me and my position on the steps also gave me some kind of advantage. Or was it such an advantage, I wondered? I might be able to see Criccoli or any of his partners, but they could equally well see me, especially Criccoli, six-feet two or three.

The crowd's murmuring softened into an awed whisper as,

presumably, the rumour of the Pope's approach moved along them. I have no religious convictions, but I am fascinated, as any psychiatrist must be, by all patterns of mass behaviour. Mass silence can be as impressive, although far less terrifying, than a baying mass out for blood. I suddenly and incongruously remembered that I had heard such a mob in Italy immediately after the war. I had been in a jeep in a traffic jam in a northern market square, and watched a girl's head being shaven for undue familiarity with German troops during their retreat. As if every native watcher had not shared her guilt, as James had pointed out in the mess that evening, gently causing a hearty gunner who approved the performance to think again.

Then Bianca cried out her second message, "Rupert! Rupert! They have seen you. They are coming to you!"

Terror drives out embarrassment. I said, "Scusa" and quickly turned with the preposterous, impossible intention of escaping from that crowd. Only terror or madness could send a man upon such a hopeless errand. I began to shove my way into the crowd, shouldering, thrusting, battling, calling all the time, "Scusa. Vomito. Scusa. Vomito," in a dirge of distress.

I did not know where to go or what to make for. I tripped down the two or three steps and stumbled forward. Even in those first moments of terror I knew that I must not fall. To rise again would be a task beyond a Samson.

A thousand images assailed my mind. Two above all others drove me on. Fear of falling beneath the crowd and fear of steel within my body.

So I stumbled forward, calling my war-cry of "Scusa! Vomito!" like an uncouth beggar, seeing before me only a mass of faces, featureless, expressionless, distaste transforming and distorting their glazed sightseers' eyes as they realized how easily their Sunday best clothes could be soiled by sudden sickness from this unknown, unwelcome intruder. Their hatred and disgust that anyone so beastly should break into their awed assembly may well have saved me. My cries, like a blunt and ancient scythe, opened a grudging, narrow path.

Does one ever know, afterwards, what really happened in a time of terror? I doubt it. We recall, I suspect, a series of impressions, greatly blurred yet somehow with us for all our

236

days. And perhaps a dozen impressions as sharp and strange as a cinematic "still". So with me then. I recall the antagonistic glutinous face of the mob, a mob I hated with unreasoning terror as I thrust against it. I recall, above all, my sudden image of escape: the colonnade.

With the pressure of fear and this sudden association of ideas—colonnade, escape—I moved towards the great pillars, calling aloud my plea to make a way as I made my stumbling approach.

Then a great silence fell on the crowds around me. The Pope had appeared, I judged, as I plunged on.

In the silence I heard only my monstrous breath. Perhaps to rid themselves of such a sick intruder the crowds seemed to give way more readily to my calls and endeavours.

Then I was within the shelter of the colonnade, just beyond the exit from the Musei Vaticani. Yet, even as I gained the shelter, I was almost winded and knocked out as I went round one man straight into a chest-high stone bollard. I stumbled and choked and almost went down in a heap. Fortunately, the crowd was just as pack-jammed there as it was out in the piazza and I was supported by the mobs even as I slumped amongst them.

I took a deep breath, partly regained my wind and went on, keeping to the outside row of pillars, but well within the colonnade.

The ground beyond the colonnade is rubbled and uneven. That I had noticed, unknowingly, an hour before. Now that knowledge clicked into place in my mind like a faraway signal. I must keep away from there.

As I went on, the crowd seemed less solid. At each step I seemed to push against only twenty bodies instead of fifty. That memory also I recall most vividly.

Then away to the right, beyond the line of the colonnade curving slowly on its segmental course round the piazza, I saw, as clearly as I see a patient come through the door of my consulting-room, the man in the brown suit I had seen that morning at the station. He was thrusting his way firmly into the crowd within the colonnade.

I wondered momentarily whether to stop and try to hide

myself within the crowd. Fear, however, will almost always drive us into movement if movement is possible. Then, too, if I were to get to the airport I had to go on. So I went on, even though I saw, in that split-second, across the intervening dozen bodies, that he had also spotted me, an unknown man but the only moving man in that vast stationary crowd. I watched him as he seemed to change course and began to clear a way ahead diagonally, plainly trying to head me off. I could not go out beyond the colonnade, for there were the steps, the rough ground and the base of the towering cliff of the Vatican City. There I would be trapped. And I could not return to the shelter of the crowd. There, too, I should be trapped, if I could not force a way through their solid mass. I could only keep ahead, plodding and pushing in desperation, hoping to make a way without too great a weariness in myself and without arousing too great resentment in the crowd. Already I was weakened and well-bruised from the kicking and mauling I had received in my unseemly progress. The man in the brown suit had a diagonal course to make. That gave me some faint hope. But he was smaller, tougher and plainly less respectful of the crowd. He was thrusting aside the trade unionists in his way with furious contempt, and they, so intent upon the Pope's benediction, let him pass, annoyed perhaps but possibly cowed by the fury of his thrusting. My own sickening, half-whining, half-apologetic passage merely made them react against me, not wilt before me. They let him pass and then turned once more towards St Peter's. So he moved ahead, gaining on me. I could see that, inevitably, he would soon have cut my path.

He came at me as I reached the side of one of the pillars. As if in a fixed trance I had watched him thrust aside, almost cleave the last three or four of the crowd who separated us. Then he was by the only intervening human. He almost hurled him aside, and then, a foot away, he tried to grab me. As he reached out for me, the near-by crowd, especially those he had come through, crushed against each other and fell away, sensing trouble, leaving possibly a free square yard. He clawed at the lapel of my jacket, but I hit his wrist hard, bringing my fist down with frenzied force. He winced and came again. As he lunged forward two trade unionists, seeing that he was the

238

aggressor, sought to hold him back, but they were bulky family men and had no chance against his squirming, maddened, rough-house tactics. He shook them free as if they were over-fed puppy-dogs. With a desperate punching and pushing I managed to thrust him off. As I did so, I saw the flash of a blade. He wanted quick results, hoping, presumably, to escape in the ensuing shambles. A woman shrieked "Coltello!" as he again lunged towards me, mouthing meaningless words. The crowd crushed against itself like animals in panic.

Without thinking, I acted as all men desperate for their lives have always acted. By instinct and without a thought for the aftermath. He was twenty years younger than myself, stronger, tougher and more ruthless. As he lunged I kicked him in the genitals. He gasped and screamed and fell. As I plunged on I had to step across his body. He was writhing and crying like a broken child.

I think now, in retrospect, that the crowd was so appalled by the horror and swiftness of this sudden fracas that they were shocked into silence and inaction. I have a sickening memory of the cries of women and men as I left them, the cries of "Polizia! Polizia!" Then the crowds were again about me like a self-sealing protective skin.

I went on, knowing now that I dare not give up. Terror at the vengeance that would be exacted for the man I had left crippled drove me on. I was sickened, leaden-footed, thick-throated, choking with despair.

In a haze I saw the Vatican post-office lodge beyond the pillars at my left. Away to the right, I spotted the high spray of the playing fountain, and the upper limits of the piazza obelisk. These objects were framed by the pillars of the colonnade. I must be somewhere half-way along the colonnade, I judged, but by then I knew myself to be defeated, trapped within an endless colonnade. Dim memory told me that I must have a chance of escape if only I could get to the great gate of the Porta Angelica. But the distance seemed too vast to cross, as, I suppose, the last ten yards in a four-minute mile seem impossible to cross.

Then I saw the two men in dark suits I had seen at the station break through the crowd by one of the pillars ahead, and knew that this would be the nightmare's end. The great arms of the bull-necked one could seize and break me as I might break a child. I was desperately weary and sorry for myself and was at breaking point, almost ready to welcome the ghastly end to the whole sorry tale. I was in no mood for teen-age tackles. I knew I stood no chance. Yet one of the horrors of our age had seized my mind within those moments. The memory of the thud of my brogue catching the brown-suited man gave me a sudden remorseless access of strength. A sadistic and sickening sense of power, without a doubt, but had it not worked? So begins the storm-trooper's nauseating philosophy, I daresay. The crack of the toe-cap in the other man's teeth. Then, just as suddenly, I was spent and finished and could not go on. I would have to stand and take what was coming.

I stopped and leaned against a pillar, the back of my head against the cooling stone. I heard my breath leaving my body in spewed-out thuds. Then, as the men approached, seeming to part the people about them as giants might thrust aside a field of corn, I acted with the viciousness of despair. The older man was within a yard of me, his arms out-thrust, preparing to engulf me, when I stepped back on to the low plinth of the pillar, leaned back against the unyielding stone, balanced so that my right foot was free and kicked again.

I took a terrifying risk. I might have slipped. He might have seized my foot and dragged me down. But then there was no risk because there was no alternative. I had to do just that. Instead he took my boot partly on the side of his chin, partly in his throat. I heard the crack of the jaw-bone, his dull cry as he went down. In falling he lumbered against the younger man. Arms reached out and they were both down. I kicked again as I went on. I caught the side of the younger man's head, brutally, retchingly.

These, I suppose, are scarifying admissions for an Englishman to make, but I am no hero in a schoolboy's story of adventure. I was a panic-stricken, middle-aged medical man caught into events utterly outside all his limited experience. I used the only weapons available to me—my heavy brogue shoes. I stumbled on, reeling, I think, my legs like spearmint. I could still hear the horror of the crowd behind me. But nobody tried to hold me back.

Perhaps the odds were in my favour. The crowds were there to hear the Pope. They were so thick on the ground that what happened in one spot was wholly hidden from those five yards away. And the columns of the colonnade are so close, no more than six or seven feet apart, that each group of four made almost a self-contained compartment. And the construction of the colonnade doubtless helped to seal off almost all sounds made in one compartment from another. I have thought often upon that nightmare in the sun, and doubtless I shall never cease to speculate upon its horrors so long as I shall live.

The colonnade is perhaps three hundred yards or more along its curving length. I think I had taken almost an hour to cover the distance from the steps. At last I reached the Porta Angelica, staggered across the piazza there, moving wearily past two carabinieri, and, by the bus-terminus, found a taxi, I stumbled in and gasped "Ciampino! Quick! Quick!" He said, "Si, si, Signor," and was away.

I looked back and saw, in peaceful anticlimax, the empty square, a line of waiting empty buses under the unrelenting sun, two men at the tables of a café playing a game of cards.

43

ALL that remains to be written is simple and could be quickly done, but it will take me many hours and the writing will be a pain almost beyond bearing. That I know: for I shall be writing part of my life away.

I reached Ciampino forty minutes before the plane was due to leave. I sent a cable to my housekeeper, Mrs Seabrook, ostensibly addressed to my daughters. Then I had a long whisky, scarcely touched by water, and wandered off to buy my daughters and Mrs Seabrook presents from amongst the gaudy selection of dolls and jewellery in the airport kiosks.

By then I was beginning to breathe again, although deadly weary and dishevelled.

For once I found an unaccustomed reassurance in the company of fellow-travellers. I stayed amongst them, wishful to become part of their herding instinct. A sense of security possessed me from the moment we were gathered into our group for BEA flight 131. As we entered the customs shed and were shut off from the world beyond the barrier I began to look towards England, towards the securities of that much abused island. No sound I have ever heard, not even the purring of a hearth-rug cat, gave out such an air of homeliness as the roar of the engines of the Elizabethan shattering into life on the runway. The flight was uneventful. I slept throughout the journey, awaking only to wave away the plastic tray of food. We were in England before five o'clock and I was in Wimpole Street before seven.

44

FOR many minutes after arriving at the flat I was overcome by emotions too deep for words as I was caught into the boisterous greetings of my daughters. Somehow I felt that they should know already of my ordeal, and the warmth of their welcome almost persuaded me for a moment that by some chance they did know. Then, too, I had been so engulfed by passion of a different kind that their exuberance almost bowled me over by its intensity and innocence.

Finally, I banished them, saying that I must ring the hospital in Vicenza, for James had had an accident. They were immediately contrite and silent, before bursting again into a cross-fire of questioning. What kind of accident? asked Joan. Was it serious? Could they write to him? Would he come here when he got back? asked Peggy. And so on and on.

I went into my consulting-room and booked two calls to Italy: a personal call to Doctor Dolci at the hospital at Vicenza, and another to Bianca at the Hotel Tolfa in Rome. An hour's delay, I was told.

242

By then I was trembling with fear and trepidation. The inevitable anticlimax had caught up with me. I was weary, lonely, bruised and utterly sick at heart.

I went upstairs to the kitchen and asked Mrs Seabrook to make supper for eight-thirty. Then I bathed. Lying in the hot bath I went over the direful happenings of the preceding twenty-four hours in my life. I could not relax. The exquisite soporific effects of a bath eluded me that evening. I was as jumpy as any of the nerve-edged patients who had ever entered my consulting-room below.

I got out and towelled myself down, dressed quickly and went to say good-night to Joan and Peggy, now almost ready for bed. For a time their chatter kept my own fears away. I had never thought to find some kind of soothing influence in their non-stop anecdotage. Then, at last, the telephone interrupted their tales and I went across to the sitting-room, closed the door and took up the receiver with the deepest forebodings.

Doctor Dolci wasn't at the hospital, the operator said, would I speak to another doctor, a Doctor Albani, assistant to Doctor Dolci? I said I would.

Albani might have been speaking from St George's Hospital at Hyde Park Corner so clear was his voice. He spoke in Italian, swiftly and to the point. James had died at three o'clock that afternoon without regaining consciousness. Yes, Mrs Sandford was still in Vicenza. She had returned to her hotel, the Villa Rosa, and would be remaining there for a day or so. The police had requested her to remain and she had also wished to do so. I thanked him and rang off.

I sat back in my desk chair, stunned and sick. I cannot write now of my thoughts. My mind was too full of memories, too poignant and saddening to record. And I was beset by an agony of self-recrimination that I knew would never dull. James's death would be a stabbing part of my conscience for every day of my life.

I sat there in the slowly gathering dusk without a light and waited on my call to Bianca. Ten minutes later the telephone rang once again and the operator said nobody of the name of Signora Colleoni was registered in the Hotel Tolfa.

"Let me speak!" I said and waited desperately until the

243

voice of the night-porter answered. I asked him whether he was the one who had shown the English doctor from the hotel that morning.

"Si, Signor," he said.

"And when did Signora Colleoni leave?"

"This afternoon, sir, I believe."

"Where to?"

"We do not know."

"She left no messages? No address?"

A long pause and then "No, Signor, there is nothing here."

"Thank you."

I put another call through to the Villa Rosa at Vicenza. I was benumbed, as I suppose all those whose worlds begin to collapse about them are benumbed. I had had the same feelings when Helen died, but then I had been expecting the final moment for many months. These events had swept me into their momentum too swiftly.

I must have sat there for a long time. Mrs Seabrook knocked on the door and said, "Supper, sir," and I called, "In a moment, Mrs Seabrook," but I stayed on in the darkening room, knowing that I must wait until Georgina rang. Around nine o'clock she was on the line. Her gay, high-pitched, enlivening voice was now a sad whisper, like a tearful girl's. She could tell me little more than Albani had told me. There was no need for me to return, dearly as she would like me there. She would see that James's body was brought back to England. Soon she must start to think. Did the Italians believe in cremation? Surely James would rather his beloved Fells should receive his ashes than the Veneto? I agreed. She would fly back with James's body or his ashes, probably on Tuesday. Would I please meet her if she rang me first and make all London arrangements? The Italians had been so kind, but she was still stupefied. She began to cry again. In her tears she said that she would ring me again the following night and tell me more. I said, "Of course, of course, Georgina," and we rang off in a ghastly moment of having no more words to utter.

I went slowly down to supper. Mrs Seabrook asked no questions. I took up *The Sunday Times* and tried to read, but I could think only of dear James and of Bianca and speculate to

244

no avail. Soon my head was in a hammering whirl. I wanted
her and she had gone from my life. I began to believe that she
had gone for good. My erratic, obstinate optimism was at last
defeated. Yet my love remained, an unbearable agony that had
to be borne. James's surmises and suspicions returned. My own
defeated doubts rose up again.

I pecked at my supper and went back to the sitting-room and
put through a personal call to Bianca at the number in Naples
that she had given me that morning, fifteen hours, a lifetime
before.

Half an hour later I was rung to say that there was no reply.

45

ON MONDAY morning, before I again began to make my slow
return to the routine of my medical life, I made arrangements
for the number in Naples to be rung twice a day, once at ten
o'clock in the morning and again at ten at night. During that
day, in the afternoon, whilst I was at St Thomas's, my own
number was rung from Italy and Mrs Seabrook was asked by a
woman's voice whether Doctor Frost had returned safely from
Italy. Mrs Seabrook had hastened to say yes, and the telephone
had gone dead. "Wasn't that strange?" she said, that evening.
"I rang back to the exchange, but they said the caller had
finished."

"Very strange," I agreed and almost wept.

Only once did I get a reply from the number in Naples, and
that was from the daily cleaner, but her Italian was too verna-
cular for me and all I could learn was that Signora Colleoni
was still away and nobody knew when she would return.

By Wednesday I asked for enquiries to be made at the
London office of the *Popolo di Roma* to see whether any information had seeped through into the Press relating to any
accident in Rome on that Sunday during the Trades Union
Congress. Nothing.

My fears were resolved and dispersed on the following Saturday morning by a letter from Italy. I recognized the scrawl of

Bianca's writing and for a long second could not steel myself to slit the envelope. When at last I opened out the letter I somehow already knew the words:

My Dearest only Rupert,

This letter is a terrible letter to write, but you will by now begin to understand I believe. I did not write to you from Rome. I did not go back to Naples, but here to Capri. I know you got safely back to London. I do not think, Rupert, that I can ever come to be your wife. I am too frightened of your life in London and I know that I will not be all you think I am and all you think a wife will be to you. When you are with me I sometimes think all these things are possible, but if you are away a minute I know they are not. I am too weak. All my life is here. All my easy life and I am not strong enough to leave it. I am Italian and must keep to the sun and I am lazy and will keep to the foolish way I live which is the only way I know how to live. I cannot be the wife of a good man and in all my tears I know this is true. I love you and love you and because I love you I will not come. I know it is no good because because because. . . .

You have all my love but it is no good and you know that too and this is the end.

I shall always think of you. I have often wondered what happened to James. I tried to see the newspapers but what happens in Northern Italy is often not important in this small island. If you will write to me I will like that, but we will not meet. Perhaps one day but not soon. All these things I have thought and thought and thought about and know that they are true.

For weeks afterwards I brooded over that letter, telling myself a hundred times a day that faint heart never won fair lady. But in my own heart I knew that the issue was far more complex and could not be solved within the terms of ancient platitudes and threadbare calls to action. I could only marry a woman wishful to marry me. I had not the simple strength that takes another's doubts within its care. I needed to have assurances as well as give them. Fear in a woman implanted fear in myself. Another's doubts provoked my own. I was defeated, perhaps by circumstance, but mainly, I suppose, by myself, as each man is ultimately triumphant or defeated by himself alone.

I have never been able to see life in simple, clear-cut patterns. A man more certain of himself might (indeed, would) have gone straightaway to Naples, determined to return with a wife—a wife he had, if needs be, virtually abducted. I could not do this. Why? Why? Why? I ask myself incessantly throughout the day, and in the night, rise from my bed determined upon action in the morning. But the dawn comes and determination withers. And there are patients and the recurring routine of my consultations, and the hospital.

Millions will understand my dilemma, I think; the millions of irresolute accepters. Thousands will scoff; the thousands quick to action, to seize this nettle danger.

So there it is. Perhaps a record of despair, probably an inevitable record, predicated by myself. We can never escape our genes, as I have said before, and as one of my sagacious mentors once said, I remember, in a lecture in my second year at U.C.H. over twenty years ago.

46

No more than a footnote remains:

Later that week I saw Professor Hankinson at the Ministry of Supply and gave him the two envelopes.

He was a vigorous, clean-shaven, iron-grey-haired man in his early fifties, looking more like a gardener than a physicist. Perhaps he was both. He was quiet for a while at the end. Then he said, "Partly I blame myself, Doctor Frost. I should have known or, at least, begun to suspect. He harangued me no end sometimes when we got on to the indivisibility of knowledge and so forth. He was an idealist. I'm not. Too insular, I suppose. Also I'm not particularly suspicious. The English aren't as a rule, are they? I never suspected him for a minute. Perhaps as a departmental head and all that I come out of all this rather badly. I hope this business didn't put you to overmuch bother, by the way?"

I shook my head. How could I begin to try to explain anything in that high-ceilinged, cream-painted Civil Service office? Even now, I wonder, have I begun to explain anything, even to myself?

Throughout my days I make my endless reservations . . . if only I had drawn a piece of pasteboard with C.F. upon it instead of G . . . if only Georgina had not chattered so gaily in the coach . . . if only Greenaway had sat elsewhere . . . if only I had not espied Bianca on the Molo that afternoon . . . if only I had returned to London at James's first gentle behest . . . if only . . . if only . . . our eternal lamentation for our failures.